W9-BCA-627

"Would you answer something for me?"

Luke asked. "Is it always so difficult for you to accept help? Or is it just me?"

"I think it's just you," Emily answered.

"Are you always so honest?"

"When I have to be."

Her glance was steady. His own was no less certain as he realized there was nothing he could say that wouldn't complicate an already complicated situation. The simpler the relationship between Emily and himself remained, the easier it would be for everyone in the long run.

That was what Luke told himself as he breathed in the half-wild scent she wore and felt the tension escalating in his body. That was what he believed as his glance caressed her translucent skin and the shape of her very kissable mouth. It wasn't what he wanted, though. Not at all. And it had been a very long time since he'd really wanted anything without feeling that he was trying to prove something by getting it.

Dear Reader,

Welcome to Silhouette **Special Edition** . . . welcome to romance. Each month, Silhouette **Special Edition** publishes six novels with you in mind—stories of love and life, tales that you can identify with . . . as well as dream about.

We're starting off the New Year right in 1993. We're pleased to announce our new series, THAT SPECIAL WOMAN! Each month, we'll be presenting a book that pays tribute to women—to us. The heroine is a friend, a wife, a mother—a striver, a nurturer, a pursuer of goals—she's the best in every woman. And it takes a very special man to win that special woman! Launching this series is *Building Dreams* by Ginna Gray. Ryan McCall doesn't know what he's up against when he meets Tess Benson in this compelling tale. She's a woman after the cynical builder's heart—and she won't stop until she's got her man!

On the horizon this month, too, is MAVERICKS, a new series by Lisa Jackson. *He's a Bad Boy* introduces three men who just won't be tamed!

Rounding out the month are more stories from other favorite authors—Tracy Sinclair, Christine Flynn, Kayla Daniels and Judith Bowen (with her first Silhouette **Special Edition** title!).

I hope that you enjoy this book and all the stories to come. Happy 1993!

Sincerely,

Tara Gavin
Senior Editor
Silhouette Books

CHRISTINE FLYNN

LUKE'S CHILD

Published by Silhouette Books New York

America's Publisher of Contemporary Romance

If you purchased this book without a cover you should be aware that this book is stolen property. It was reported as "unsold and destroyed" to the publisher, and neither the author nor the publisher has received any payment for this "stripped book."

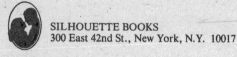

SILHOUETTE BOOKS
300 East 42nd St., New York, N.Y. 10017

LUKE'S CHILD

Copyright © 1993 by Christine Flynn

All rights reserved. Except for use in any review, the reproduction or utilization of this work in whole or in part in any form by any electronic, mechanical or other means, now known or hereafter invented, including xerography, photocopying and recording, or in any information storage or retrieval system, is forbidden without the permission of the publisher, Silhouette Books, 300 E. 42nd St., New York, N.Y. 10017

ISBN: 0-373-09788-3

First Silhouette Books printing January 1993

All the characters in this book have no existence outside the imagination of the author and have no relation whatsoever to anyone bearing the same name or names. They are not even distantly inspired by any individual known or unknown to the author, and all incidents are pure invention.

®: Trademark used under license and registered in the United States Patent and Trademark Office and in other countries.

Printed in the U.S.A.

Books by Christine Flynn

Silhouette Special Edition

Silhouette Desire

Silhouette Romance

CHRISTINE FLYNN

is formerly from Oregon and currently resides in the Southwest with her husband, teenage daughter and two very spoiled dogs.

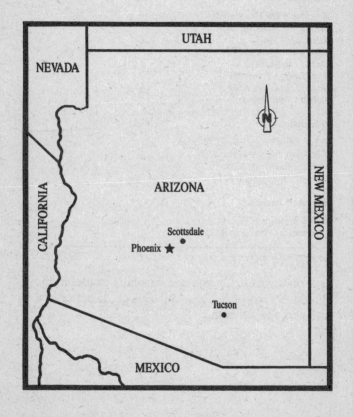

Prologue

Fifteen-year old Emily Russell sat among the colorful stuffed animals on her bed, her legs crossed Indian-style and her grandmother's guitar cradled in her arms. In the other room, beyond her bedroom wall, with its posters of graceful ballerinas and baby animals snuggled against their mothers, her parents were once again engaged in battle. It seemed to Emily that the fighting should have stopped once they were divorced. But now they just fought about different things.

It was her father's weekend to take her to his house, and he'd shown up late. Her mother was having a fit, which made no sense at all to Emily, since her mother hadn't been going anywhere and Emily was the one who'd been waiting. Now she didn't even want to go. Her father's mood would be terrible, and he'd just rag on her mom all evening. Then, tomorrow, he'd try to make it up to her by buying her a bunch of stuff her mother would later spend hours criticizing, because she was sure he was only trying to buy Emily's affection.

Emily couldn't have cared less about the things he bought her. She didn't want more clothes or records or makeup. What she wanted was to talk to her dad. Maybe she could even tell him how excited she was about being put in an honors English class with the seniors. She was dying for him to be proud of her. For *someone* to be proud of her, anyway. When she'd told her mother, the woman had only told her she could take the class but she wasn't to socialize with older kids—she was only fifteen, after all. Then she'd said to remind her father when she saw him tonight that he was late with child support.

From the sounds of the angry discussion taking place on the other side of the wall, it seemed that her mom had reminded him herself. Her mother was never in better form than when the issue was money. Unless the topic was Emily's father's lack of participation in their lives. She had that one aced, too. They were old themes. Ancient, actually. And Emily knew all the accusations and recriminations by heart. Even when her parents had been married, her father had been on the road most of the time. Her mother had had to give up her once-promising dance career to stay home with Emily. Now Joyce Russell was too old to pursue her dreams, Emily hadn't needed "supervision" in a long time, and she was left with little for company beyond a bitterness she nurtured with far greater care then she had her daughter.

The voices grew louder—her mother's more strident, her father's angrier. Soon, one of them would start throwing things. Emily had been forgotten, as she so often was.

She hugged the guitar over her churning stomach. Strumming the chords helped block out the sounds coming through the walls, so she played louder. Loud enough that she could no longer hear the accusations and the names they called each other and the warnings and the insults. She closed her eyes. The notes from the guitar were dissonant. That didn't matter. She wasn't playing music, anyway. Not like she usually did when she sought escape from her parents' fighting. She was only making noise to drown out more chaotic sounds.

Some people weren't meant to be parents. Her own never should have been. They certainly didn't want her. From the time she'd been born, she'd just been in the way. Someday, though, someone would want her. Someday she'd have a child of her own, and she would love it so much it would have to love her back.

Chapter One

She'd blown it. Emily was absolutely positive of that as she hurried through the school parking lot to pick up her son before after-school care charges kicked in. Her one shot at a promotion she desperately needed, and she'd quite probably been knocked out of the running by her own past. The gentleman she'd interviewed with had zeroed in on the one item on her résumé she'd hoped he'd overlook, and all but ignored everything she'd accomplished since.

Yes, she'd had to admit—twice, because he hadn't heard her the first time—she had dropped out of high school. And, yes, it had been a while before she'd gone back. She had pointed out, however, that she had obtained her GED—omitting the circumstances of the disastrous year and a half before she'd managed that—and then gone on to get a degree in library science. Her track record as an assistant librarian was excellent.

He hadn't seem at all impressed. He'd merely steepled his fingers, leveled his bespectacled glance at her, and announced that he had several other candidates to interview before a decision would be made. It was, after all, a very responsible position.

She didn't doubt for a moment that he'd have dropped his dentures had he known that she'd once had a police record.

Since that record had been acquired as a juvenile and no longer existed, Emily didn't spend any time dwelling on what might have transpired had he known about it. She was concerned only with what might have affected her interview. Being her usual inwardly less-than-confident self, she had been picking apart her performance ever since she'd left the Scottsdale library system's administration building. Having exhausted everything she'd said or done, she started in on her appearance, certain now she should have worn a suit rather than the blouse and neat straight skirt she'd so carefully selected this morning, and that she should have worn her hair up instead of tied back. She tended to look younger than her twenty-nine years, and wearing her hair up added a certain sophistication that might have gained her a more favorable impression.

Wishing she could do it all over again, Emily headed for the main walkway leading through the campus of the private school she'd enrolled Cody in just last month. Casa de los Niños was outrageously expensive, but it was the best. And the best was what she wanted for the little boy who, nearly four years ago, had stolen her heart the moment he'd curled up in her arms. Like her, he'd once had a less-than-even shot at a future.

The warm, dry breeze tugged wisps of auburn hair from the clip controlling her shoulder-length curls. Brushing the strands from her face, she noticed a man emerge from the

building ahead of her. He paused as the door closed behind him, looking back over his shoulder, as if thinking to
go back in. He must have decided against it. A moment
later, he started down the walkway.

He was a tall man, broad-shouldered, lean-hipped, his
bearing betraying no hint of the hesitation she'd seen. He
had a presence about him that a person would respect—or
envy. Whichever feeling he incited, he definitely wasn't a
man to invite indifference. His strong, even features spoke
of Nordic ancestry, of brawn refined by sophistication.
The European cut of his suit was cosmopolitan, and his
urban polish seemed more suited to a boardroom or
country club than to a school yard. Yet, there was that hint
of the rogue beneath the polish. A kind of ruggedness that
defied the trappings of civility. But as attractive as he was,
it was the way he pushed his fingers through his hair as he
looked back toward the doors of the building behind him
that gave her pause.

He seemed shaken by something. Deeply so. When he
turned around again, raising his eyes to her now that she
was directly in his path, she was touched by what she saw
in his expression.

His eyes were the color of old pewter and shadowed with
a desolation so raw, so real, she could have sworn she felt
it herself.

For a moment, she thought she might have embar-
rassed him by witnessing his distress. His pain was that
plainly evident. But he didn't appear to give her much
thought at all. As the distance between them decreased, his
heavier footfalls alternating with the light tap of her heels,
he simply stared at her—through her, it seemed—until her
own worries gave way to a soft, empathetic smile.

Her smile must have seemed incongruous to him, troubled as he was. He seemed puzzled by it for a moment.

Then his unfocused gaze sharpened. Perhaps encouraged by what he saw in her green eyes, he acknowledged her with a nod of his head.

The next instant, he looked away and continued past, no longer looking back. No longer seeming vulnerable.

Emily watched him go. He'd just come from the special ed building; the one where children with special needs spend much of their day. He seemed too troubled to be anyone but a parent. A parent with either a special-needs child already attending the school or one he wanted to get into the program. She remembered how difficult it had been seeing all those children in the beginning. Some parents had more trouble than others admitting that their child wasn't perfect, that their offspring needed special consideration, either in his or her education or in simply learning how to function from day to day.

Some truths, Emily knew, could be pretty devastating. It was that kind of pain she'd seen in his eyes.

I hope you'll be all right, she silently told him, and continued to watch as the driver of a limousine, a dusky-skinned gentleman with a mustache like a well-used scrub brush, emerged from the vehicle's air-conditioned comfort to open the rear door.

The stranger slipped inside, his movements as athletically graceful as his long strides had been. Moments later, with its occupants shielded behind smoke-colored glass, the long black limo silently slid away from the curb.

Emily could only stare after it, wondering who the man inside was. She wondered, too, at how strongly she'd felt his desolation. What bothered her most, though, as she turned to the special ed building herself, was that something about the man had seemed almost . . . familiar.

Why that should be, she had no idea. She'd certainly remember having run into him before, though she couldn't imagine where it might have been. Unless, perhaps, she'd seen him at the hospital or the clinic. Her recollection of names left a lot to be desired, but she never forgot a face.

A slow smile removed the soberness from her features. Even the matter of her less-than-promising interview was temporarily forgotten when she saw a towheaded child in leg braces and a Terminator T-shirt maneuvering a wheelchair through the door ahead of her. Nothing seemed quite so bad when she saw her Cody's lopsided grin. There had been a time when he hadn't smiled at all.

"Mom! Guess what?"

"What?" she called back, waving at Mrs. Kramer, the snow-haired teacher holding the door open for him.

"Billy's having a birthday party, and he wants me to come."

Her smile never faltered, even though this month's budget didn't include extra money for birthday gifts. "When is it?"

"I dunno. But he said his mom 'n' his dad are getting him a pony."

The pony was all Cody talked about all the way home. He wasn't clear as to whether the pony was just for rides during the party or if Billy Bartell was getting a horse of his own. Knowing Jan Bartell as she did, Emily was sure the horse's presence would only be temporary. The Bartells had plenty of acreage for a horse, but they'd moved to Arizona because of Billy's asthma. Unfortunately, his condition was aggravated by allergies to just about everything, including animals. That was why he had a turtle for a pet. And because Billy had a turtle for a pet, Cody had one, too.

Emily didn't remind Cody about his little friend's difficulties. She simply kept her conclusions about the animal to herself and let him go on about how cool it would be to ride a real horse. His enthusiasm was a balm for Emily; his innocent excitement was almost contagious. So it wasn't until she turned her dependable old Volkswagen bug onto the quiet little street where she and Cody lived that her smile faded. And then only because a limousine was pulling away from the curb in front of her house.

Cody sat too low in the seat to notice. Even if he had seen the long, black vehicle, he wouldn't have paid much attention to it. Now that he was so close to home, his thoughts had turned to food. He wanted macaroni and cheese for dinner.

"You had macaroni and cheese last night," she reminded him, and frowned at the brake lights of the limo as it slowed a block farther down. A moment later, it turned the corner and disappeared.

The appearance of a limousine on her street was merely a coincidence. She was sure of that. It couldn't possibly have been the same one she had seen just fifteen minutes ago at Cody's school. All limousines looked alike to her, anyway. They were long, rather pretentious things, in black, white or silver, and were as familiar as city buses on Scottsdale's streets. Some streets, anyway. Her quiet neighborhood, with its maze of cozy little patio homes, was hardly on the beaten path to resorts and golf courses and glitzy shopping malls, but she supposed drivers had the right to get lost once in a while. Or maybe the passenger had just wanted to do a little slumming.

Coincidence, she reiterated to herself, thinking of the man she'd seen at the school. It disturbed her a little that she could picture his face so clearly. Disliking the feeling, she tried not to think of him at all. Perversely, the effort only made her think of him more. Even as she went through her late-afternoon routine, preparing Cody's supper and cajoling him through his hated leg exercises, the haunted look in the man's eyes remained with her. She thought it odd that she should have empathized so much with someone she would undoubtedly never see again.

But she did see him again. At least she thought she did, that evening, in the park across from her house.

Emily had taken Cody to the park, as she often did, because the bribe of an hour or so on the play equipment usually got him through his exercises with a minimum of grousing. At the moment, Cody was on the swings. A few other children from the neighborhood played nearby, their mothers or fathers no doubt hoping to exhaust them before bedtime. Occasionally Emily visited with a parent while their children shared a teeter-totter or played on the merry-go-round. More often, she and Cody simply endured the stares; the curiosity from the other children; the sympathetic looks from the other parents. Or, worse, the quick shunning, as if by being ignored, they—and thus their affront to what was "normal"—could be made not to exist. Most people weren't deliberately cruel, but it never ceased to amaze Emily how insensitive some could be.

She was being rude herself at the moment, though she didn't wish to be. She just couldn't help staring at the man she'd noticed watching them.

Beyond the teeter-totters and slides, a row of relatively short palm trees delineated the picnic area. Standing next to one of those palms, shaded by its graceful fronds, was a man with hair the color of wheat, wearing slacks and a white shirt with the sleeves rolled up.

There was no one around him. No child. No other adult. There was no limo in sight, either—though when she found herself looking for one, she decided it could well be in the parking lot by the baseball diamond. She wouldn't be able to see it from where she stood.

Was it the same man? she wondered. Or had she just been thinking about him so much that she was imagining things?

Whoever he was, he just stood there. Watching.

Cody, his fine blond hair flying, twisted in the swing to see what had happened to his last push. "Come on, Mom. I want to go higher."

Absently Emily gave him another shove and glanced back over her shoulder.

It was impossible to tell for sure, but the man's attention did seem to be on the swings. Since she and Cody were the only ones at the swings, that meant he had to be watching them. Emily glanced back at her son, following his high arc as his little fingers gripped the chains of the swing. Cody's metal leg braces flashed in the fading afternoon sun. His wheelchair sat in the grass behind her. Not quite sure why she was doing it, she pulled it closer.

A moment later, keeping her eye on the stranger, she grabbed the chains and pulled Cody to a stop. As she did, the man moved from the tree.

Her heart lurched.

"Cody?" Deliberately she kept her odd apprehension from her voice. She was most likely only imagining things. The guy was probably perfectly harmless. After all, there was a police station not two blocks away, and no self-respecting weirdo would hang around with cops that close. "There's a man over there by the trees. Have you ever seen him before?"

Cody looked to his right. Then to his left. He also checked out a cricket making little dust puffs in the dirt as it hopped past the swing.

He looked back to his mom and shrugged. "I don't see any man."

"Come on, Cody. Over my shoulder. By the picnic tables."

"Oh," he said, and squinted in that direction.

After a couple of seconds, he mumbled, "I don't know. Push me more. Okay?"

It was entirely possible that the man was simply too far away for Cody to see well. She wasn't even positive it was who she thought it was herself.

Promising she'd push him again in a minute, Emily finger-combed Cody's silky flax-colored hair away from his big gray eyes. Because it was becoming imperative that she know, she asked him if there had been any strangers at school today. "Think hard, honey. Was there anyone there that you don't usually see?"

A frown flitted over the freckles on Cody's nose at the question. Emily knew why, too. He didn't want to think. He wanted to swing. But he also realized he wasn't going to get pushed until he really did think about it. Finally he remembered the man the principal had brought to his classroom this afternoon. Though Cody didn't sound too happy about having to waste his time recalling it, he told her that the man had looked at the pictures on the wall and stared at some of the kids. Then he'd talked to Mrs. Kramer, staring at Cody for a while longer, and left.

Cody hated being stared at.

And that was precisely what the stranger near the trees was doing. She could almost feel his eyes on them as she straightened and ruffled Cody's hair.

For the briefest moment, she even thought he might approach. That same moment, she recalled the desolation she'd seen in his dark gray eyes. It was him. It had to be— and because of that, her vague sense of unease didn't fit at all with the sympathy she also felt. Yet the unease was there. Definite and undeniable.

It faded when, after a moment of what looked very much like indecision, the man pushed his fingers through his hair—and walked away.

The next morning, Emily stopped by the administrative office at Cody's school when she dropped him off. Cody's teacher hadn't arrived yet. The principal wasn't available, either. The secretary had no trouble remembering the gentleman Emily inquired about, though. A Mr. Montgomery, she recalled. But the woman had no idea what he'd wanted when he'd come in yesterday. He'd asked for the principal, and she'd turned him over to her immediately. She did, however, remember that he'd said he'd only be in town for a while, that he had a six-o'clock flight to catch.

That information eased Emily's mind considerably. If the man she'd seen yesterday had been on a plane at six o'clock in the evening, it would have been pretty well impossible for him to have been in her neighborhood at seven.

An hour later, Emily had finally stopped chastising herself for letting her imagination get the better of her at the park. It was difficult to think of anything else, anyway, during the preschooler's story hour at the library. As the children's librarian, she truly enjoyed working with the under-three-foot-tall crowd. Even if the children did sometimes demand the patience required for canonization.

Anissa had already been to the bathroom twice. Shane had finally stopped teasing Brittany. And Jason was no longer picking his nose. All eleven children sat on the bright red carpet in the reading room, their eyes trained on "Miss Emily" as she began to read one of the less grim of the Grimms' fairy tales.

She hadn't finished the first paragraph when eleven little heads turned with the sound of the door opening. Thinking it a late arrival, Emily, too, glanced up.

In the space of a heartbeat, her easy smile faded. Vanessa Sheldrake stood facing her in the doorway, her perfectly coifed silver hair gleaming in the overhead lights. Vanessa was head of the branch, a quiet, methodical woman whom Emily greatly respected and whose job she hoped to get when the woman retired in two months. It wasn't Vanessa's perpetually stern expression that had her attention. It was the man behind her—the one she'd seen yesterday at Cody's school.

"May I see you, Emily?" Vanessa asked. "Susan will take over here."

Emily barely noticed the young woman entering the room. She was aware only of how the man's glance moved from her to the children gathered at her feet. She handed Susan the book, knowing his eyes followed her every movement as she rose from the small stool and moved to the door.

This Mr. Montgomery suddenly struck her as a formidable-looking man. Powerful, actually, she thought, and the vague sense of unease she'd felt at the park settled firmly in her stomach. He obviously hadn't left town yesterday, after all.

Luke Montgomery was out of his element. He freely admitted that to himself as he looked into a room filled with miniature tables and chairs and pint-sized beanbags. The feeling of having fallen into a rabbit hole was compounded by the wide-eyed expressions on the well-scrubbed little faces staring up at him from a square of apple-red carpet six feet below. Somehow those children were infinitely more intimidating than anything he would find at a boardroom table or among any construction crew.

The only expression of any real concern was that of the slender young woman now walking toward him. Her movements were fluid, graceful in the way of a woman at ease with her femininity. She held her head high, and her arms, bared by the black cotton sleeveless shell she wore, swung loosely at her sides. Her eyes were on his, direct and assessing—and he thought them the most amazing shade of green. He hadn't been able to to tell their color in the photographs he'd seen, but then, the photos hadn't done her justice at all. He hadn't even recognized her when he'd first seen her at the school yesterday.

She stopped in front of him. The top of her head barely reached his shoulder. As she tipped her head back to meet his eyes, the overhead lights caught shades of topaz and ruby in her thick auburn curls. Her skin was flawless, her mouth full and tinted the color of pale pink tea roses. He hadn't been prepared for her to be beautiful. But then, he hadn't been prepared for a great deal of what he'd learned in the past few months.

"I thought you might be able to help this gentleman, Emily." Vanessa stretched her polite smile between them. "He's inquiring about material on coping with a handicapped child. Since you've read everything in that section, you'd be in a better position than I to make recommendations."

"I didn't mean to interrupt."

His voice was husky, deep, and saved from gruffness by the apology in his tone. The apology surprised her, mostly because there wasn't a hint of it in his hard and handsome face. There, surprisingly, she saw defensiveness, and maybe a little hesitation. She had the feeling he wasn't terribly familiar with the combination.

Emily chose to address Vanessa, telling her that helping him wouldn't be a problem. Vanessa hadn't thought it would be. Or so she said before she left Emily to indulge equal measures of curiosity and caution.

Ignoring the two patrons watching them from the book stacks, and blocking Susan's soft voice as she led the children into the land of make-believe, Emily shamelessly studied Luke Montgomery's naggingly familiar features.

"I don't know if you remember," she quietly began, "but we ran into each other yesterday afternoon. At the school where my son goes. I had the feeling that maybe you were checking it out yourself."

His assessment equalled hers, though his had somehow taken in the entire length of her slender frame. Somewhere in the process, his defensive edge had softened.

"That is what I was doing. I'd never been there before." He extended his hand toward her. From beneath the cuff of his charcoal-gray suit jacket his crisp white shirt cuff extended the proper half inch. The cuff link in it looked suspiciously like real gold. "The name's Montgomery. Luke," he added, as if he wanted her to call him that. "You're..."

"Emily Russell." She took his hand, holding it only long enough for its heat and its strength to register, then pushed both her hands into the pockets of her black-and-pink flower-print skirt.

"I saw you at the park last night, too," he told her, because he knew she'd seen him and he wanted that out of the way. "I watched you with your little boy on the swings. I hope I didn't frighten you," he added, because she looked suddenly wary. "I just wanted to talk to you about him."

"Why didn't you?"

He suddenly seemed reluctant to answer, which surprised Emily, because the reluctance really didn't suit him. But then she saw pain shadowing his eyes, the same pain she'd sensed in him as they had passed at the school.

"I didn't want to intrude. That's one of the reasons I came here. To get reading material," he added because he didn't want it to sound as if he'd followed her. "I thought I'd try to figure out what I needed to know that way." He wasn't quite telling her the truth, but it was close enough to it for his purposes at the moment. "Can you recommend anything?"

Warily she considered both him and his inquiry. "Maybe if I knew what you were looking for. What kind of questions do you have?"

"Things like how well he can get along with the braces he wears? I mean, can he do regular little-kid things? Will he ever be able to play ball? I have no idea what a kid like that can do."

"A kid like that?"

Drawing his fingers through his hair—a gesture of recent acquisition—he let out a long, unsteady breath. This wasn't going well. But then, Luke hadn't expected that it would.

"A child with a birth defect," he said, though he knew she knew perfectly well what he meant. "That's what my son has. I don't know what the defect is, exactly. I don't even know *him*. I mean, I've seen him, but we don't know each other...." His voice trailed off, becoming quieter when the two patrons at the stacks frowned at them. "There's a possibility that he may come to live with me. And I have no idea what to expect. When I saw you in the park, I thought I'd just walk over and introduce myself, but..."

He'd lost his nerve. He didn't say that though; he simply let his words trail off with a shrug.

It occurred to Emily, as she stood there watching him try to hide his distress, that this conversation wasn't really as confusing as it seemed. He was simply asking for help. Rather ineptly, to be sure, but that was why he was here. He'd seen her at the school, then happened upon her and Cody at the park. That had to be it. As certain as she felt of that, she was also certain enough to bet her potential promotion that Luke Montgomery had never asked for help in his entire life—which might explain why he was bungling the job now.

Compassion cracked her caution. A smile, soft and encouraging, touched her mouth.

"Would you like a cup of coffee?"

Relief. She was sure that was what she saw in his eyes.

"Yeah," he said, and almost smiled.

He breathed in her scent as she passed—something musky and dangerous and a bit wilder than a woman should probably wear around small children—and followed her directions down a short hall while she disappeared down a very long row of books. As he entered what was little more than a small cubicle filled with books and posters, he faced a child's handwritten "I Love You, Mom" inside a crayon-drawn heart tacked on an overflowing bulletin board.

A pang of guilt hit as he looked away from that childish scrawl. Even though he was treading on sensitive and unfamiliar ground, and he was the one at a disadvantage here, Luke decided he might really be the bastard he'd so often been accused of being.

"Sorry there's no cream or sugar to offer you. Everyone here drinks it black." Emily watched him turn from where he was reading the fine print on a poster for literacy week and handed him a foam cup of steaming coffee. "You never said how old your little boy is. Mind if I ask?"

"He's six."

"So's my little guy," she said with a smile. "And you said yours might be coming to live with you?"

Luke ignored the chair she'd indicated by her crowded desk, moving instead to the window overlooking the parking lot and the mall beyond. His jaw bunched as frustration warred with reluctance. "His mother died a couple of months ago."

"I'm sorry."

"It's all right." He lifted his hand dismissively, his expression hard and strangely distant. "We hadn't seen each other for a long time. What I'm concerned about is the boy. I know very little about him." He paused, the quick anger she'd sensed in him overshadowed by a deep sadness that seemed to take him even farther away. "I didn't even know he was handicapped until a while ago," he said in a voice so quiet she barely heard him. "I really don't know quite what all's wrong with him. She didn't mention it at all."

From the tension in his stance, it was easy to see that Luke was dealing with enough without having a stranger pry into his marital life. Emily, therefore, quashed the questions that came to mind and pulled a book from behind her desk.

The wisest thing to do would be to give him a list of books to read on the subject, wish him luck and send him on his way. The man definitely had problems, and she had enough of those herself without taking on anyone else's. She couldn't turn her back on him, though. The fact that he'd approached her—a complete stranger—told her that he cared very much about his child. Approaching her hadn't been easy for him. Obviously he was desperate.

"One of the books I had in mind for you has been checked out. It deals generally with parents' attitudes and acceptance. Without knowing what your son's disabilities are, I can't direct you to anything more specific. You can take this one, though. It's a listing of agencies and support groups where you can get information on just about every disability there is."

She watched him take the book and stare at the title on the cover as if the words were foreign to him. Perhaps they were. Foreign and frightening.

"I have my own copy of the other book at home, if you'd like to borrow it."

He glanced up at her offer, his eyebrows dark slashes of skepticism.

"I'm not far from the park where you were last night," she said encouragingly. "If you'd like, you could stop by to pick it up after I get off this afternoon. You could meet my son, too. Maybe the idea of being around a child with a physical problem wouldn't be so difficult for you if you knew they were basically just like other children."

"Basically just like other children." The nature of his problem seemed to grow by the moment. "Kids in general are kind of a problem. I don't know anything about them at all."

"Maybe you *had* better come by, then."

The woman had a smile as gentle as spring rain. Soft, warming, rejuvenating. She seemed like a good person. Decent. And Luke felt like a fraud for letting her draw the conclusions she had. But she was making it easier than he'd hoped it would be, and God knew he could use a break. He just had never expected to get one from her.

"Seven o'clock?" she asked, writing her address on a notepad.

There was no response as she lay the pen down and tore the sheet from the pad. Holding the paper out, she turned to hand it to him.

She didn't know anything about the man, other than that he appeared well-off and that he had a son with a disability. It was the latter that kept her guard down. They had something in common that no one who was not in their position could truly understand, and it made her feel good to know that she and Cody might be able to help.

He was watching her, his eyes intent on her upturned face. "Are you sure?"

"I'm sure," she returned, and saw something like thanks enter his eyes.

Chapter Two

Luke didn't need the address Emily had given him. He drove right to her quiet little neighborhood from his hotel, remembering the route from yesterday, when he'd checked out the small beige stucco house with the tiny patch of lawn for a yard and the wind chimes hanging by the front door. Sitting in front of the house now, he reached for the manila envelope on the passenger's seat. He withdrew two typewritten sheets. The one on top had two black-and-white photographs clipped to the upper right-hand corner.

He'd checked out everything in the private investigator's report. Where Emily Russell lived. Where she worked. The school where she sent the boy. The latter was remarkable only because he didn't think librarians made enough to afford such expensive tuition, and he couldn't help but wonder where she got the money. There didn't seem to be a boyfriend in the picture. No male friends at all. And even though he knew she was divorced, she didn't get alimony or child support. According to the information gleaned from court records, her marriage to James Edward Ashton IV had ended after six months some twelve years ago. She'd adopted the child on her own.

The child. This little boy called Cody Russell.

Luke looked at the top photograph, at the image of the child with the pale hair and the shy smile. The picture had been taken with a telephoto lens, capturing the boy through the window of an ice-cream shop.

His son.

Closing his eyes, Luke drew a deep breath. A moment later, releasing it, he pushed the photo beneath the second picture. The one of Emily Russell. It had been taken as she'd stood beside her car in some parking lot, the lens catching her full face.

He frowned at the grainy snapshot. The PI his attorney had recommended to check out Ms. Russell really should find another line of work. There were a few glaringly obvious facts missing from his report, and his skills as a photographer were equally inept. The man had failed completely to capture a decent likeness. Yet, to be fair, Luke knew no photograph could capture a person's essence. Essentially, Emily Russell was a generous and sympathetic woman; those were qualities that were somehow lacking in most of Luke's female acquaintances. The empathy in her smile had touched him even before he'd realized who she was.

It was still hard for him to believe that she'd offered to help him, a total stranger, just because she sympathized with his situation. People weren't usually so selfless.

Deception was a lousy way to repay such generosity.

To keep his conscience from shifting into overdrive, Luke stuffed everything back into the envelope and shoved it under the front seat. He knew he was taking advantage of this woman's kindness, but he'd have to be a fool to tell her the truth just yet. If he told her at all. She was the one who'd allowed the facade, so he might as well take advantage of it.

"She might not let you get anywhere near the kid without a court order," his attorney had warned. "Unless she goes the other way and decides to bleed you dry once she finds out who you are. She was used to nice things at one time. Her folks had a little money, and being married to that society kid, she no doubt refined her tastes. She's got next to nothing now. You watch your back pocket, buddy."

Since Luke paid Jeff to worry about his back pocket, he would remember his attorney's advice. For the moment, though—and despite his longtime associate's assessment of female behaviors—he would avail himself of Emily Russell's willingness to oblige him. He'd rather learn about his son with her cooperation than without.

The front door opened before Luke was halfway up the toy-strewn walk. Emily stood at the threshold, a towel in one hand and a soft smile of welcome on her lips. The gauzy-looking oversize white cover-up she wore left the shapeliness of her curves entirely to the imagination. Though it was not daring garb by any means, Luke found the shapeless thing remarkably provocative as she stepped out to hold open the screen door and a shaft of sunlight backlit her long, slender legs. Her feet, he noticed, were bare.

Her glance slid toward the street. "Your car shrank."

He looked over his shoulder, more to avoid meeting her eyes than to check on the rented black Jaguar he'd left at the curb.

"I think I like this one better," he heard her add, a smile in her voice.

"Me too. Not as practical as a limo when I'm traveling, though." He found it far more efficient to use a driver familiar with a city than to waste time reading street maps. "I can get a lot of work done between airports and meetings by having someone else drive."

Tugging at the knees of his gray worsteds, he bent to pick up a bright yellow dump truck from the walkway. While he was there, he grabbed a miniature backhoe, too.

"You don't live in Phoenix?" he heard her ask.

He reached the open door. From where he stood, an arm's length from her, he caught her scent. That blend of eroticism and innocence he'd noticed this afternoon—and somehow hadn't been able to forget.

"Denver. That's where my house is, anyway. Here." He held out the toys, as much to keep from staring at the chips of turquoise in her green eyes as to be rid of the dusty objects. "I seem to have something in common with your son." He inched the miniature earth-moving equipment higher. "We're both in construction."

Dirt smudged his broad hands. Noticing it when she took the toys, she handed him her towel with a smile.

"You're a contractor?" It sounded to him as if she'd been wondering what his occupation might be. "What do you build?"

The terry-cloth towel was damp, as if she'd been drying something with it. Luke kept his eyes on his hands as he wiped them. "I rebuild, actually. Most of the projects I design are for urban renewal."

"Then you're an architect?"

"That, too."

"Sounds busy."

"It is."

He handed her back the towel and watched her smiling gaze turn to the smudges he'd made on it as she invited him inside.

"Go on in and make yourself comfortable," she said as the screen closed behind them. "I'll just be a second. Can I get you something to drink? A cola, or some iced tea?"

He'd have preferred a Scotch. A double, actually. Neat. But liquor hadn't been offered, so he settled for the tea and, after being directed to the living room, watched her disappear into a bright but narrow kitchen. From where he stood, beside a beige sofa strewn with blue pillows, he could hear the muffled thud of a cupboard door closing and the clink of ice into glasses. He could also see the dining room table, which was spread with files and forms. One of the forms was in a typewriter she had set up at the nearest end, and a stack of what looked to be completed files sat on the floor.

The little boy was nowhere in sight.

Relieved—and not sure why—Luke pushed the sides of his suit jacket back and shoved his hands into the pockets of his slacks. "This is nice," he said for the sake of conversation, and glanced back toward the files. The names on them all seemed to be different, but the forms all bore the name of a local insurance agency. From the looks of it, she was doing their typing for them.

From the kitchen she asked, "What is?"

"Your place."

Feeling like the intruder he was, he let his glance continue on around the room. Her furnishings were modest, basic and sparse. But what was there seemed well cared for, as if the owner took pride in their possession despite their lack of value. The people he knew—his friends, his family—didn't simply own things, they displayed them. In their homes, the invitation was to view, not to touch.

That was definitely not the case here. His glance was first drawn to an open album of photographs on one of the end tables. As he then looked from the book-lined shelves to the stylized prints of children dancing in pastel swirls of color, he couldn't help but think that this room invited a person to live in it, to relax.

He moved toward the books covering most of the far wall. "You like to read," he observed, then was grateful that she hadn't seemed to hear him.

Of course she liked to read, he told himself. She's a librarian.

She was also, apparently, a musician. A modest collection of sheet music, classics mostly, was stacked beside a tape player. But it was the guitar in the corner, partially hidden by a huge and healthy potted fern, that drew his attention.

"My grandmother gave that to me when I was a little girl. It had been hers, but her arthritis got so bad she couldn't play it anymore."

The sound of her voice jolted him. He withdrew his hand, not realizing until he did that he'd been about to touch the instrument's lovingly polished wood.

"A twelve-string guitar is a difficult instrument to play. Are you very good at it?"

"Cody thinks so. Here," she said, offering him a glass of tea with a slice of lemon balanced on its lip. "Do you play?"

"Not the guitar. I was only forced to abuse the piano."

She smiled at that. "What about your son? Does he show any interest in music?"

The inquiry in her eyes was gentle, undemanding. Dangerous.

"I have no idea," Luke said, and, thanking her, took the glass before turning away.

He didn't turn quickly enough. She saw the bleakness he'd meant to hide.

Without thinking, Emily reached for his arm. Her fingers curled just below his elbow, her touch an automatic response that would have been triggered by any parent in his situation. But something about the way his glance jerked to her hand before meeting her eyes told her he didn't want her empathy.

Or maybe, she thought, as he waited for her to pull away, he just didn't want her so close.

Self-consciously she let her hand fall.

She focused her attention on her own glass. "It's okay if you're feeling unsure about being here," she assured him, because she was afraid he might be. She didn't want anyone feeling uncomfortable in her home. Or with her. "A sense of insecurity seems to go with the territory. I've met a lot of parents in our circumstances. Having a child with a disability gives us something in common that no one not in our position can really understand."

"I'm not exactly crazy about the feeling."

She smiled at his understatement. "I have a feeling that you probably hate it. You strike me as the type who doesn't like not being on top of a situation."

"Any other observations?"

The corner of his mouth tipped slightly. The expression seemed as much an apology for what had happened a moment ago as an attempt at a friendlier manner. What Emily noticed most, though, was the faint familiarity in that small smile. There was no reason his smile should be familiar to her at all.

"Only that you don't seem comfortable with the idea of having to turn to someone you don't know for answers. But don't worry about it. Okay? When you're in a clinic or in a hospital waiting for the results of endless tests, it's not unusual to find yourself sharing your insecurities with someone you'll never see again.''

"That's because some people find it easier to tell such things to a stranger. Ask any bartender.''

She met his cynicism with absolute agreement. When it came to admitting what made a person vulnerable, strangers were safer. They weren't so apt to abuse the knowledge as someone who supposedly cared. Yet all she said to him was that parents who had a child with disabilities weren't strangers to the insecurities he might be feeling about his son. Or his doubts or his fears. "We all have them. All of us.''

"Even you?'' he asked.

She smiled. "Especially me.''

He said nothing then. He simply stood there, studying her upturned face until she felt it heat. There was nothing bold in his glance. Yet beneath his quiet perusal she suddenly felt far less sure of herself than she had only moments ago.

This wasn't like talking with just any other parent of a child with special needs. With Luke, it was different. He was the kind of man who could make a woman feel feminine just by standing next to her. The kind of man whose masculine presence dominated and taunted, yet somehow reassured. At that moment, standing close enough to imagine how it would feel to be held against his very solid-looking chest, she realized how attracted she could be to him. That knowledge shook her. It had been a long time since she'd been attracted to a man. Longer still since she'd allowed herself to be intrigued by one.

Stepping back, she cleared her throat and grasped for something to fill the sudden silence.

"I only asked about the music,'' she said, since it was all she could think of, "because it's not unusual for a handicapped child to make up for his disability by excelling in some other area. I thought maybe your son..."

"Is that him, Mom?"

At the timid inquiry, Emily turned to the little boy in the doorway. Cody sat in his wheelchair, his freshly washed face betraying his shyness. He had wanted to finish getting himself ready for bed all by himself. It was a task that took just short of forever for him to accomplish.

Luke stood stock-still, his heart hammering. He wasn't sure what he felt at that moment. Curiosity was high on the list. Anxiety was up there, too. And concern. The little guy was so...little. And he looked so fragile, sitting in the small wheelchair with his too-short legs encased in the hip-high braces.

"Hi, honey," Emily said, and crouched beside him to fasten the button he'd missed on his blue-and-white-striped pajama top. "This is Mr. Montgomery." She leaned closer, her voice dropping a notch. "You're supposed to shake his hand. Remember?"

Recollection flitted over Cody's freckles. Then a frown. "What am I supposed to say?"

"Nice to meet you," Emily quietly coached.

Luke remained motionless as Cody's hands gripped the top of the push rings on the wheels and started to push himself toward him. Realizing the coffee table would block the little boy from reaching him if he stayed where he was, Luke set his glass down and moved forward himself.

The moment he stopped in front of the boy, he wasn't at all sure what to do.

As Cody had done only moments before, Luke looked to Emily. Her attention was on Cody, who had raised his left hand.

"The other one, honey," she whispered.

"Oh, yeah," he muttered. Dropping his left hand, he lifted his right. "Hi."

The rehearsed greeting had been forgotten, but as little fingers disappeared in his grip, Luke scarcely noticed. The child's hand was so small, so warm, and the shy, slightly crooked smile on the boy's face made Luke's shirt collar feel a size too small.

"Just call me Luke. Okay?"

Cody didn't acknowledge the request. He just stared up at the stranger towering over him and pulled his little hand back to grip his wheel again. Pushing the right wheel forward and the left wheel back at the same time, he expertly spun around to look at his mom. Having done as she had instructed him to do, he now wanted only to be dismissed. "Can I play Nintendo now?"

"Not tonight, honey." With the grace of a dancer, Emily scooped him up from the chair, braces and all. Her voice, already soft, became quieter. "We have company. That means we'll sit out here and visit."

"Do I hafta?"

"Yes," she whispered, though Luke could easily hear every word. "You do."

Cody didn't frown. His expression looked more like one of resignation to Luke—who then wondered as Emily carried the boy to the sofa, if a six-year-old even knew what resignation was.

Despite her slenderness, she'd picked up her son as easily as she might have a sack of flower petals. Cody looked solid, easily forty pounds plus hardware. Watching her, Luke couldn't help but wonder how firm she might be beneath the shapeless dress she wore. Odd how something so plain could be so provocative.

"Mr. Montgomery came to visit with us," she went on, sitting Cody down. "I told you that he has a little boy your age who has to wear braces, too. Remember? His little boy might be coming to live with him soon."

Looking a little more interested now, Cody wiggled himself into the corner and stuffed a sky-blue throw pillow between his braces to lean his elbows on. With his fists scrunching up his cheeks, he blinked up at Luke. "What's his name?"

His name? Luke thought, watching the little boy watch him. Geez. A name, he repeated, mentally running his hands through his hair. Of all the questions to be hit with first.

"Junior." Luke had always assumed that if he had a son the child would have his name. "His name's Junior."

Cody seemed to think about that for a moment. Then, in a leap of logic understandable only to those familiar with small children, he shyly said, "I have a turtle named Michelangelo. He's green."

Luke had assumed most turtles were. The choice of name seemed a little unusual, though. "Michelangelo?" he repeated, pleased at the change of subject, though he had no idea how they'd come to it. "Why did you name it that?"

" 'Cause Billy got Leonardo."

"That was his first choice," Emily explained when she saw Luke looking a little lost. "They're Teenage Mutant Ninja Turtles," she went on, then found that she had to explain that, too.

"Interesting," was Luke's only comment when, a few moments later, he crouched down to bring himself eye-level with Cody. "Do you have any other pets?"

"Nope." A loose thread on the pillow had the bulk of Cody's attention now. He picked at it as he talked, seeming a little intimidated by the big man's attention. "Mom won't let me have a dog or nothing. She says we're gone too much to take good care of a puppy, and puppies need lots of hugs and stuff, an' it's better not to have one than to 'glect it." His head came up. "Does your boy have a dog?"

"No," Luke answered, quite honestly. "He doesn't."

"Did you adopt him?"

"My little boy?"

Cody nodded.

Luke looked to Emily. "No," he said, not sure why he thought she'd help him out here. "He's my own."

"Mom adopted me. She picked me. She said that makes me special."

Luke didn't know what to say. Not because it was news to him that Cody was adopted—though Emily obviously thought it was—but because the boy seemed so content with the idea.

This child was his. This child, with the gray eyes so like his own and the imperfect little body. He couldn't seem to get past the fact that his son was less than perfect. For the most part, Emily dealt in euphemisms. Specials needs. Physically impaired. The fact was, the child he had sired was crippled. Disabled. Not normal.

Dear God, he didn't want to think in those terms. But faced with the reality, he could hardly deny his disappointment—and the extraordinary guilt that came with it for feeling as he did. Compounding it all, as he stood there numbly listening to Emily explain that she'd adopted Cody when he was three, was the overwhelming need to do what was right.

The problem, however, was that he didn't *know* what was right. He'd come to Arizona with no clear plan beyond seeing his son. Ever since he'd learned of the child's existence, that had been his goal. But in his drive to ac-

complish that goal, he'd had no idea of how truly difficult seeing the boy would be.

Except for his bowed little mouth, which even now
showed strong signs of Luke's stubbornness, the boy bore
little resemblance to his natural mother. Andrea Benning-
ton had been a striking woman with dark eyes and hair the
color of midnight. But the child they had produced had
gray eyes much like Luke's own and the same corn-silk hair
Luke had seen in photographs of himself as a child. The
boy's physical similarities, while notable, weren't necessarily so compelling. What drew him to Cody had more to
do with the child's attempts to master the social graces
Emily had encouraged—as when the boy politely asked
Luke if he'd like to see his fort.

Cody's bedroom was a mess—or at least Luke thought
so until he realized just what the mess was. Until that moment, he had forgotten how, as a child, he, too, had built
forts from bed linens and chairs before graduating to a
precarious wooden structure built—to the gardener's cha-
grin—in a majestic old oak on his parents' estate in Connecticut.

Cody had built a fort out of his red bedspread. Protected beneath it was a town built of blocks housing a collection of plastic dinosaurs. Showing it to Luke, Cody was
just as proud of his creations as Luke imagined he might
once have been—had there been anyone other than a
nanny around to admire it. Anyone like Emily.

With her long legs tucked beneath the folds of her skirt,
she sat beside the child on the floor of the room, with its
low shelves of books and toys and a terrarium holding an
amazingly alert-looking turtle, and listened to Cody tell her
how he was going to make a garage next for his stegosaurus. Luke listened to him, too, impressed that Cody even

knew what a stegosaurus was, but Emily had most of his attention.

She seemed totally absorbed with the child. Her hand lay on his leg, her slender fingers tucked beneath one of the long metal sidepieces of the brace so that she could touch Cody's soft-looking skin. Luke had the feeling she was scarcely aware of how she always seemed to be touching the child, smoothing his hair, patting his shoulder. He doubted, too, that she knew how appealing she was when she smiled at the little boy who clearly adored her. Once, as the three of them sat there—Emily and Cody on the floor and Luke perched on the edge of the twin bed crowded with stuffed animals—Cody even put his arms around Emily's neck and gave her a hug for no apparent reason at all.

A strange ambivalence filled Luke at that innocent show of affection. He hadn't had to know the child to be concerned about his welfare. And Emily, so far, seemed to be everything a mother should be. Yet the bond between this woman and his son somehow made matters that much more difficult to deal with. The conclusion made little sense. But then, very little had made sense to him lately.

He stood, uneasy with watching this woman play with his son.

Emily glanced up as he rose. Luke suddenly looked uncomfortable, anxious to be gone. It was also past the time for Cody to be in bed. Telling Cody to "Say good-night to Mr. Montgomery," she picked him up, quietly sucking in her breath when his brace banged her knee, and told Luke she'd be out in a minute.

From the middle of the living room, he could hear her quietly coaxing Cody with his prayers. When she got to "and a special blessing for Mr. Montgomery and his little boy," Luke wondered if the answer to that prayer might not be in the form of a lightning bolt zapping him on the spot.

As if to avoid the possibility, he moved from where he'd stopped and took to pacing the bare tile floor.

He wished he'd listened to Jeff's advice and stayed the hell away. Since he had disregarded his attorney's advice, however, the next wisest course—according to Jeff, anyway—would be to walk out the door and never come back. Luke had a plane to catch in less than two hours. He'd already postponed his meeting in San Diego twice, chasing after the boy. Now that he'd met his son, there was nothing to do but get out of his life.

Those were the thoughts creating Luke's brooding frown when Emily found him at the front window, staring at two moths chasing each other around a street light.

"He tends to be a little shy around strangers."

Luke closed his eyes. He was a stranger to his own son. "He's a neat kid."

"Thank you."

He checked his watch again, then turned to see her standing with her hands clasped in front of her, her expression strained despite her lovely smile. He wondered if it was only after the child was tucked in for the night that she allowed the stresses of raising him to show.

She moved closer, crossing her arms beneath the swell of her breasts. "I worry about him, though. Just as I'm sure you'll worry about your little boy. I don't know if your meeting Cody helped you or not."

He didn't, either. "Is there any chance he'll ever be okay?"

She picked up a stuffed elephant, a pathetic-looking thing with a missing eye and threadbare patches on its gray velvet. Hugging it to her, she suddenly looked terribly fragile—and very much in need of being held.

Who takes care of her? Luke wondered, and then he wished he hadn't, because he had the uncanny feeling there wasn't anyone.

"He'll never be without braces, if that's what you mean. The doctors hope he'll be able to get around on crutches in the next few years, but he has a lot of surgery to go through before that can happen. They think they can lengthen his legs, you see. It's been done before for children with similar problems. But there are never any guarantees." The elephant got an extra squeeze. "You'll discover that soon enough with your son."

There were any number of excellent reasons Luke should leave right this moment. He could walk out the door, and she'd be none the wiser. No harm done. It would be the decent thing to do. For her, anyway.

Luke could no more walk out the door right now than he could stop breathing. He needed to know more. He needed to know everything.

"Is he normal otherwise, Cody, I mean?"

Her gentle smile slipped back into her eyes, letting him know she appreciated his interest—or, possibly, that she was grateful for it—as she answered with a little laugh. "Most definitely. Except for the hip displacement and having legs that are too short for his body, he's a typical six-year-old. He was having it kind of rough when I first met him, and he was awfully withdrawn. But he's doing okay now."

Luke's chest expanded with the deep breath he drew. All evening Emily had wondered at how contained he seemed, at how tightly he held himself in. He'd watched Cody's every move, always staying at arm's length. Always keeping his thoughts carefully masked. Now his agitation was beginning to show.

She watched as he glanced at his watch for the second time in less than five minutes. In Cody's room she'd thought he might be getting pressed for time. The thought occurred again, but he made no move to end their conversation.

"Would you mind telling me why you would adopt a child, knowing he was born handicapped?"

Of all the questions he could have asked, that was one she hadn't expected. Not that it hadn't been asked before. She just hadn't expected it from him. That he had asked, gave her an impression she sincerely hoped was wrong. Not everyone could accept a child's disabilities.

"Because I cared about him," she said, remembering how long it had taken the little boy to respond to her. He hadn't responded to anyone, really, because the faces in his life had been constantly changing. "I used to read to the children at the county hospital, and Cody was a patient there. It took a while, but eventually he let me hold him while I read him a story. And then it got to the point where he'd cry himself to sleep unless I was there." She shrugged; it was a simple, understated movement. "He needed me."

The truth of the matter was that she'd needed Cody as much as he'd needed her. She mattered to the child. That was far more than she'd ever meant to anyone else.

Luke began to pace; his hands in his pockets, his head bent. His path took him between her and the dining area off the kitchen, where she and Cody would watch the hummingbirds at the feeder just outside the window as they ate their meals.

Following his measured strides, she wondered if Luke had ever eaten a bowl of cereal while trying to count the beats of a hummingbird's wings. It was impossible to do— both to count the blurred wing strokes and to imagine Luke Montgomery entertaining himself in such a way.

Though some of his agitation could undoubtedly be assigned to his present situation, he didn't strike her as a man
who tended to spend much time relaxing. Quite probably
he didn't know how. Even with his present concerns
weighing on him, he had that stress-driven energy that
marked those bent on success. Now that she thought about
it, she couldn't quite picture him having cold cereal for
breakfast, either. He was croissants and fresh-ground
coffee, perhaps with strawberries—but not in season. A
man who had his initials on the buttons of his dress shirts
could have his flown in from somewhere exotic.

"Doesn't it get pretty expensive?" she heard him ask.
"There must be medical bills. And you mentioned surgery."

"It can get expensive." It could bankrupt some people,
actually. But she didn't think he had to worry about that.
Not that she thought he was even thinking about money as
his glance moved over the objects in the room. She might
not have much, by his standards, but she'd be willing to bet
everything she owned that she was a lot happier with her
situation at the moment than Luke was with his.

"Are you able to manage all right?"

She frowned at his bluntness. "We do okay."

"But it's not easy."

"No. It's not always easy," she said, and sat the elephant back down on the sofa. Now seemed as good a time
as any to get the book she'd wanted to loan him.

Luke watched her reach for one of the top shelves. He
knew she thought he'd overstepped some boundaries by
asking about her finances. But there were things he had to
know. Money was something Luke took for granted. He'd
been born into it, raised with it, and he earned more than
he knew what to do with. When he wanted something, he
simply bought it. He only had to look around the room to

know that Emily didn't indulge herself in any luxuries. Money she could have spent on herself was sacrificed instead for her child. For *his* child. That knowledge hit him hard.

She turned, her hands on her hips and her expression mildly annoyed. "I could have sworn that book was here," she said to herself. "I wonder where I put it."

"It doesn't matter."

"Yes, it does. It goes into things like reasonable expectations, and how to handle disappointments and such. I think it might really help you with your son."

Reaching up again, she ran her fingers along the titles.

"Emily."

"And there's a chapter on clothing. You'll never believe how hard braces can be on pants. What you'll need to do is have his pants reinforced in the spots where the braces rub...."

"Emily."

He said her name again, wondering at the gentle sound of it as she finally stopped talking. She glanced toward him, waiting.

Now that he had her attention, he wasn't at all sure how to begin.

He pushed his fingers through his hair. "I don't have any idea how to do this."

"Do what?" she asked, and let her arm fall as she turned to face him fully.

"Before I say anything else, I just want you to know I'm sorry." He suddenly knew that everything was about to change. Everything. He was sorry about that, too. "I never thought it would go this far."

A knot formed in her stomach at the bleakness in his expression. "What would go this far? I don't..."

She fell silent when he shook his head. "Just let me say this. Okay?"

Warily Emily nodded.

"I told you that my son's mother died a few months ago. What I didn't mention was that I hadn't even known we'd had a child until then. Andrea wrote me after she found out she had cancer. She left instructions with her attorney for the letter to be delivered after her death. She wanted me to know that she'd given my son up for adoption."

He paused, looking everywhere but at the green eyes that were so intent on his face. "I had no idea she was pregnant when she broke our engagement. She knew I'd have pushed the marriage issue if she told me, so she kept quiet about it. What the letter didn't mention was that the child had...problems."

Emily hesitated. Uncertainty warred with a sickening hint of foreboding. Hadn't he told her this morning that he'd just found out his child was handicapped?

"I didn't know until I saw him yesterday. God," he muttered, rubbing at a spot on the bridge of his nose. The damned investigator hadn't even put it in his report. "I'd no idea. When I saw him sitting there in those braces, I don't even know what it was I felt. Sick, I think."

Oddly, the only anxiety Emily felt was his. Maybe because it was safer than acknowledging the very real sense of panic coiling in the pit of her stomach.

Her fingers were pressed to her mouth, and her eyes were huge over the tips of her unpolished nails. She remembered the first time she'd seen Luke, the desolation in his eyes as he'd walked away from the special ed building yesterday. That same haunted look shadowed his handsome features now, turning the tension in his body into something almost tangible. She could have ached for him, if the sense of foreboding hadn't finally taken shape.

"Cody," she whispered. "Cody is your son?"

"There is no doubt in my mind."

"No. No," she whispered, because she needed there to be doubt. She wanted him to have made some dreadful mistake by coming here. The boy in the letter wasn't her Cody. It was some other little boy he was looking for. Someone else's son. But even as she wanted him to have found the wrong child, she knew that he hadn't, that there was no mistake. There had been a disturbing familiarity all along about Luke Montgomery. Now that she knew why, the resemblance to Cody was easy to see. It was there in the stubborn set of their lean jaws, the sharp intelligence in their gray eyes, the slightly crooked way they both smiled.

Her voice sounded unsteady. "What are you going to do?"

Luke swore under his breath. He didn't want her to be frightened.

"I don't know." He hated indecision. In others it was annoying. In himself it was intolerable. "All I know for sure is that he's my responsibility. That's not something I turn my back on."

"Any responsibility for him is mine." The reminder was spoken quietly; the steel behind it not all that surprising. "I adopted him."

"I was never notified of my rights."

The last thing he wanted to do was argue or threaten. But the threat hung there, anyway. Luke's attorney had already told him what it would take to obtain custody of his son. Because Luke hadn't been notified that his child was being put up for adoption, there was precedent for having the adoption overturned.

Luke kept that to himself as he watched the little remaining color drain from Emily's face. This woman loved his son. The son Luke scarcely even knew. Never in his life had he known a woman to care as much for a child. Not his mother. Certainly not his ex-fiancé.

He stepped back, giving Emily her space. He had no idea what she would do. He knew only that he could no longer expect her compassion. He felt its loss more than he could ever have anticipated.

In her eyes now was the fear of losing the child she thought of as her own. He hated that he'd put that fear there. But he couldn't walk away from his son. Not now that he'd found him.

"You had no right to deceive me."

"I never said one word to you that wasn't the truth."

"What about what you forgot to say?"

Her chin tipped up, challenging, despite her vulnerable position.

"You can't tell me you'd have been so willing to invite me over if you'd known who I was. I needed to find out about him. How much would you have told me? How close would you have let me get?"

"You're very perceptive."

Immediately Emily regretted her sarcasm. She regretted a lot of things in those few seconds. That she'd been so quick to assume she knew what he wanted. That she'd ever invited him here. That she'd ever laid eyes on him.

She needed more distance than he'd given her. Moving to the center of the room, hugging her arms around herself, she focused on the rigid line of his jaw.

"Look. I'm sorry. You walk in here and tell me my son is your son. Then you tell me you don't have any idea what you're going to do about it. You'll have to forgive me if I don't feel like being gracious. I just don't know how I'm supposed to handle this. Okay?"

"That gives us something else in common."

His words were barely audible, muffled as they were by the clench of his jaw. But the truth in them kept her silent. They had Cody in common. *He* was who they had to think about.

Luke, it seemed, shared another trait with his son. It was a trait she fostered in the child but definitely wasn't crazy about in the man. Determination. It was etched in the weary lines of Luke's face, and audible even in his subdued voice. "I want to know what he needs."

"He doesn't need anything."

"Fine. Then tell me what you need. You said yourself his care is expensive. Do you have medical insurance?"

"I don't think that's any of your business."

"I happen to think it is. He's my son. I have the right to see that he's properly taken care of."

He hadn't meant to insult her. But he knew he had when he saw heat rise in her cheeks. Her voice turned deliberate and deceptively soft. Velvet over steel, he thought, and wondered if she had any idea how the combination challenged a man.

"I take damn good care of my son, Mr. Montgomery. He has everything he needs. We manage just fine."

"Right." He waved his hand toward the dining room table. He'd been wondering how she could afford Cody's tuition. Now he knew. "By working two jobs."

The look in her eyes wasn't quite a glare. But it was close enough to make the point.

"Emily," he said, resigned to the fact that she'd take exception to just about anything he said right now. "I have every intention of contributing to Cody's welfare. This obviously isn't the best time to discuss exactly how I'll do that. I have a plane to catch for a meeting I've already postponed twice, but I'll be in touch with you. I won't just walk away from him."

Chapter Three

The door had no sooner closed behind Luke Montgomery than Emily headed for the telephone. Her hand trembled as she snatched her address book from beside it and began looking for the name of the caseworker who had handled Cody's adoption. She had to talk to her. She had to know there was nothing Luke could do to take Cody away.

At the moment, that was Emily's only concern. Nothing else mattered. Not how Luke had found Cody. Not that he hadn't been honest with her. Not that she was shaking so hard she could barely hold the small book still enough to read. Nothing.

She kept turning pages, heard them rustling in the silence. But when she found what she was looking for, she didn't pick up the phone.

It was precisely because her son mattered so much that Emily couldn't make the call. In the moments it had taken her to find Olivia Martinez's name, she'd slowed down enough to realize that contacting the caseworker might not be such a hot idea after all.

Even if she could reach the woman at this hour, telling her about Luke might not lead to the assurances Emily was seeking. If a problem existed with the adoption's validity, she didn't want that problem called to the attention of anyone who might not be aware of it. She had no idea how these things worked, but the last thing she wanted to do was create a situation where temporary custody of Cody could be given to Luke while the matter was worked out.

Still frantic for reassurance, Emily turned back to a number she'd passed moments ago. That of Dr. Cleo Hamilton. Dr. Hamilton was Cody's orthopedist, and the closest thing to a true ally Emily had when it came to Cody and his welfare. The doctor knew all about her and Cody. But to bother Dr. Hamilton at home for a nonmedical emergency was something Emily just couldn't do.

Emily closed the book. What she needed was someone to tell her that everything would be all right. That Luke Montgomery was not a threat to her and her son. Better yet, she wanted someone to tell her that this was all a bad dream, that when she woke up in the morning she'd discover that the man didn't even exist. Dr. Hamilton couldn't tell her any of that. The physician wasn't the sort to sugarcoat reality.

The book was returned to its place next to the phone on the counter. There was no one to offer the assurances she needed. No one to lean on. The only thing for her to do right now was what she'd always done—handle the problem alone. Panicking wouldn't solve anything.

Checking on Cody did seem rather necessary, though.

So she peeked in on him and pulled his blanket to his shoulders. Then checked on him again two minutes later, just because she needed to touch his soft little face.

"I love you, precious," she whispered to the sleeping child, and made herself back away, because what she wanted to do was pick him up and rock him, and it wouldn't have been fair to wake him just to make herself feel better. Aside from that, it had been a while since Cody had liked to be rocked. He thought it too babyish. Except when he didn't feel well. That was also the only time he called her "mommy" anymore—when he was sick, or when a growth spurt was causing pain to his hips. And when he was scared.

Like all the times he'd been in the hospital.

Like all the times he would be again.

Emily didn't want to think about that now. Not that she ever wanted to think of the surgeries Cody faced. But she could only cope with so much. Between worrying about the unpredictable results of her interview yesterday and Luke Montgomery's arrival in their lives, she had all she could handle at the moment. So she left the room to pace until she simply couldn't bear the uncertainties any longer.

Her pacing brought her to the corner of the living room where her guitar stood propped against the wall by the bookcase.

For nearly a full minute she stood there, staring down at the scarred instrument, before she reached for it. The wood felt good in her hands. Warm and solid. It felt even better when she pulled the braided leather strap over her shoulder and hugged the guitar to her chest like the old friend it was. Using the guitar to escape was something she hadn't done in a very long time. She wondered if it could still make her forget.

She'd closed the door to Cody's room. Now she curled up on the sofa with her legs tucked beneath her and closed her eyes. The first chords joined the tinkle of the wind chimes. Soft, peaceful sounds, like Cody's gentle breathing. She deliberately chose a ballad, thinking the melody relaxing, for she needed such a melody to drown out the voice that kept telling her she should have known better. She should have known that no matter how hard she tried she'd never have the stability she'd always craved. Her security was threatened again. The little family made up of herself and the child—a child she couldn't have loved more had he been her own flesh and blood—seemed in danger of being torn apart.

Who would ever have thought his father would appear out of nowhere? she wondered. From the time he'd been born, Cody had lived in the limbo of being a ward of the state. His mother had given him up, and no one else had wanted him. Until Emily had come along. According to the caseworker, the mother hadn't even known who the father was.

But, apparently, the mother had known. And now, so did Emily. And anyone who could see beyond the end of her nose could see the resemblance Cody bore Luke Montgomery.

The music wasn't working.

Emily closed her eyes tighter, curling closer into the cushions and increased the tempo. She tried to concentrate on the complex fingering required to play the twelve-stringed instrument, letting the music become more driving—for driving thought from her mind was all she wanted to do.

No matter how she tried, no matter how intricate the music became, the thoughts remained.

Cody was Luke Montgomery's son.

And Luke Montgomery wasn't going to simply disappear.

He's my responsibility, he'd said. *I won't just walk away.*

Her palm flattened on the strings. "He's mine," she whispered into the suddenly silent room. "Mine."

"Mommy?"

Emily's head came up at the sound of her name. Setting the guitar aside, she scrambled for the bedroom door just as she heard Cody call her again.

The light from the hallway fell across his bed. He was on his elbow, unable to sit because of the night brace that kept his legs apart while he slept. Brushing his hair back from his sleep-warmed forehead, Emily sat down beside him.

"What's the matter, honey?"

"The guitar woke me up."

He sounded accusing, irritable, as he tended to be when wakened from a sound sleep. But he reached for her anyway.

She gathered him close, loving the sweet soapy-clean scent of him and the feel of his small arms, so much stronger than the smaller limbs he tried to push himself closer with. She hugged him tighter.

Dear God, she thought, burying her face in his soft downy hair. What was she going to do?

The panic increased with her next thought.

What was *Luke* going to do?

He didn't make her wait long to find out. That he didn't keep her in suspense for long would have seemed commendable, she supposed, were she inclined to think of Luke with any generosity. But as she stood in the workroom of the library the next morning, staring at a stack of interlibrary requests, she was thinking of him only as the threat he was. It was hard to be charitable on only three hours of sleep.

The telephone rang. Sue Shroeder, one of the library's volunteers, answered it. "Line two, Emily," she said, then picked up the bundles Emily had already put together and hustled out to catch the van driver before he left.

With a nod that did little more than acknowledge the disappearance of the woman's head around the edge of the door, Emily picked up the extension on the cluttered worktable. In the process, she knocked over a mason jar holding pencils, two of which rolled onto the floor and under a chair. If she hadn't been so preoccupied, she'd have noticed the darn jar and moved it.

She was reaching for the pencils, receiver pressed to her ear, when the voice on the other end of the line made her slowly straighten up.

There was no preamble. "Emily. It's Luke. I've got to get back to my meeting in a minute. Is Thursday night good for you?"

"Good for me for what?"

"For dinner. I want to talk to you about setting up some sort of visitation schedule."

Emily's chest suddenly felt tight, her heartbeat seeming to clog her throat. "Visitation schedule?"

"You know. So I can come see Cody on a regular basis. I think that would be better than my stopping by unannounced. Don't you?"

She certainly did. But she also refused to be railroaded. "I don't mean to be rude, but I don't even know you. I can't agree to anything like that until I get some questions answered."

"All the more reason for us to get together."

She didn't know what to say—except that he was right. For some reason she didn't care to name, she didn't want him to be right. She also didn't want him to sound so reasonable. It gave him an edge she could easily have resented, had she not been so grateful for it.

If it killed her, she would sound reasonable, too. "I'll have to see if I can get a sitter. I don't leave Cody very often."

She thought she heard him swear under his breath. But it sounded as if he'd moved the mouthpiece down to his chest. From somewhere near him, Emily heard a male voice inquire how long he'd be, and Luke's reply for him to get the others together and he'd be right there.

"I'd appreciate it if you would see what you could do," he said when he came back to her. "I'll have my secretary call you to make the arrangements. How late do you work?"

"Until four."

"Fine. I'll see that she reaches you before then. See you Thursday," he concluded, and was off the telephone almost as abruptly as he'd come on.

The sound of the dial tone competed with the thud of her heart. Emily replaced the receiver. Taking a deep breath, barely aware of the smell of book glue always present in the room, she set the pencils she'd retrieved back into the jar. She hoped to heaven that she'd done the right thing.

Dinner sounded safe, after all. A civil meeting. Neutral territory. Public place. And the more she thought about it, the more she realized how necessary it was to accept his invitation.

It was not necessary however, to accept the offer of a car he wanted to send for her when his secretary called later that afternoon. That was why she told the efficient-sounding woman she'd simply meet Mr. Montgomery at the restaurant he'd chosen, asking her to thank him any-

way. Then she stopped by Bartell's Insurance Agency to
drop off their typing on her way to pick up Cody and asked
Jan Bartell if Cody could play with Billy for a while
Thursday evening.

Emily had met Jan at the Children's Clinic a year ago.
Billy's respiration therapy and Cody's physical therapy had
been scheduled on the same days, and Jan had come rush-
ing in late for an appointment because the agency's secretary had quit and she and her husband were trying to keep
the office running all by themselves.

"You wouldn't know anyone who could do some typing, would you?" had been the harried question that had
led to both a part-time job and a friendship based on their
children. Jan actually intimidated Emily a little; mostly
because she was a whirlwind of efficiency and so good at
everything. But since the boys had started attending the
same school, and Cody had become Billy's best friend, she
was also good to Cody. The clincher was that Emily really
didn't know who else to leave him with.

"No problem" was Jan's offhand comment as she
gratefully accepted the work Emily had done. The one
thing Jan couldn't do well was type. "I'll warn you,
though. I've still got my sister's little boy staying with us.
If Cody comes home with a couple of phrases you've never
heard before, that'll be where he got them."

The embellishment of Cody's vocabulary was a concern, but learning a socially-unacceptable word from a
nine-year-old troubled by his parents' divorce was pretty
far down the list of Emily's worries two nights later. As she
stared into her closet trying to come up with something
appropriate to wear, she was thinking only that she'd come
to resent Cody's father a lot in a remarkably short period
of time.

She pulled a simple short-sleeved black sheath off a hanger. She wore black well. Another reason for the selection was that she'd read somewhere that black was a power color.

A person shouldn't necessarily believe what she reads. Emily didn't feel at all powerful. She felt like mush inside when she stepped into the quiet restaurant at five minutes after seven for the seven o'clock reservation. The five-minute delay had come from driving around the block twice while talking herself out of going back home.

Feeling like Daniel being led to the lion's den, she followed the waiter past tables set with silver and crystal and stands bearing enormous bouquets of exotic flowers. Wood paneling polished as smooth as satin reflected the light of the brass chandeliers. The nap of maroon carpet scattered with a design of vines and pink cabbage roses padded her footsteps. Emily scarcely noticed the refined atmosphere, let alone took time to appreciate it.

She didn't notice diners turning their heads as she passed, either. But Luke did. He noticed both Emily and the people watching her and wondered again why a woman as lovely as she would take on the burden of his son. He needed to know more about her. And not only because she had his child. He hadn't been able to get her off his mind.

Luke's glance narrowed as she approached, analytical, appreciative. He liked the way she looked. The simple dress she wore accentuated her slenderness, its knee-skimming length perfect for her long, coltish legs. She was a striking woman, and with her rich auburn curls combed back from her face she appeared rather elegant. But what Luke remembered as he stood when she reached the table was the sensual, earthy appeal she'd held for him when she'd appeared in her doorway, drying her hands on a dish towel, with a loose, gauzy dress flowing around her incredible legs.

A chameleon, he thought, and wondered if she was indeed everything she appeared to be. He'd long ago discovered that few people were.

Luke greeted her with a nod, but she kept her lashes lowered until she'd been seated. A vaguely haunted look shadowed her eyes when she finally glanced across the table. With the uncomfortable feeling that he might be responsible for robbing them of their spark, he propped his elbows on the table and looked at her over his clasped hands.

"How do we do this?" he asked.

"Do what?"

"Begin." His smile was strained. "Under other circumstances, I'd tell you how lovely you look. If I said that now, you'd probably think I was trying to make points, or remind me that this is hardly a date. On the other hand, for me to simply ask you how you are would put you in the position of having to lie, were you to be polite and say 'fine.' I think I can guess how you are, anyway. It doesn't look like you've slept much better than I have the past few nights. No offense," he added, "but I don't remember those shadows under your eyes from the last time I saw you. And now that I think about it, I do remember your eyes." He'd be absolutely honest with her. No hedging. No bull. "So, would you settle for 'I'm glad you came, Emily'? I was afraid you might not show up."

Emily had thought she was prepared for anything. She was wrong. He remembered her eyes? "I had to come." For Cody's sake. Cody was all that mattered.

Luke seemed to sympathize with her. "You said you had some questions." He spread his hands. "Do you want to start now?"

There was something about him. An openness she hadn't expected, an openness that could too easily disarm her if she trusted it. She couldn't let that happen. Not with the stakes as high as they were.

He wanted to know if she wished to start. Wondering how to begin, she glanced up just as a waiter appeared to see if she wanted something to drink. Luke had already ordered. An untouched cocktail sat beside his water goblet.

She asked for a glass of wine, and when the waiter departed she reached for the menu he'd left on the corner of the table. She wasn't the least bit interested in the offerings penned between the heavy blue brocade covers. She only wanted something to hug to relieve the knot in her stomach.

"Would you mind telling me how you found us?" she quietly asked.

He didn't even hesitate. "I hired an investigator."

"How did he find us?"

Ice cubes tinkled as Luke somberly toyed with his drink. "I didn't ask him. His instructions were to find my son. How he did that was his concern." Luke didn't like the way he'd made himself sound. But he'd known from the beginning that the matter of finding his son couldn't be resolved without bending rules. "From the information he gave me," Luke added, because it hadn't been too hard to figure out the investigator's methods from his report, "it appears that his initial source were court records."

"Of the adoption?"

His eyes remained on his glass.

Emily felt herself lean forward. Her voice fell to just above a whisper. "Those records are supposed to be sealed!"

He couldn't fault her indignation. He'd have been angry, too, if he'd discovered that his personal life had been rifled as hers had. And she didn't know the half of it yet.

"I imagine they still are." He met her eyes, his gaze direct. "The files in the office of Andrea's attorney weren't though. Once the investigator got your name from one of the secretaries, finding you was a piece of cake. Even if your address hadn't been in the file, he could have traced you through the motor vehicles department or the tax rolls or a half-dozen other ways. It's not hard to find someone who isn't trying to hide."

"And my job?" She didn't want to know this. She felt very sure of that as her fingers tightened around the thickly padded menu. "How did he find out where I worked? Was that in the file, too?"

"I don't know if it was or not. I gather he found that out the same way he learned where Cody went to school. He just followed you. You seem to have a very predictable schedule."

The thought of having been followed almost made her ill. "What other information did your investigator give you?"

"The name of your ex-husband, and the date your divorce decree was entered."

"That's it?"

"Pretty much. He wasn't terribly thorough."

Emily had to agree. It seemed there were a few pieces of her past that he hadn't uncovered. Pieces that mattered only to her and wouldn't have done Luke any good even if he had discovered them. It would almost have relieved her to know she had retained some modicum of privacy—if she had been able to feel anything like relief.

There had been a vaguely familiar feel to the knot in her midsection. Now she knew why. It was the same feeling she'd had when her parents had been fighting each other for custody over her—not because they'd wanted her, but because each had thought the other did. It was the same feeling that had been there when she'd figured out why Jimmy had married her, when he'd let her be picked up for the car he had stolen, and when his parents had made him divorce her. It had been a long time since she'd felt so completely powerless over the events in her life.

With great care, Emily set the menu on the white damask. Its gold tassle dangled over the edge of the table. She now knew why Luke was so willing to answer her questions. He knew there was nothing she could do about the answers. "I don't think I'm very hungry."

Luke swore under his breath. The woman looked as pale as the *crème brûlée* being served at the next table. "Please, Emily. I just did what I had to do."

"I don't doubt that, Mr. Montgomery."

From Luke's point of view, the waiter's timing stank. Emily, however, regarded the arrival of her wine as a most welcome interruption, though she scarcely heard the recitation of the chef's special selections for the evening and had to be asked twice if she cared to order.

More to avoid making a scene by not ordering than because she wanted it, Emily chose the last item he mentioned, since it was all she could remember hearing. Luke did the same, and the faint edge in his tone had the waiter departing a little more quickly than he might have had the air not been so chilly around that particular table. Emily rather wished the waiter could have hung around a little longer. The silence he left behind was filled by the strains of baroque music filtering through quiet conversations and a tension thick enough to choke on.

A good thirty seconds passed before Luke spoke. When he did, his voice was low, and his words were deliberate. "You won't keep me from my son."

Gray eyes locked with green. His were cool and unyielding. Hers revealed more desperation than she wanted him to see. Still, her tone was just as certain as his.

"You won't take him from me."

Refusing to release his visual hold, Luke leaned back. "Now that we have that out of the way, do you want to discuss what we *are* going to do?"

The size of the knot in her stomach had doubled. The energy in her voice had all but died. She didn't see that she had much choice.

Desperately wanting this evening to be over, she coached herself to take it one step at a time. The way she and Cody did his exercises. "I'm at a disadvantage here, Mr. Montgomery."

"Luke."

"Luke," she conceded. "You know far more about me than I know about you."

"I'm decent people, if that's what you're concerned about. Decent enough to want to do what's right where Cody is concerned, anyway. Isn't that what you want for him, too?"

He knew exactly which buttons to push. She held his glance, refusing to let him know that. "Are you married?"

Her bluntness was a little unnerving. "No," he said, thanking whatever saint guarded over that sort of thing that he didn't also have to deal with a wife right now. "The closest I ever got was to Andrea. She called it off when she decided I was already married to my work. I guess I was late for one too many dinner parties."

"Were you? Married to your work, I mean?"

If Luke was to be perfectly honest with himself, Andrea had been right. He'd been married to his work then. He still was. His work was what he loved. What excited him. What motivated him. He was rather surprised at how easily he opened that private part of himself to the woman watching him so warily across the table, but he felt he owed her nothing less under the circumstances. He could appreciate that she would want to know about him. After all, she cared about what influenced Cody. Had she not been skeptical about him, Luke might have been more concerned about her.

He just wished he could get past her wariness now. As the conversation settled down and he told her about his projects in Seattle and Dallas and San Diego, he noticed that her wariness wasn't in her expression so much as it was in the way she worried a crease in the tablecloth into one big wrinkle, then rearranged her salad without taking a single bite before the waiter took it away.

She wasn't enjoying dinner any more than he was.

She also wasn't paying any attention to what she was doing. She'd buttered his croissant.

Picking up her wine, he moved it closer to her. "If you're not going to eat, at least drink your wine. It might help you relax."

Emily glanced at the beautiful meal she'd scarcely noticed the waiter setting before her. "I'm sorry, Luke." She took the napkin from her lap and placed it by her plate. "I can't relax until I know what you're going to do about Cody."

Luke leaned forward, his hand coming down on top of hers on the napkin. There wasn't a trace of an expression on his face. Not a hint of any emotion in his eyes. Just a deep, dark intensity that was as alarming as the warmth of his palm seeping into the back of her hand.

"Emily," he said, in a voice as dark and smooth as aged whiskey, "I promise you, I'm not going to do anything about Cody without talking to you first. Okay?"

He was close enough for her to see that he really wanted her to believe him. At the moment, she almost did. But situations changed. Promises could be broken. No one knew that better than Emily. "How do I know that? I don't know you," she said. "I can't trust you."

His eyes narrowed. "Do you trust anybody?"

"Let's just say that, for the most part, I believe people tend to be loyal only to themselves."

The quality of his speculation seemed to undergo a subtle change, almost as if she puzzled him somehow. But it wasn't puzzlement she noticed in his glance as it moved from her mouth to where her heart pounded between her breasts. Deliberately, he raised his eyes back to hers, and the intensity in their smoky depths tugged at something deep inside her.

Unnerved, she pulled her hand from beneath his, surprised to find that he'd held her there with only his touch. He'd exerted no pressure at all.

"It seems you and I have more in common all the time," came his quiet observation.

Emily saw him reach for his drink. A moment later, he shoved it aside, his expression resigned.

"Come on." He rose from the table. From inside his suit jacket, he removed a small leather folder. Tossing several bills onto the table, he reached for her elbow to guide her from her seat. "Neither one of us is hungry. Let's go for a walk."

She wouldn't have thought she would be relieved to be alone with him, but away from the other diners and the watchful eyes of the waiter, some of the awful tension actually seemed to dissipate. Not that she was truly alone with Luke as they stepped out into the dark and balmy evening. The plaza where the restaurant was located was filled with shops and fountains and little sitting areas with trees and benches. There were others strolling about, but it wasn't crowded, and it seemed easier somehow to talk to Luke when she wasn't facing him.

"Thank you," she said to him as they made their way past the orange trees threaded with twinkling lights in the center of the promenade. "I think I was about ready to climb the walls in there."

"I could tell."

She almost smiled.

So did he.

That made talking easier still.

"Have you told anyone about Cody?" It was a question she'd been wanting to ask all evening. "Your family or friends?"

Luke's hands were in his pockets, and his attention was on the patterns pressed into the walkway. "My family, at this point, is only my mother and some aunts and uncles back in Connecticut. No. I haven't told them. Or any friends, either." Only Jeff knew. "I couldn't see any point in it."

"Until you figure out what you're going to do," she added for him.

"Something like that."

An elaborate display of chocolates beckoned from a window they passed. Emily, who adored the stuff, didn't even notice. "Is your family pretty straitlaced? I mean, would you get ostracized for things like divorce or flunking out of school or having babies out of wedlock?"

"Hardly. My father ran around on my mother for years. Having a child out of wedlock might raise an eyebrow, but it wouldn't be a problem."

That left only two other possible reasons for his not wanting anyone to know. Either he didn't want to claim responsibility, which Emily knew was not the case, or he hadn't accepted Cody himself. "You don't want them to know he has a disability, do you?"

There was really no question behind her words. No accusation, either. For that Luke was grateful.

"I just think the fewer people who know right now, the better it will be for everyone."

Translation, she thought, watching the muscle in his jaw work, you're having trouble coming to grips with the fact that your child will never be "normal," so how can you admit it to anyone else?

If he would only say that he was having difficulty accepting Cody's limitations, she could tell him that she sometimes had problems with the idea herself. And she'd chosen the situation. She didn't mention that, though, because he said nothing else about Cody. He just asked where she'd parked her car. The question seeming to stall the conversation again. So she didn't tell him, either, that he was probably right in not telling his family until he was better prepared. He might not have any problems with them at all. Lots of people lovingly accept their disabled grandchildren. But there were plenty who had real trouble with the idea. Her own mother had been one of them.

"You've totally ruined your chances of finding a decent husband, you know," she'd pointed out, but since Emily ignored everything else her mother said, she'd ignored that, too. Since her mother had moved to Orlando, she never saw her anyway. And she hadn't seen her father since she'd turned eighteen and the custody situation was no longer an issue.

"I'd like to see him this weekend," she heard Luke say. "Will that be a problem for you?"

"This weekend?"

She didn't know why it took her so long to say it would be all right. After all, she'd already drawn the only conclusion her basic sense of fairness could allow. She couldn't risk alienating the man. If she did, and he decided he wanted Cody with him, she might jeopardize her chances of ever seeing her son again. That decision wasn't based so much on what she would do, however, as on what she couldn't do. She couldn't afford a legal battle, either, though she knew she'd sell everything short of her soul to meet him in that fight. A fight that would probably be doomed from the beginning, because she could barely afford to hire an attorney, and he probably had a whole firm on retainer. She knew from witnessing her parents' long and bitter divorce that justice was not only blind, it could also be deaf and dumb.

But the most important consideration was Cody himself. Legalities aside, Cody had the right to know his father. And his father had the right to know him. She was the only one who stood to lose. She'd already been deprived of her peace of mind.

Chapter Four

"That's two in a row, man. What's the matter with you?"

Jeff Eller grinned as he palmed the ball and headed for the service box. He loved it when Luke's handball game was off. It was the only time he could beat him.

"Quit gloating and serve, Eller." Luke was breathing hard as he picked himself up from the gleaming hardwood floor. "The game's not over yet."

Determined to get his timing on track, Luke moved into position. The fact that he was off irritated him. It also made him that much more determined to get control of his game. Not because he needed to beat the stocky, balding and bearded attorney lofting the ball for a serve. He didn't care who won. He only cared that he wasn't doing his best.

The ball whizzed past, hitting low on the back wall of the closed court. Luke dived sideways, hard muscles straining, as the blue rubber ball ricocheted toward him.

The ball connected with the padded palm of his out-stretched glove with a solid *thwack,* and he sent it careening off two walls before Jeff got it. A split second later, Luke cut him off to drop down for a kill shot.

Another point, this one Luke's. The next was Luke's, too, as, shoes squeaking, the thud of the ball echoing off walls, ceiling and floor, he brought the score nearly even.

His son would never be able to do this.

The shot sailed past his head. He hadn't even reached for it.

Determined to concentrate, he sprinted forward, nailing Jeff's serve. He wondered if Cody would ever be able to walk.

He'll never be without braces, Emily had said.

Luke completely missed an easy lob.

The game was Jeff's.

For Luke, it would have been a shallow victory to win over an opponent who hadn't given the game his all. For Jeff, winning was all that mattered. The attitude endeared him to few, but it made him a very successful attorney.

Grinning, he threw Luke a towel. "It was probably your jet lag that gave me the edge, but I prefer to think my game has improved. You want to take on Collins and Jaffe next week? They're at the top of the board right now. Might be kind of interesting. Just a friendly game," he went on, wiping the sweat from his face. "With a friendly little bet. I can reserve the glass court."

It was just the kind of thing Jeff lived for. Four competitive people going for the jugular in front of other members of the exclusive club. Even in college, where Luke and Jeff had both played football, the then prelaw student had been predisposed to grandiose displays of competition.

Luke, however, lacked his longtime associate's thirst for blood.

When Luke said he'd pass on the match, Jeff, true to form, proceeded to pester him about it all the way to the locker room. He wanted to know why Luke wouldn't play—why, when he was as good as he was, he didn't want to show off his stuff. "Come on, buddy. Between the two of us, we could beat their socks off."

Luke wasn't interested in beating anybody's socks off. "I've told you before, I'm not into competition."

"I don't know why not." Exasperated with trying to get Luke to agree, Jeff jerked open his locker door. "You're the most competitive person I know."

Luke said nothing. It was true, after all. Compared to Luke, Jeff looked like a wallflower when it came to competition. But Luke's competitive streak didn't involve anyone but himself. Every effort he made was an attempt to top his own last accomplishment, to beat his best time, his best distance, his best game. When it came to his work, each project had to be that much more innovative, that much larger, than the last.

Jeff's tenacity was showing. "We could schedule it toward the end of the week."

"I won't be around this week."

"The weekend, then. It'll be harder to get a court, but there's bound to be a cancellation...."

"I won't be back this weekend." Luke draped a towel around his neck and grabbed another towel off the stack at the end of the bench. "I'm going to Arizona."

That finally punched a hole in Jeff's balloon. Disapproval replaced exasperation as he snatched up a towel of his own. "You're still looking for the kid?"

"I found him."

Luke started for the showers.

Jeff was right on his tail. "What have you done, Montgomery? Have you talked to anybody? The kid? That Russell woman? Tell me you didn't tell her that the kid's yours. You didn't, did you?"

Luke turned on his heel.

Nearly slamming into him, Jeff swore. Then, catching the warning in Luke's stony expression, he went dead silent.

Deference to the other men in the facility kept Luke's voice low, but there was no mistaking his displeasure. "The kid's name is Cody. And, yes, I told her he's mine."

Jeff was not to be deterred. He was right behind Luke again. "I've warned you, Luke. She's going to start thinking about all the 'sacrifices' she's made raising your child. I'll bet you two to one she's going to want everything you've got."

"I don't think she's like that."

"They're *all* like that."

Luke was accustomed to his friend's cynicism. In many respects, he probably even shared his views. But something about Emily had crept past his harder edges. "You have too many ex-wives, Jeff," Luke muttered, and headed for the showers.

Luke didn't hold Jeff's opinions against him. Still, he wasn't sure he appreciated the doubts the man kept planting in his mind. They were doubts that probably *should* be there, since he really didn't know the woman, but for some reason, Luke just couldn't take them too seriously. The lady he'd met for dinner just didn't seem the type to manipulate or take advantage.

He remembered how restrained she'd been, and how protective of Cody. He remembered, too, her tentative acceptance of the situation after they'd finally gotten past the positioning and the power plays and more or less established that it would be easier working together than against one another. There was nothing simple about having a total stranger crash your life. He appreciated that. But what he appreciated more was that she was willing to give him a chance, when she could easily have made seeing Cody difficult. She hadn't had to be so accommodating. She could have made him go to court to establish the right.

He wasn't considering any of that when he pulled up in front of her house Saturday morning. He was thinking only that he was in no way prepared for whatever might happen in the next few hours. When Emily had asked what he had in mind to do when he visited Cody, Luke had told her he'd leave the choice of activity up to her. There had been no question as to whether or not she would accompany him and Cody. Luke wouldn't have known what to do with the child alone. And she hadn't had to say so for him to know that she didn't want the boy out of her sight.

He climbed out of his rental car, relieved to stretch the kinks remaining from his early-morning flight. Having no idea how much time Emily had allotted him, he had already checked into a hotel on his way in from the airport. All Emily had said about the day was that they'd be going to a very special park.

From down the street came the sound of a lawn mower, and the pungent scent of freshly cut grass drifted on the gentle breeze. Next door, a woman holding a baby on her hip smiled at him as she picked up a newspaper from under a shrub. But Luke was most aware of Emily.

As with the first time he'd come here, he was struck again by the sight of her standing at the door holding the screen door open for him.

She wore shorts. Some sort of washed-out denim things with pink patches that matched her T-shirt and the pink socks she'd rolled down to her tennis shoes. What he noticed most, though, was her smile. That first time, it had been warm, welcoming. Now, it was guarded and wary.

The breeze caused the ceramic birds of the wind chimes to knock into each other, filling the citrus-scented air with their gentle tinkling. "Cody's almost ready. He slept in this morning, so he's moving a little slower than usual." The screen door groaned as she pushed it wider. "Come on in. I'll go see how he's coming along."

"Could that wait a minute?"

He touched her shoulder to stop her when she stepped inside. Beneath his hand, he felt the smooth play of muscle as she stiffened. When she backed up so that his hand would fall away, she looked distinctly uncomfortable.

She had to know he wasn't comfortable with this, either. "Did you tell him who I am?"

Emily shook her head, auburn curls swaying gently against her cheeks. "I thought we'd see how today went."

Luke didn't know if he was relieved or disappointed. He did know he should stop staring. Now that he was closer, he could see that her hair was still damp, her skin free of makeup. She smelled of soap and powder, as if she'd just come from the shower, and he couldn't help the faint tightening in his midsection at the thought of how soft her skin might be.

He saw her glance back out the open door toward his car, a black Jaguar similar to the one he'd rented before. "That thing have a trunk?"

"It does. Why?"

"Cody's wheelchair has to fit in there. And there's a basket on the counter in the kitchen. That goes, too."

He assumed she wanted him to get the basket, since she then turned to go to Cody's room. Luke, grateful for something to do, headed into the kitchen. He wasn't ready

to see his son yet. He had no idea why. The boy was only
one-sixth of Luke's age and less than half his height, yet he
intimidated Luke as if he were twice his size. Maybe it was
because the feelings Cody evoked weren't particularly
pleasant. Luke had always thought that a child would
make a guy feel proud. What Luke felt most was guilt.

She'd packed a picnic. Cold chicken, potato salad and
brownies, from what Luke could determine of the containers covered by a blue-and-white-checked tablecloth.

"You didn't have to bring lunch," he said from the
archway between the living room and the short hall. "I'd
planned on taking you both out."

A striped T-shirt dangled from her hand as Emily poked
her head around Cody's bedroom door. "It's not necessary for you to feed us. There's a blanket on the arm of the
sofa," she added as her head disappeared again. "It goes,
too."

Luke frowned toward the doorway. He hadn't been sure
what to expect of today, but as he loaded the basket and
blanket into the car and headed back inside, he had the
strange feeling Emily already knew exactly what he was
going to get.

One thing he didn't get was a greeting from Cody when
Emily called him into the boy's bedroom to ask if he'd get
the thermos from the kitchen, too. The little boy sat in his
chair while Emily, kneeling in front of him, pulled his shirt
over his head. He didn't smile at Luke when his head
popped through the collar. He didn't say a word. He did
nothing but fix his big gray eyes on Luke as Emily tucked
his shirt into his shorts, smoothed his hair and wheeled him
out. Cody didn't look happy.

He didn't look any happier three minutes later, when
Emily insisted on pushing him out to the car herself. Em-

ily usually encouraged Cody to do as much as possible for himself. But moods were mercurial.

Wanting to help when he saw that she was about to put Cody into the back seat, Luke offered to lift the boy for her.

"I'd better do it," she muttered, then grimaced when one of the metal joints of Cody's braces knocked against her leg as she picked him up. A moment later, she had him in the seat and buckled up.

Relegated to the rear, Luke folded the wheelchair—after Emily showed him how—and loaded it in the trunk. He couldn't remember the last time he'd been on a picnic. He wasn't even sure this one was a good idea, given Cody's enthusiasm level. But Emily told Luke that Cody loved picnics. If he did, Luke sure hated to think how the kid acted when he had to go to the dentist. Something definitely wasn't right. When he'd met him before, Cody had seemed more shy than unfriendly. But he definitely wasn't having a good time now.

It was easy enough for Luke to see that his mother wasn't very pleased with his behavior, either. Emily's lovely features were drawn, and her smile, guarded as it had been, completely missing. He wished she'd smile again. Just give him a glimpse of the smile he'd found so healing when she'd first offered to help him out—back when she'd thought he was just a guy with a son like her own.

With an inward sigh, Luke asked which direction they were headed and pulled away from the house. He knew full well that it wasn't only her son's attitude that had her so tense. His own presence was why her hands were knotted so tightly in her lap as she stared out the side window. He could count the time she'd made eye contact with him in milliseconds.

At least Cody would look at him. The kid was practically staring holes in the back of his head from the backseat. "Have you finished building the house for your dinosaurs?" Luke asked, thinking to draw the boy out, since Emily was being so quiet.

About three phone poles later, Cody mumbled, "No."

A question requiring more than a simple answer seemed to be in order. Luke, therefore, asked Cody to tell him what he was doing in school. The response this time was nothing more than the protrusion of his lower lip. Even Emily's disapproving glance failed to gain a more favorable expression. So Luke, not having a clue as to the nature of the kid's problem, gave up and decided to ask Emily about the weather. The report—sunny and in the seventies, typical for February in Phoenix—lasted as long as it took for Luke to catch a glimpse of Cody in the rearview mirror, looking more sad than sullen. The kid's eyes were as big as saucers, and the lower lip that had looked almost belligerent a moment ago now seemed to be trembling.

He wanted to ask Emily what was going on. He didn't want to discuss the boy in front of him, though. He'd hated it when his father had done that to him—spoken about him as if he weren't even there. Yet, even if Luke were to ask, he didn't know if Emily would tell him. The scenery out the side window seemed to hold an inordinate amount of interest for her. Not knowing what else to do, Luke swore under his breath and turned on the radio to fill the silence.

She wasn't supposed to hear the muttered oath. She didn't, actually. What Emily caught was the motion of his lips and the hardening of his jaw, but she'd caught the gist of what he'd muttered. And why. As she tucked her arms around her middle, she felt grateful that at least Cody hadn't heard it. Swearing was the last thing she wanted him picking up from his father. Billy's cousin gave her enough to worry about on that score.

They hadn't been together twenty minutes, and already Emily was wishing the weekend was over. For her sake. For Cody's. Even for Luke's, she supposed, except it was his fault they were all so uncomfortable.

From the minute he'd awakened this morning, Cody had done everything he could to delay getting ready. Every time she tried to hurry him, he'd slowed down that much more, dawdling over breakfast, playing in the sink instead of washing, watching television instead of getting dressed. Finally, he'd come right out and said he didn't want to go—which threw her completely, since the Telephone Pioneers of America Park was one of his favorite places. He wouldn't tell her exactly why he didn't want to go, either. Yet the moment she'd seen him staring at Luke, she'd known it had something to do with him. Her attempt to talk to Cody about it while Luke loaded the car had netted her nothing. Cody had simply clammed up and given her a decidedly accusing glare.

She hoped to heaven she was doing the right thing.

"Take a right at the next light," she said. "The park's down a few blocks on the left."

She looked toward Luke then. Not at his expression, for she had the feeling it would be far from welcoming. What had her attention was the play of muscle on his thigh when he shifted gears, and how the brown hair on his strong forearms picked up glints of gold from the sun. She'd thought him attractive in a very sophisticated way before. In a suit he exuded power, authority, and a refined sort of sexiness that was alarmingly appealing to her. Wearing worn jeans that delineated his well-muscled legs and a knit shirt that exposed the breadth of his chest, he was attractive in an entirely different way. One that was raw, faintly uncivilized and very... physical.

Dear heaven, she thought, she had no business noticing such things. Not about him. All he wanted from her was access to his son.

His thigh flexed again as he stepped on the brake. Forcing her glance up, her heart bumped in her throat. He was watching her. From the faint glint in his eyes, he knew she'd been studying him.

The light had turned red.

Hoping to heaven than she hadn't done the same, Emily immediately turned to check the prices on the pumps at the gas station on the corner. "Unleaded is up again," she said. "How much is it in Denver?"

"I'm afraid I haven't noticed. How much farther?"

The park was less than six blocks away. For that, Emily was truly grateful. Once they got there, the business of parking and unloading the car finally gave them all something to do other than wish they were somewhere else. For about two minutes, too, she thought Cody's attitude might have straightened out.

When there was a lot to carry, Emily usually had Cody hold things for her while she pushed him. Thinking he could carry the small picnic basket and blanket, she set them in his lap, then stepped back to let Luke push while she grabbed the thermos.

Cody didn't want Luke to push him, though.

Finally, he deigned to speak. "I'll do it myself," he announced. Elbows pointed skyward, he pulled away from Luke by giving the silver push rings on his wheels a hard shove.

Luke let him go. Not taking so much as a single step, he shoved his hands in his pockets and watched Cody head toward the entrance leading into the park.

At a loss, Emily went after Cody herself, stopping him to grab back the blanket and basket. Crouched low, she frowned at his disgruntled expression. He frowned right back.

"What's the matter with you, Cody? You know you can't push and carry all this. Let Luke push you."

"I don't want him to."

Luke had followed. "It's okay," he cut in.

"No, it's not. He's being rude."

Luke felt bad. Cody looked absolutely lost in that chair, his big gray eyes filling with tears. He hadn't meant to upset him. And he didn't want Emily getting upset with him, either.

Not knowing what else to do, he took the basket from the woman scowling up at him. "I'm going to put this on one of those tables over there. You two come over whenever you're ready."

"We're ready now. Aren't we, Cody?"

Cody didn't look as if he wanted to be. "I'll push myself."

"Fine."

"Can I go to the sandbox?"

That was fine with Emily, too. It was Luke who had the misgivings as the boy pushed away.

"Should he go alone?" There were an awful lot of bigger kids crawling around the various pieces of equipment. Kids big enough to knock over a little boy in a wheelchair. "I mean, does he need help getting into the sandbox or anything?"

"The kids don't get into this one." She pointed to where Cody was headed, missing the concern in his voice. "See how high it is? They just pull their chairs up to it and dig in. Cody builds castles. Or tries to build them, anyway.

The sand is really dry, and his pile always collapses when he goes to put holes in it for windows.''

A smile, oddly sad, touched her mouth. "At least he has the ability to do what he does. A lot of children who come here can't build anything at all. The best they can do is let the sand run through their fingers. But that's good, too," she added, brightening. "Tactile sensations are really important to a lot of these kids.''

At first, Luke wasn't sure what she meant by "these kids.'' But it didn't take long for him to figure it out. The Telephone Pioneers of America Park was unlike any he'd ever seen. At first glance, it was simply an ordinary park, with children of all ages playing in it. There was a baseball game going on in one of the two diamonds, two racquetball courts were in use, and a couple of teenage boys were going hard at a game of one-on-one at the basketball court. Everywhere Luke looked, there were children climbing over or on or through colorful playground equipment. Squeals of delight and, sometimes, annoyance filled the warm spring air.

Then he noticed the difference—the number of children in wheelchairs. Two were being pushed up a ramp to a specially designed slide. Another was alternating laughter with frustration as she and a friend played tic-tac-toe with huge spinnable blocks. Swings, exercise equipment, play areas—everything in the park had been built and laid out with the special children in mind.

They staked out a picnic table. With Cody occupied at the sandbox, Emily sat down on the bench, her eyes on Cody but every other sense tuned to the man sitting down beside her. He had questions about Cody, she was sure. And she'd give him nothing but straightforward answers. Like Dr. Hamilton, Emily didn't believe in sugarcoating reality.

The question he asked, however, had nothing to do with Cody or any of the other children. When she looked over at him, he was studying her legs.

They were stretched out in front of her, her ankles crossed. From the frown creasing his brow, he apparently didn't like what he saw.

She started to straighten. His touch stopped her.

"What did you do to yourself?" With his index finger he slowly traced a small red bruise at the top of her knee. Another bruise—older, judging from its greenish cast— marred the top of her thigh.

There was a bruise on her other leg, too. But it was only the one his fingertips brushed that she paid any attention to. The feel of his fingers left behind far more heat than such a gentle touch should have created.

"They're from Cody. His braces bang into my legs sometimes when I pick him up."

"Isn't he a little heavy for you to be handling?"

"It doesn't matter if he is or not. There are some things he can't manage alone."

"Like what?" Luke wanted to know. He watched her swallow as he pulled his hand away. She hadn't moved away from him, as she had when he'd laid his hand on her shoulder before. That mattered to him, but he was too distracted to wonder why as she met his eyes.

Almost immediately, her glance shied away and her focus turned toward the sandbox. The movement of her head caught the sun in her hair. Her thick auburn curls looked as silky as her skin had felt. Would they be that soft? he wondered, then tried to imagine what they would feel like in his hands if he were to run his fingers through them to cup the back of her skull.

He wondered, too, if she ever missed not having a man around, a husband or a lover to share with, to help.

Disturbed by the divergent and dangerous paths his thoughts wanted to take, he glanced back at the sandbox himself. He needed to know everything he could about his son, and his thoughts were best kept trained in that direction. Fortunately, this woman whose inherent gentleness was betrayed by the softness of her voice seemed to understand that. She told him how Cody needed help getting in and out of his bath and the car and up and down stairs. He'd mastered chairs and his bed long ago, and could swing himself from one to the other if he positioned his wheelchair correctly. But his favorite way of getting around in his room was still to simply scoot around on the floor. He liked to play that way outside, too. Especially in the dirt with his trucks, which she didn't let him do too often, because then she had to wash his braces.

She was pragmatic and practical and curiously at ease with so many things that Luke found alien. When Cody came up to them a few minutes later, frustrated that his castle had collapsed, Emily asked if he'd like to get on the swings. The little boy's face lit up like the sun, and he wheeled around so fast, he nearly fell over. Emily didn't scold him or tell him to be more careful or fuss that he'd almost hurt himself. She simply waited until he figured out that he couldn't get decent traction in the sandy area where they were and he let her push him over to where he wanted to go. A few minutes later, she was back, having lifted him onto an isometric swing that Cody could pump by himself by pushing and pulling on the swing's vertical handles.

Cody liked to swing. It made him feel like a bird, Emily said. He liked birds. And he liked Billy Bartell, she told Luke, to familiarize him with his son. Billy was his best friend.

"Is Billy in a wheelchair, too?"

"No," she told him, sensing a hesitation to the question, but missing Luke's relief to her answer because she was watching the swings. She also didn't notice the hesitation returning when she explained that Billy had severe asthma, or realized how quiet Luke became after she mentioned that Billy's illness didn't allow him to run or play rough-and-tumble games, which was probably why he and Cody got along so well. Luke grew quieter still as she began to tell him about the disabilities of some of the children playing with Cody, whom she recognized from other visits to the park. The kids all seemed to be having a great time. She was glad Luke could see that—even though he had gone almost completely silent by the time they'd finished lunch and Cody had taken off again.

Thinking Luke was bored, certain he was accustomed to much more exciting pastimes, Emily called Cody to come back from the sandbox so that he could throw their paper plates away. Cleanup detail was his contribution to all picnics.

"Do you ever take Cody to ball games?"

With most of her concentration on Cody, who was ignoring her anyway, she missed the tightness creeping into Luke's voice. "He's seen a couple of beep ball games, but that's about it."

"Beep ball?"

"It's a game the blind play. The softballs and bases are equipped with beepers. The electronic signals sound loud enough to guide the players around the diamond. It's the diamond over on the other side of the park. Do you want to go see it?"

She was being as helpful as she knew how to be—mostly because she didn't want him to think her uncooperative—and so far she thought she was doing okay. It would be easiest for Cody if they all got along, after all—though Cody had a ways to go himself on that score.

It seemed Luke thought she had a ways to go, too.

She raised her hand to wave again at Cody.

Luke caught it midair.

"Let him play," he said, then eased his grip when he saw her looking at his fingers circling her wrist. Her hand looked like a child's compared to his much rougher one, her bones delicate, her skin so much paler.

His jaw clenching, he let her go.

"Why did you bring me here? Why didn't we go to a regular park, or a zoo or something? There have to be a hundred places to take a kid on a Saturday afternoon in a city this size."

He hadn't raised his voice. Actually, he'd lowered it so that no one else could hear. But his eyes pinned her. Accusing. Hard.

She clearly didn't understand his annoyance. "I suggested this because we don't get to this park very often. It's a long way from our house, but we like it because Cody can play without me having to be right with him. I thought, too, this would be a good place for us to talk if you had questions about him, because he's always off doing something here and he wouldn't overhear us."

"You didn't bring me here to scare me off?"

The accusation, though quietly spoken, had her chin coming up. "This is a normal part of Cody's life."

"And you thought if you showed me just how different that life is I'd walk away. Right?"

Hurt robbed her voice of the venom he deserved. "If I'd wanted to scare you off, there were other places we could have taken you. The rehab center. Or the hospital. If it bothers you to see these children playing, you should see them when they're so weak they can't move. Or when they're hurting from surgeries and therapies and their own muscles are seizing up on them so bad that even drugs won't really relieve the pain."

Her hand arched toward the swings and sandbox. "These are the good times, Montgomery. These are just kids having fun. That's why I thought you should come here first. I know it hit you hard to realize your son has a disability. And I know it can't be easy for you, trying to adjust to his problems. But I can't make you accept them. And I won't be the scapegoat for whatever anger you're trying to deal with because of them."

Turning away, Emily shoved her fingers through her hair. He truly had no idea how hard it was for her to let him into their lives. She'd be damned if she'd stand there and let him attack her for doing what she'd honestly thought best.

"Come on, Cody," she called, slapping plates into a stack. "We're going home now."

Luke swore. Quietly, because Cody was only a few feet away when he turned around. A moment later, not stopping to think about anything because it was all getting too complicated anyway, he crouched down in front of the boy.

He could feel Emily's eyes on his back. "Have you ever built a drawbridge on a sandcastle, Cody?"

The little boy looked over toward his mom, then back at the big man in front of him.

"I don't know how."

"Well, come on then, and I'll show you." Two steps and he was at the picnic basket, taking out items Emily had just put in. The lid from one of the containers. Three straws. A napkin and a cup. "This should work. You hang on to these while I get something to hold water."

A hint of excitement, tempered by inexplicable distrust, danced in Cody's eyes. "You really know how to build a drawbridge?"

"Sure do." He smiled. Almost. The expression seemed to cost him. He pointed to the wheelchair. "How fast will that thing go?"

Cody shrugged.

Luke swallowed. "Think you can get to the sandbox before I do?"

For the first time all day, Emily saw Cody grin. There was nothing he loved better than a race. He never cared that he didn't win. He only cared that he went faster than he had the last time.

He was giving it everything he had as, elbows pumping, he headed down the walk while his dad took a quick detour by the water fountain.

Chapter Five

He'd blown it. There was no doubt in Luke's mind as he paced between the pool of light created by the lamp on the desk and the open French doors leading to the veranda of his hotel suite. He would never have dreamed of beginning a project as unprepared as he had been today. Certainly, he would never have approached a business proposal with a closed mind. Yet today, with his son and Emily, he had done both.

Running his fingers through his hair, he retraced his steps through the puddle of light on the thick mauve carpet. He didn't know how to cope with a lot of what he'd been hit with lately. But one thing was for sure. Lashing out at Emily was not the answer.

He glanced toward the telephone, wondering if he should call her. Wondering if she'd even speak to him if he did.

To her credit, she had been fairly gracious to him when he'd dropped her and Cody off a couple of hours ago. She'd said the boy was tired, that she was a little tired herself, then thanked him for the ice-cream cone he'd bought at Cody's request on their way back from the park. She'd said she'd see him tomorrow, very politely, for she had too much class to be rude. Then she'd waited at the door without asking him in until he'd taken the hint and said goodbye himself.

What would he say if he did call her? That he'd like to try again? That this was all a little overwhelming, and that he'd get the hang of being a father eventually, if she'd just bear with him? That he was sorry he'd behaved like such an ass?

It was a start.

His briefcase sat open on the desk. Scattered around it was the correspondence he'd been answering until he realized he'd spent more time thinking about what had happened today than about renovations, expansions and design flaws. Reaching across the papers, he picked up the phone.

She answered on the third ring.

"Emily," he said, pushing past her quiet hello. "It's Luke. Before you say anything, I just want you to know I'm sorry." How many times had he said that to her in the past week? "I had no business coming down on you the way I did this afternoon. It won't happen again."

At the sound of Luke's voice, Emily closed her eyes, took a deep breath and sat down at the kitchen counter. It seemed he, too, had been thinking about their little altercation in the park.

She closed the yellow pages on the hotel listings. "I was just going to call you."

"To tell me to go to hell? Or was there some other reason?"

He had no idea how many times she'd wished she could do the former. "Some other reason," she said, liking that he didn't take himself as seriously as others probably did. "I wanted to ask if you'd mind spending time here with Cody tomorrow instead of taking him to the zoo." The visit to the zoo had been Luke's idea.

The pause on the line sounded uncertain. "Doesn't he like the zoo?"

"Oh, it's not that." Cody loved the zoo. Especially the things with scales and claws. "I'm just afraid that playing so hard at the park one day, then going to the zoo the next, might tire him out too much."

"As long as I get to see him," came Luke's reply. "Was today too hard on him?"

A vague sense of jealousy taunted her at the concern she heard in the deep, smoky tones of Luke's voice. The emotion was the same unpleasant one she'd encountered every time Cody had mentioned Luke's name tonight. She tried hard to ignore it. She tried to ignore, too, the conflicting sense of welcome she felt at Luke's concern because there was now someone other than herself who had more than a professional interest in what affected her son.

"He's fine," she assured him, hating her ambivalence. "He's asleep now, but it took him a while to wind down. All he could talk about through supper and his bath was the castle you two built and how smart you must be 'to build whole buildings and stuff like that.'"

To her surprise, Luke actually chuckled at Cody's description of his work. The husky sound reverberated over the wires, reminding her of when she'd first heard it that afternoon. A small crowd of children had gathered around Luke and Cody while the two had constructed a fantasy of paper cup-shaped turrets, complete with straws for flag-poles and foil gum wrappers for flags. They'd even built a moat that, with the help of the other children, had been filled with water.

The memory might have been pleasant had it not been tainted with the recollection of how she'd felt as she'd watched them. How she still felt just thinking about it. All the while Luke had been involved with the children, with Cody, Emily had looked on from her place at the table, silently noting the similarities between father and son—and fighting the awful feeling that she was the outsider. Not Luke.

That wasn't his perception, though.

"I still don't think I've redeemed myself where Cody's concerned," she heard Luke say. "When I left tonight, he wasn't treating me like a pariah anymore, but he didn't seem unhappy to see me go, either. Would you mind telling me what you told him about us getting together? I'm not accusing you of anything," he added hastily. "I'm just wondering why he wouldn't talk to me. He wasn't like that the other night."

Emily knew he hadn't been, and she was as troubled by Cody's behavior as Luke. What she did know, however, was that it was easier for her to talk to Luke when she was safe from his disturbing gray eyes. When she was face-to-face with him, he always seemed to understand far more than she was prepared to share. "All I said was that the man who'd come to see us the other night was going to take us to the park on Saturday. He seemed fine with the idea until this morning."

"And how were you with it?"

"With what?"

"With the idea of my coming to see him."

The question surprised her. Or maybe it was the fact that he didn't have to be in the same room with her to pick up on her insecurities. She coiled her finger around the cord, choosing her words carefully. "A little nervous," she admitted.

"Maybe it won't be so bad tomorrow."

"Maybe."

He paused. "I don't want to leave tomorrow without him knowing who I am, Emily. How are we going to tell him?"

We. He wanted to do this together.

She had no idea why she should feel grateful for that, when she could easily have told Cody herself who Luke was by now. She knew exactly why she hadn't told him, though. Once she did, nothing was going to be the same.

"Emily?"

"I think it would be best if he heard it from me," she finally said, "with you in the room. After I tell him, you can answer his questions. As curious as he can be, I know he'll have them."

"Any idea what kind of questions he'll ask?"

"He's six, Luke. Who knows?"

"True," he muttered. He was only beginning to appreciate the workings of a child's mind. "Have you had dinner yet?"

Caught off guard, thinking, too, that kids hardly had a lock on inexplicable leaps of subject, Emily hesitated. "I ate with Cody." After four seconds of silence, she asked, "Why?"

"I thought maybe we could have this discussion in person. Guess I'll have to settle for room service. Do you know anything about the food at this place?"

"This place" was one of the ritzier hotels in Phoenix. But Luke didn't care about the food. The question was merely an attempt at some sort of conversation that didn't threaten or anger or otherwise remind either one of them exactly why it was that, at eight-thirty on a Saturday night, two virtual strangers were spending their evening together on the telephone, trying not to upset each other.

But just as important as not upsetting her was simply keeping her on the line. And not only because she was the woman who'd adopted his son. His reasons had more to do with how she moved, the hint of seduction in her smile. And maybe, mostly, the vulnerability that she was usually so careful to keep out of her eyes.

If he were to be honest with himself, talking to her wasn't really what he wanted. He wanted to see her. That was why he'd been pacing the nap off the carpet in his hotel room. He wasn't sure he trusted the reasons why seeing her felt so necessary, though, so he settled instead for asking her to tell him again how she and Cody had found each other, and simply let the gentle tones of her voice ease some of the tension in his soul.

It was almost nine o'clock before he finally ran out of excuses to keep her on the line.

Twelve hours later, when she opened the front door for Luke, Emily was looking for excuses herself. Excuses for why, along with the trepidation, she had actually felt a hint of anticipation when his car pulled up outside. As he gave her a smile and offered a quiet ''Hi'' on his way in, she settled for believing that anticipation was there only because of his apology last night. With it, a truce of sorts had been declared and she was simply looking forward to a day that had to be better than the one that had preceded it.

Determined to meet him halfway, she asked if he wanted a cup of coffee and let him follow her into the kitchen. The cozy space felt even smaller when filled with his very male presence.

"I'd better warn you," she said, praying the truce would last when he found out what he was in for this morning. "Cody's mood isn't any better than it was yesterday when you got here. He doesn't want to come out of his room."

She filled a fresh mug, thinking he'd have to forgive her for the happy face on the yellow ceramic as she handed it to him, added more coffee to her own mug, and slid a carton of two-percent milk down the counter to him in case he wanted it.

Leaving him to frown at the carton as he picked it up—a fair indication that he preferred either cream or a pitcher—she went back to folding the clothes she'd carried in from the dryer and dumped them on the free end of the kitchen table. The far end was, as usual, occupied by her typewriter.

"I've been into his room twice in the past half hour trying to get him to tell me what's wrong. This isn't normal behavior for him," she said wanting Luke to understand. "Usually he's very sweet. But I'm not going to make him come out if it's something he really doesn't want to do."

Emily kept her back to Luke and her attention on the blue towels she was folding. He didn't have to see her expression to know she was braced for a challenge. After what he'd said to her yesterday in the park, she probably had every right to expect one.

"You said he never wants to do his exercises," he pointed out mildly. "You make him do those."

"That's different. His exercises are for his health."

Luke couldn't argue with her there. He didn't want to argue with her at all. From what he understood of her so far, he didn't think she wanted to, either.

The phrase "peace at any price" came to mind as he glanced toward the stained-glass hummingbird hanging in the window. The morning sun shot through its clear colors, painting streaks of lavender and rose and green on the floor. It wasn't so much those brilliant splashes of color that Luke noticed, though. It was the way the morning sun shining through the window touched Emily's hair, her skin. When she glanced over at him, that golden light made her skin appear almost translucent.

Still studying her as she gave a towel a snap to smooth it, Luke sipped his coffee. "We won't ask him to come out, then. Do you think he'll talk to me if I go in to see him?"

She shrugged. "You can try. You're not going to tell him, though, are you? Not now, I mean." Her brow furrowed.

Seeing her consternation, Luke set his coffee down near the morning paper on the counter. From the slightly harried look of her, he'd bet she rarely found time to linger over the editorial page.

"We already decided we'd do that together. Remember?" He knew she did. Just as he knew, when he saw her gaze shy away from his that she didn't believe he would necessarily keep his end of the bargain. "He's hearing it from you. All right?"

With a nod that was as much relief as acknowledgment, she turned to a drawer to put the towels away. She hated that he could so easily sense her distress, her doubts. She hated even more that she was grateful that he could.

Behind her, she heard Luke's footsteps fade as he moved through the living room and down the short hall. There was a solidness about him, a steadiness, that she found far too appealing. He took command, did what had to be done. He'd done it yesterday, when he'd taken Cody to the sandbox. He'd done it when he'd first discovered he had a son. He was doing it now.

Dear heaven, she thought with a sigh, it would be so nice to have someone like that take over once in a while.

Knowing that a person had to be careful what she wished for, Emily quietly followed Luke. Eavesdropping wasn't nice, but she had given up scruples of one sort or the other in the past, and she was pretty sure God would forgive her under the circumstances. Stopping just outside Cody's room, she hung back, far enough not to be seen, but close enough to hear. When it came to Cody, nice or not, she had a right to know what was going on.

Luke's voice was the only one she heard.

"Your mom says you don't want to come out. Do you want to tell me why?"

Through the open window of her own bedroom down the hall, she heard the bark of a dog from somewhere down the street. From Cody's room, she heard only silence.

"You know, Cody, I thought we did pretty well together building that castle. Do you want to try to build something else today?"

Emily thought that would elicit a response for sure. Cody said nothing.

"O-kay," she hear Luke mumble, and could almost picture him running his hand through his thick hair. "If you don't want to tell me why you want to stay in here, and if you don't want to build something, what do you want?"

"I want you to go away."

At the absolute conviction in the small voice, Emily moved into the doorway. Her glance darted straight to Luke.

He didn't seem at all surprised to see her.

He was sitting on the edge of Cody's bed, his elbows resting on his spread-apart knees and his hands clasped between them. Cody had pulled his wheelchair up to the play table next to his nightstand, and his attention was focused on two building blocks he was snapping and unsnapping with almost rhythmic clicks.

To his credit, Luke's voice betrayed only patience, and not the hurt he was entitled to feel. There was nothing so blunt as the honesty of a child. "Would you mind telling me why you want me to leave?"

The blocks snapped apart again. "Because she's my mom."

"I'm afraid I don't understand, Cody. What does your mom have to do with my coming to see you?"

"That's not what Billy's cousin says you come here for. You don't come to see me. You come to see her."

"What makes you say that?"

He shrugged, still snapping and unsnapping the blocks. "'Cause Billy's cousin says when men come to see moms they have to be nice to the kids so they can sleep in the mom's bed."

Cody's sullen expression remained fixed on his blocks. Luke's glance flew to Emily. Not for clarification or guidance, as it had before. By the glint in his eyes, it was apparent that he'd caught the gist of Cody's apprehension.

"I see," Luke said gravely. "You think the reason I'm here isn't because of you. It's because I want to see your mom, and I'm only spending time with you to make points."

Again, a grave and sullen nod.

"Did Billy's cousin say why that would be so bad?"

"'Cause the kids have to stay with baby-sitters all the time and the moms aren't home anymore. Joel gets to stay at Billy's house sometimes, though."

"Joel is Billy's cousin?"

"Uh-huh."

"So you think your mom's going to leave you with a baby-sitter because I'm around? Is that it?"

Cody didn't seem to know if it was or not. The whole matter seemed to be more then he could truly understand. He just knew what he'd heard from a nine-year-old whose mom was apparently going out a lot, and, being six, he wasn't really sure what it all meant.

Hands on his knees, Luke rose from the edge of the bed. "Don't go away, sport," he muttered. "I'll be right back."

Two strides and he'd dwarfed Emily in the doorway. Three more strides and he had her back down the hall, out of earshot of a pouting little boy.

"Don't you ever go out?"

"What?"

"He's acting like you're going to disappear if he gets left with a baby-sitter."

"I told you I don't leave him very often."

"Well, he seems to think something's going to happen. I don't know what you've told him about sharing beds, but I've got the feeling we're not all talking about the same thing here. He needs to know this has nothing to do with you."

Emily knew what Luke wanted. She also knew he wanted it now. There was something so irrevocable, though, about telling Cody that this man was his father.

Once he knew, she would have to share him.

She looked up, wanting to ask for a little more time, and knowing that she couldn't have it. Luke's face was near enough for her to count the tiny lines feathering from the corners of his eyes. Close enough for her to breathe in the scent of him. And when she met his eyes, she felt the intensity in him touch her clear to her soul.

For a half-dozen seconds, he said nothing. He simply stood there, his face devoid of expression, his glance shifting from her eyes to her mouth and back again.

When he spoke, his voice held the restlessness of a hot summer night. "We have the perfect opportunity to explain to him why I'm here, Emily. As it stands right now, he thinks the only reason I'm here is because I want to sleep with you."

Luke didn't move, even though there wasn't a doubt in his mind that the only smart thing to do was back away before he said another word. The temptation to tell her just how appealing he found the prospect of bedding her was entirely too great at the moment. Almost as great as the temptation to taste the lovely shape of her mouth.

His glance skimmed downward, past the smooth line of her throat. The T-shirt she wore was loose, like a blouse, concealing the shape of her breasts. He was absolutely certain the gentle swells would fit perfectly in his hands. She would fit him everywhere, he thought, mentally spanning the slenderness of her hips, the length of her legs.

"Well?" he asked, inordinately pleased that his voice didn't sound as thick as parts of him felt.

Her eyes held awareness. He recognized it in those incredible green depths, because he was feeling it himself. Yet, as surely as she felt it, she denied it, replacing it instead with an anxiety he didn't understand.

She backed away, lowering her head to conceal the distress in her fragile features. *He needs to know this has nothing to do with you.*

"I'll tell him," she said, and slipped past Luke before he could stop her.

Emily was shaking when she claimed the spot on Cody's bed that Luke had vacated only minutes ago. She was shaking on the inside, anyway. On the outside, she maintained as calm a demeanor as possible. For Cody's sake. Cody was who was important here, after all, and the way she presented the news about Luke could easily affect the child's attitude. It wouldn't be fair to prejudice the boy toward his father without giving his father a chance.

Cody knew something was up. A distinctly guarded look flitted over his freckles when Luke sat next to her on the bed.

Emily tensed.

Taking Cody's chair by the arm, she unlocked the brake and turned him around to face her. She didn't look at Luke. She didn't dare. He was too close. Instead, she concentrated on the uncomprehending frown in those young eyes that were so incredibly like those of the man beside her.

"Cody," she began, her voice as calm as if she were reading a bedtime story. "The reason Luke has been coming to see you has nothing to do with me. I don't care what Joel says," she cut in because Cody had just opened his mouth to protest. "Billy's cousin might be older, but he doesn't know everything." Though she had to admit that he'd certainly been exposed to a lot more than she'd expected.

"The reason Luke is here is strictly because of you." She leaned forward and slipped her hand under his brace to touch his soft skin. "Honey," she said very quietly. "Luke is your father."

She knew she wasn't breathing. She wouldn't have been surprised to learn that Luke wasn't, either, as they both watched the little boy's face crumple in a frown. The frown was one of incomprehension, though. Not displeasure. For the moment, at least.

The frown deepened as Cody's six-year-old mind attempted to make sense of what he knew and of what his mom had just said. The revelation required clarification. "You mean, he's my dad?"

Emily nodded. "He's your dad."

Cody's lower lip twisted as he considered the implications in those words. When a few more seconds passed, his glance bounced to Luke.

"Really?" he wanted to know.

"Really," Luke said.

The strain in Luke's voice brought Emily's glance to him. He sat very still, the whole of his attention centered on the child in the wheelchair. As concerned as Emily had been about having to share Cody, it didn't occur to her until now that Luke could have been just as concerned that Cody might not want to have anything to do with him.

Some of her own trepidation eased. The first time she'd seen Luke, she'd been struck by how easy it was for her to feel what he felt, the desolation she saw in his eyes. Now, so close to him that she could feel the tension in his body, she was again aware of how very susceptible she was to him. She didn't know why that was, or even if it was very wise for her to acknowledge it, but she couldn't seem to let him bear his anxieties alone.

Knowing even as she did it that she stood to lose the most, she laid her hand on Luke's arm. The flesh was hard, the hair surprisingly soft. She didn't say a word. She didn't have to. When she met his eyes, the gratitude was there.

When she looked back to her son—to Luke's son—the boy's skepticism had been replaced with a child's practicality. "Are you going to live with us?"

"No," they both said so quickly that Cody frowned again.

Emily leaned forward. "He lives in Denver, honey. He has his own house there."

"But I'd like to come visit you," Luke put in.

"Can we build stuff?"

With that question, and Luke's slow, slightly lopsided smile, Cody no longer seemed interested in Emily's presence. His attention turned completely to the man who was concentrating closely on the animation in Cody's innocent features. The boy timidly admitted he didn't know how to finish his dinosaur house, and that Luke could help him if he wanted.

Listening to Cody, seeing Luke's relief, Emily rose from the bed. Cody's pajamas and a stray sock lay on the floor near the closet. She picked them up, both disconcerted and relieved that the little boy didn't seem to care about any of the things she'd thought he might be concerned about—such as where Luke had been all his young life, and what Luke's presence in his life meant now. He seemed interested only in the fact that Luke hadn't been hanging around just because of his mom, and that Luke knew how to build things.

It seemed Cody was also pretty impressed with the fact that he now had a dad, just like Billy did. At least that was what he said to Luke. Emily knew how important it was for Cody to be like his best friend. What Emily knew, too, when she later saw Cody sneaking peeks at the man helping him draw a design for his dinosaur village, was that the acquisition of a father made him a little less different than the other kids. That was something she couldn't have done for him herself, no matter how hard she tried.

Feeling invisible, Emily backed out of the room when she finished straightening it. With their heads bent over the play table, neither father nor son saw her leave. It was just as well. She didn't think Cody would notice how quiet she'd become. But Luke, if he'd bothered to turn around, probably would have. He was far too perceptive at times where she was concerned. That, along with everything else, was disconcerting. So she left to finish the laundry and put a roast in the oven—one of the few real meals in her limited repertoire that she couldn't screw up—and told herself to enjoy the fact that Cody was happily occupied. He easily got bored, so it was something of a relief to have someone else entertaining him.

She didn't feel relieved, though.

Not wanting to consider how she did feel, she forced herself to concentrate on the weekend tasks yesterday's outing had prevented her from accomplishing. The laundry was about finished, but she hadn't cleaned the bathroom yet, and her tiny patch of lawn needed a few passes with a mower. The flowers she'd bought to plant a couple of weeks ago sat dried up in their little boxes on the back patio, victims of another well-intentioned attempt to add a little color to her front yard. Their demise meant she didn't have to plant them now. She did, however, have to go to the grocery store. She'd intended to stop after work on Friday, before she picked up Cody. Instead, she'd stayed to talk with Vanessa, in the hope that the woman would give her some hint as to whether or not she was in the running for the promotion.

Vanessa hadn't given her a clue, and now, having blown the opportunity to shop alone, Emily would have to take Cody to the store with her. That was always a hassle. Then there was the ever-present mountain of typing to do for Jan. Tonight, after everything was done and Cody was in bed, she'd have to attack that pile before it somehow managed to clone itself.

Yes, she sighed, while checking to see if she had any vegetables to add to the roast, there were plenty of things to think about other than the man in her son's bedroom.

Half an hour later, she stood at the sink peeling some of the carrots her neighbor had given her from her enviably bountiful garden. The radio was tuned to a classical station, and she had the window over the sink open to let in the scent of the orange blossoms. It wouldn't be long before there was fruit on the citrus tree and that lovely scent was gone. So she opened the windows whenever she was home to gather in as much of it as she could. She'd learned long ago that if a person didn't appreciate the little things she could go through life missing a great deal.

She was finishing the last carrot, humming along with the radio, when she heard Luke come up behind her.

"Cody's asleep."

She glanced over her shoulder. "He is?"

Luke nodded, looking as if he wanted to smile but didn't know how she'd take it. "He started yawning while we were working out the details on his sky garage. By the time we got to the hover ramp..."

"The hover ramp?"

"It's where his pterodactyls will land."

"I see." Amazing, she thought, seeing how serious Luke looked. This man who redesigned urban centers and built skyscrapers and subterranean supermarkets spoke of Cody's extinct flying reptiles as if the things were as common as houseflies.

"Anyway," he continued, "he was yawning, so I started rubbing his back while we drew. He put his head on his arms on the desk, and in two minutes he was out. I imagine his back gets awfully tired from sitting in that chair."

Cody had let him rub his back? That was how *she* sometimes helped him go to sleep. "I'd better lay him down."

Luke stepped in front of her before she could move. "I can do it. Just tell me if there's anything I need to know about picking him up. Do I have to support his legs any certain way?''

Emily was sure he didn't want her to know how eager he was, or how uncertain. Yet, behind the seeming indifference in his expression, she could see that he was both as he waited for her to tell him what to do.

"His hips," she said, more impressed than she wanted to be by his need to care for his son. "When you lift him out, be sure his hips don't twist. Or that his braces don't catch on the chair."

"You want to watch to make sure I do it right?"

He smiled now. Openly. And Emily felt the impact of his slow grin nudge something inside her. He was learning what he had to do for his son, and the knowledge pleased him. Whether she wanted to be pleased or not was beside the point. She couldn't deny him her smile in return. This was his little victory. And no one knew better than the parent of a child with a disability how precious little victories could be.

Emily wasn't surprised that Cody had fallen asleep. Despite his insistence that naps were babyish, he still needed them once in a while. Especially if he'd awakened during the night and had a hard time getting comfortable enough to go back to sleep. She mentioned that to Luke as she dried her hands, because he seemed hungry for whatever she would tell him about his son, and she felt like a miser for giving him so little when she realized how much even that small bit meant to him.

She would make a point of including him, she promised herself, and thought that this afternoon's exercise session would be just the place to start. In the meantime, she could show him the baby book she had kept for Cody. The first few years were missing, but she'd carefully watched for and charted his progress and accomplishments since then. She didn't mention any of that just yet. Instead, she stayed in the doorway of Cody's room and watched Luke lift the child ever so carefully from his chair.

Emily stood back, forcing herself not to pull down Cody's shirt when it rode up or reach for Cody herself when his head lolled forward. Luke was perfectly capable of getting the child from the chair to the bed without incident; certainly he was more physically suited than she to handling the growing child's weight.

Luke had gripped Cody under his arms. She watched now as he slowly straightened to slide one arm under Cody's bottom for support as the boy's head fell forward to rest on his shoulder. Holding him against his chest, braced legs dangling against his hard thighs, Luke slipped his free hand up to cup the back of the little blond head.

It was the first time he had ever held his son. As Luke's eyes closed, Emily could only imagine the thoughts going through his mind.

He turned away from her, and several seconds passed before he spoke. "Back or stomach?" she heard him say, and wondered if she only imagined a huskiness in his voice that hadn't been there before.

"Back," she quietly told him.

He stood so still that, for a moment, she wondered if he was going to move at all. Then she saw his broad shoulders flex as he gently lowered his son to the bed. Several moments passed before he pulled his arms away, and several more after he'd straightened to look down at the sleeping child. He didn't seem to want to go.

It wasn't until they were out in the kitchen again that Emily realized she hadn't fully understood his reluctance.

"Will he sleep very long?"

"Probably until it's time for dinner. A couple of hours, anyway. That's good," she added, because Luke scowled.

"He does his exercises better when he's rested. It's easier on everybody if he's in a good mood."

"I'd wanted to learn about his exercises."

"You can. After dinner."

Luke's glance darted over her shoulder. Chopped vegetables sat on a cutting board by the sink. From the oven came the delicious aroma that had been taunting him for the past half hour. Roasting beef. The plain old-fashioned kind his parents' housekeeper had fixed for him when his parents were out of town.

"I hope you didn't think I was staying. I'm going on to Dallas this afternoon. I've got a four-o'clock flight."

She hadn't thought to ask how long he'd be around today, and he hadn't said. It was no big deal, then, that she'd forgotten to take a pie out of the freezer. She really had no idea why she'd thought he'd want to have oven stew with them, anyway. He was a busy man. For a while there, watching him in the park yesterday and seeing him playing with Cody today, she'd forgotten that.

"When did you want to see Cody again?" she asked, refusing to admit that she was at all disappointed to see him leave.

"Is next weekend all right with you? I'm not sure where I'll be on Friday, but I'm sure I can be in here by noon Saturday."

He was really going through with it. As she watched him gauging her reaction, she knew he truly wasn't going to let go of his plan to see Cody as often as he could. She doubted he ever did let go of something once he made up his mind what he wanted.

The knowledge intrigued even as it intimidated.

"For a couple of hours on Saturday, then?" she proposed.

"Sunday, too. I'm not flying all the way back here to see him for just a couple of hours. I want to spend time with him doing whatever it is he normally does. And I want to take him to the zoo."

She wouldn't insist on less time. She couldn't. As long as Luke was willing to come here to see Cody, she needed to be as amenable as possible. If she made things difficult, he might decide he wanted Cody in Denver. Permanently.

Oddly, she didn't feel that threat at the moment. What she felt was curiosity. Luke had mentioned the zoo before. Several times, it seemed, though she really hadn't paid much attention until now. That was where he'd wanted to go today. He'd mentioned it yesterday, too. "Cody's been to the zoo, Luke."

The slightly crooked smile that looked so cute on a young boy looked incredibly sexy in the adult version. Sexy, appealing and rather endearing, and she didn't want Luke to be any of those things to her.

"I haven't."

A frown skittered over her face. "You mean you've never been to the Phoenix zoo?"

"I mean I've never been to one anywhere."

"You're kidding."

He shook his head. "Look on it as a flaw in my development. My parents weren't into that sort of thing when I was a kid. Once I got older, it never occurred to me to go."

But it was something he wanted to do with his son. There were other things Luke wanted to do, too. Things he hadn't thought about in years. Things he'd never even realized he'd missed until he'd seen the children playing in the park yesterday. There was a lot he couldn't do, too. Could never do. But he wasn't going to think about that right now.

Luke would have liked to tell Emily all that. He'd have liked to thank her for today, because the few hours he'd spent with Cody had made him feel a sense of accomplishment unlike any he'd ever felt before. He didn't say anything, though. He wasn't comfortable enough with his thoughts just yet. He wasn't yet sure what she thought of him, either. Or how she felt about his presence in her life. Just as it would take time to get to know his son, it would take time for her to trust him.

He had the uncomfortable feeling that her trust would be far harder to earn than Cody's acceptance. In the meantime, he'd just do as she did with Cody—take one day at a time. Which reminded him of another little matter that had been nagging him. The problem was how to approach it.

Chapter Six

Luke stood at the counter watching Emily add the vegetables to the roast. A few tendrils of her rich auburn hair
had escaped the length of pink ribbon she'd tied at her
nape, and they curled in soft corkscrews by her cheek. The
errant curls intrigued him. They seemed to rebel at being
held back like the rest of the thick waves that remained
obediently restrained. The style suited her well, he thought.
Little bits of rebellion held in by a lot of self-imposed restraint.

"I'd like to stay until Cody wakes up." The newspaper
he'd noticed earlier was now spread over the counter. Idly
he moved toward it. "I don't want to leave without saying
goodbye to him." A pair of scissors lay on one section,
along with her grocery list. He pulled the list toward himself when he saw her turn to the sink for another handful
of vegetables.

"I'd appreciate that," he heard her say. "He'd want to know where you went, and it would be better for you to explain than for me." Potatoes were added to the roasting pan. "It's important for him to understand that you work a long way from here. Or have you already told him that?"

Her expression remained impassive, her movements uninterrupted, as she waited to hear how much he had told Cody about himself. Beneath her softly spoken words, though, lay an inference Luke didn't at all appreciate. What she wanted Cody to understand was that his father wouldn't always be here for him. That was the last thing Luke wanted to say to the boy.

The quick stab of annoyance had his eyes narrowing dangerously. An instant later, a jolt of conscience had him turning from her before she could question his irritation at the truth.

"Cody and I haven't talked much about anything other than his project in there." He pushed the list on the counter aside, still feeling annoyed, whether or not it was justified. "I was ready to answer any questions he had, but he didn't ask."

Luke told himself to let it go. Emily hadn't accused him of anything, after all. She'd merely stated a fact he couldn't dispute. He did live and work a long way from Phoenix, and he couldn't always be here for Cody. The fact that she'd hit so close to home was his problem. He was not like his own father. He would not make the same mistakes.

Taking a deep, steadying breath, he forced his irritation deeper, burying it as he always had. For now, there were other matters to attend to. Starting with the condition of her finances. The section of the paper she'd mutilated with the scissors held manufacturers' cents-off coupons. Apparently she used them quite extensively.

Luke knew better than to quiz her about money. Most people would rather admit the intimate details of their sex lives than discuss what they held in their savings accounts. While Luke had to admit that her preferences in bed intrigued him far more than the balance of her checkbook, he had to stick to the matter at hand.

The direct approach had failed miserably before, and he was trying to come up with a way to address the subject without appearing crass when a grinding sound came from the room off the kitchen. The noise reminded Luke of a malfunctioning cement mixer.

Emily seemed to know exactly what it was.

"Not again," she groaned, and let the oven door slam shut as she turned to the opposite end of the kitchen. The god-awful grating grew louder when she pushed open the door of the small utility room.

Luke was right behind her, frowning at her back as she reached for the lid on the washing machine. The noise stopped the instant she flipped the lid open. Water and soap suds had already leaked from under the machine. Foam moved like lava across the tile floor.

He'd never heard her swear. She did so now. Most proficiently, and mostly under her breath.

"I just spent forty bucks getting this thing repaired. The guy who fixed it *promised* it would last this time." Barefoot in the suds, she reached into the hamper behind her for a towel. "This is just terrific," she muttered. "Now I get to go to the Laundromat this afternoon, too."

She glared at the mess, still muttering. She was disgusted and annoyed, and for all practical purposes she didn't remember Luke was there until she knelt down and found him at eye level with her on the floor.

He had a towel of his own. It dangled between his knees as he watched her surprise at his presence register.

"You mop up that side and I'll get this," he said. "What happened to it?"

"It looks like the tub broke off the thing in the middle that spins it around." That would certainly explain the odd tilt that had caused water to slosh all over the floor. "Or maybe there's a bracket or something that broke off."

"Do you know how to fix it?"

"Only if I had a stick of dynamite." Irritably she scooped up a towelful of suds. An instant later, she glanced over at him. "Do you?"

Luke hated to kill the look of hope in her expression. "Sorry. I send my laundry out." He wasn't sure he knew how to operate a washing machine, let alone give one first aid. "Do you want me to call a repairman?"

"Not on a Sunday. There's an extra service charge for weekends. I'll have to wait until next Wednesday, anyway."

"Why Wednesday?"

She had her head under the utility sink and was sopping up the water puddling there, so he scarcely heard her mutter, "Because it's payday."

It was all the lead he needed.

He edged toward the sink himself. "Go ahead and call the repairman. I'll take care of the bill."

She sounded as incredulous as she looked. "Why would you want to do that?"

Careful with this, Luke warned himself. "So you can finish washing Cody's clothes."

"I can finish them at the Laundromat."

"Right. Like you have time for it. You barely have enough time to do everything you're committed to."

"How do you know what all I have to do?"

The look he shot her was enormously patient. "Give me some credit, will you? You work two jobs, keep a decent house and are raising a child who requires more work than most. My guess is that you get by on six hours of sleep at best. That doesn't leave a lot of extra time to hand around a Laundromat.''

"I won't be working two jobs much longer. I hope," she concluded, then wished she had kept her mouth shut when she saw Luke's eyebrows arch. "I'm trying for a promotion at work," she felt compelled to tell him, because he was obviously waiting for her to continue. "If I get it, I won't have to do the typing anymore."

She straightened, still on her knees, and wrung out her towel as best she could in the sink. More and more she needed the raise that would come with that promotion.

"How long before you hear?"

"A couple of weeks." She hoped it wouldn't be much longer. She hoped, too, that mentioning it to Luke hadn't somehow jinxed the possibility of getting it—if, by some miracle, she was actually under serious consideration for the position.

"So let me take care of the washer in the meantime."

"That's not necessary." He couldn't tell if it was defense or pride he heard in her tone. "I said I'd get it fixed."

The thing looked as if it belonged in the Smithsonian. Luke was about to point that out—along with the fact that throwing more money into something that would just break down again hardly made good financial sense—but she was no longer paying any attention to him. She was trying to stop the flood headed for the back door.

Luke decided to let the matter alone. For now. He didn't have to like her stubbornness. He didn't even have to understand it. But he would respect it. As he was coming to respect her. Later, when she wasn't chasing down soap suds and her mood was less defensive, he'd have to ask about this promotion she was after.

Emily waited, but Luke said nothing else about paying to fix her antiquated machine. He wasn't the kind of man to let something go so easily. But as disconcerting as was his sudden silence on the subject, his proximity was even more so. The room was barely large enough for the washer, dryer and sink. Every time she moved, she threatened to bump into him. It seemed imperative that contact be avoided. Not because she didn't like the idea of touching him. To the contrary, she found the thought entirely too appealing.

"You don't have to do this," she told him, a little surprised that he'd come in to begin with. "Why don't you go read the paper or see what's on television?" With her forearm, she pushed her bangs back from her forehead and reached toward the sink again. Her towel dripped water all the way. "This won't take long."

"It'll take less time if we both do it. Here." He took her wet towel to hand her his drier one. "You wipe. I'll wring. I can get more water out than you can."

"It's okay."

"Em-i-ly."

The way he said her name made him sound a tad exasperated. He looked it, too, she thought, and felt her heart bump when she realized how close she was to him now. They faced each other on the floor, her kneeling on bare knees, him on his haunches so that he wouldn't get his pants wet. Her glance fell to his powerful thighs, straining against soft denim, then to his hand where it gripped one end of the twisted terry cloth.

Because she didn't know what else to do, she took his towel, thinking as she did how nice his hands were—wide, blunt-fingered, strong. A moment later, she discovered that their strength harbored gentleness, too.

An errant tendril of hair tickled her cheek. She started to push it back, but he caught her wrist.

"Leave it," he said, and slipped his hand upward to capture her fingers in his. His thumb lightly grazing her palm, he lowered her hand to the top of her bare thigh.

Confusion swept through her. Disarmed by the odd request, by the feel of his skin against hers, she searched his face for some clue as to what he was thinking. She saw nothing but a quiet intensity that betrayed nothing and made her insides feel like warm mush.

Luke felt her fingers, tightening around his. The movement, he felt certain, was entirely involuntary. His touch had startled her, leaving her devoid of the protective devices she relied on to keep distance between her and him— and, he suspected, everyone else over the age of ten. She looked very vulnerable without that armor. Almost like a child who has been left alone in the dark. Vulnerable and frightened and at the mercy of anyone or anything stronger than herself.

But Luke was coming to know her better than that. Emily wouldn't allow herself to be at anyone's mercy if she could possibly help it. As he saw the guardedness shadow her eyes, he had the distinct feeling that she'd been fighting her own battles for a very long time. That he had somehow breached her defenses was encouraging. There were things he wanted to know about her that had little to do with how good a mother she was to his son.

"Would you answer something for me?"

Green eyes grew warier still. "What?"

"Is it always so hard for you to accept help? Or is it just me?"

"I think it's just you."

"Are you always so honest?"

"When I have to be."

Her glance was steady. His own was no less certain as he realized there was nothing he could say at the moment that wouldn't complicate an already complicated situation. The simpler the relationship between Emily and himself remained, the easier it would be for everyone in the long run.

That was what Luke told himself as he breathed in the half-wild scent she wore and felt the tension escalating in his body. That was what he believed as his glance caressed her translucent skin and the shape of her very kissable mouth. It wasn't what he wanted, though. Not at all. And it had been a very long time since he'd really wanted anything without feeling that he was trying to prove something by getting it.

"Mom?"

Emily's breath came out in a rush. "Cody's awake," she said, quite unnecessarily.

The relief in her eyes did little for Luke's ego. "I thought you said he'd sleep for a while yet."

"The washer must have woken him up." Emily wanted to look away. She couldn't. Luke was smiling. It was a funny little smile that would have made her wonder what he was up to had it been on Cody's face. "It was pretty loud."

"So's he."

"Mom? Get me up!"

"Did you leave his chair by his bed?"

"Was I supposed to?"

She'd obviously forgotten to mention it. She seemed to be forgetting a lot of things with Luke around. He hadn't released her hand. Now, realizing she'd made no attempt to reclaim it, she pulled it away herself. "If you didn't leave his chair by his bed, he can't get out."

"I'll go get him."

"I'll finish up here."

Luke acknowledged their agreement with a nod, his glance fixed on Emily's mouth. A moment later, he drew a deep breath and rose to leave her alone with the suds.

Luke left half an hour later, after being introduced to the frustrations of video games and carrying two baskets of laundry out to Emily's car. Cody waved to him from the middle of the living room, most of his attention on the bouncing blue gorilla he was maneuvering over blocks on the television screen with a joystick. Emily said goodbye to Luke at the door, her attention focused on his faintly brooding expression as he walked away.

She had no idea what his thoughts were as she closed the door on the sound of the refined purr of his rental car. He was a hard man to read, which, she surmised, probably made him a real bear to deal with at the negotiating table.

"Is he really my dad?"

Emily turned to the little boy watching her so carefully. The joystick lay idle in his lap, his interest in the bright characters on the screen forgotten now that Luke was gone.

She knew Cody could always tell when she tried to hide something. It was a trick he'd learned long ago when faced with medical procedures that were bound to hurt. She'd never told him something wouldn't hurt if she knew it might. In those cases, she simply told him that she'd be right there with him if the doctor would let her. He looked at her now as if he were about to hear something like that.

Sitting down on the arm of the sofa, she pulled his wheelchair around to face him.

"Yes, honey. He is." She smoothed his shiny corn-silk hair. "What do you think of him?"

Cody lifted his narrow shoulders in a shrug that brought them nearly to his ears. "He's okay. But he treats me like I'm a little kid."

"You are a little kid," she said with a smile, and ruffled his hair.

He pushed her hand away. Apparently he thought he was getting too big for that, too. "Yeah, but I can do things. Like I can get in my chair from my bed by myself. He was going to carry me."

So that was the source of this slight indignation. "He just doesn't know what all you can do yet," she said soothingly. "He'll learn. But you have to be patient." Without even thinking about what she was doing, she adjusted the pads on the inside of his braces so that the metal wouldn't rub against his skin. "Do you have any questions about him?"

For a moment, Cody's frown could have been taken for deep thought. What it turned out to be was his reaction to Luke playing his video game. Children's priorities differed vastly from adults'.

"Do you know what?" he asked, looking very puzzled and not the least bit interested in the background of the man who'd fathered him. "He'd never played Nintendo before. Not ever."

Emily didn't find that hard to believe, though she did dutifully sympathize with Cody over the unfortunate oversight in the man's social development. The Nintendo was Cody's prized possession, a gift from some local firemen who every Christmas donated to the center where Cody went for therapy. Without quite knowing why, Emily hoped Cody hadn't mentioned that.

What Cody did mention was that he was hungry, which sent Emily into the kitchen after giving him a hug and reminding him that Michelangelo needed to be fed, too.

Then both of them went to the Laundromat and the store. The lawn would simply have to wait.

Libraries were always quiet. That was why Emily liked them. Quiet was the way she liked her life, too. But what one wanted and what one got often bore little resemblance to each other. Monday morning, she and Cody kept falling behind schedule, mostly because she'd overslept, but partially because she'd promised to drop off two files Jan had needed at the agency first thing in the morning. When she ran into the library twenty minutes late, the first person she saw was Vanessa. The head librarian casually said she'd been waiting to talk with her, then suggested that Emily get herself a cup of coffee and come to her office.

Two minutes later, thinking the head librarian wanted to talk about volunteer assignments, which was typical for a Monday morning, Emily stood in the doorway of Vanessa's office, steam curling over the edges of a blue mug that read Librarians Do It by the Book, while she waited for Vanessa to get off the telephone.

The meticulously groomed woman replaced the receiver of the telephone, her smooth silver hair shining in the overhead light as she glanced up. Adjusting the cuff of her lacy white blouse, she bid Emily enter.

"Emily. Please, sit down. That was the director of our Friends of the Library finally returning my call." The explanation wasn't necessary. It was just office chitchat. "I was making a pitch for some new audiovisual equipment from them, since I couldn't fit it into our branch budget for next year. I want to make sure my successor doesn't start out having to do battle with the accounting department." Her smile, oddly hesitant, stayed in place as Emily started to take the chair across from her desk. "You might want to close the door."

The suggestion gave Emily pause. Volunteer assignments didn't require a closed door. Moments later, afraid to hope this might be what she'd been waiting for, she took the chair across from the desk and set her coffee aside.

Vanessa's glasses were necessary only for reading and speaking on the telephone. She swore she couldn't hear unless she was wearing them. Taking them off, she folded them, then folded her hands on the desk as she leaned forward. "I think you know why I asked you in here, Emily."

Emily didn't move a muscle. "Has a decision been made?"

Vanessa's kind eyes were troubled, and her smile was pinched. "No. No it hasn't. It could be another week or two. I understand there are still a few candidates to interview. That's not what I was referring to."

The relief Emily wanted to feel wasn't there. As long as the decision hadn't been made, there was still hope that she might get the job. She didn't feel very hopeful, though. Especially since she was now at a loss as to the subject.

"This isn't about who will replace me, Emily. At least not directly. It's about whatever it is that's been going on with you. Is everything all right with your little boy?"

"With Cody? He's fine. Why?"

"I just thought he might be having some problems. Either at school or with his health. You've been late several times recently. Twenty minutes just this morning. That's not like you."

That was true. Emily was usually very punctual. At least she had been until a few weeks ago. "I haven't been taking a lunch to make up for the lost time," she pointed out, because she was very careful not to short her hours. "Would you rather I made it up at the end of the day?"

She hoped that wasn't what she wanted. Vanessa knew she had to leave at four o'clock to pick up Cody. What Emily had never mentioned was that she had to pay an extra charge for leaving Cody past 4:15. The new school had an excellent after-school care program, but she couldn't afford it until she was making more money—which was one of the reasons she wanted the promotion. She'd need it then, too, because she'd be working longer hours. She'd also be in a better position to afford the regular tuition.

"No. No. That won't be necessary. I know you've been making up your time. You're very conscientious, Emily. That's why I'm concerned about the changes in your work habits."

She obviously wanted an explanation. Emily couldn't easily address her superior's concerns, though. Not honestly, anyway. No one knew about the work she did for Jan. Therefore, Vanessa wasn't aware that one of the reasons Emily had been late so often was that she'd been up until all hours doing typing for an insurance agency. On the one hand, it was a perfectly logical reason. On the other, it could get her fired. She didn't know what the official policy was, but there were any number of employers who wouldn't take kindly to another employer encroaching on their time.

But even the extra job hadn't been a problem until Luke had shown up. Because of him, there had been long hours lying awake worrying about what he would do. What sleep she managed was restless at best.

"It's been a difficult couple of weeks," was all she could say. "But things are settling down."

"I'm glad to hear that," Vanessa said, meaning it. "I understand how we all run into problems once in a while, but as long as you feel you're in control, I won't worry about you. Now," she went on, having no idea how little control Emily felt she had, "I suppose we might as well talk about the promotion you applied for."

Resignation tinted the woman's tone. She hadn't planned on discussing this now. Emily was certain of that. But, since she was, Emily found herself sitting forward in her chair.

"You asked the other day if a decision had been made about who will replace me. I know you want the position, but I really think you should reconsider."

That was not what Emily wanted to hear.

Vanessa knew that, too. "As I've said, you're a conscientious worker. Easy to get along with. Creative. Pleasant. You don't get involved in the pettiness and the little personality differences that sometime arise between our volunteers and our staff, and I have appreciated that. You tend to keep to yourself, until it comes to the children. That's when I've seen you open up, Emily. You're wonderful with them. You understand them and their interests, and you're familiar with the kind of material that appeals to them. I truly feel you're suited for the position you hold right now."

Vanessa wasn't going to say it. She didn't have to. She wasn't going to recommend Emily for the promotion.

"Is there any other reason you're suggesting that I reconsider?" Emily's voice was calm, as always, the only sign of her distress the knotting of her fingers in her lap. "A lack in my qualifications?"

"It's simply a matter of time, Emily. You've been with the library for five years. All the other candidates have at least fifteen under their belt, and most have their master's degree. Actually," she added, "I understand that Orin LaFarge over at Branch Administration was quite impressed with your interview. He said you'd be an excellent candidate in about ten years. He thought you showed a lot of gumption.''

"Gumption?" Emily repeated, certain she couldn't be referring to the same Mr. Orin LaFarge she'd interviewed with.

"His word. Not mine." The woman's smile was kind. "I think of you more as tenacious. It will come, Emily. Just not now." The smile faded to understanding. "I'm sorry."

Emily picked up her cooling coffee. There was nothing left to do but thank Vanessa, because she knew the woman to be fair above all else. So that was what she did—and left the office to consider the only good thing that had come of the past ten minutes. She might not have gotten the raise she desperately needed, but at least it hadn't been because she'd blown the interview.

Her next thought was that she'd probably grow old hunched over the typewriter on her dining room table.

"Oh, Ms. Russell, there you are!" Sue Shroeder plopped an armload of books on the counter and reached into the pocket of the ghastly green smock she wore. Sue, bless her, had made green smocks for all the library volunteers. "You got a call a couple of minutes ago. I was just bringing the message to you because the lady said she needed the information ASAP." Unwadding the pink slip she'd shoved into her pocket, she held it out. "I'm assigned to you this morning, so I'll be back over in the children's section as soon as I get these books from the night drop checked in. Do you want me to take the preschoolers this morning?"

"Please," Emily said with a forced smile, then frowned down at the loopy writing on the note. "Need del time?" she read, then saw that the message was from a local appliance store.

"Need delivery time," Sue translated. "The lady who called said she's got your new washer in stock, but they can't deliver it without someone there to let them in."

The first twinge of a headache made itself felt squarely between Emily's eyes.

"I don't need this," she muttered.

"You don't need a washer?"

"Yes. I need a washer. It's . . . it's okay," she made herself say, because the woman was frowning at her. "Thanks, Sue."

Emily had never called Luke before. She had his number in her purse, only because she'd put it there the night they'd met at the restaurant and she hadn't taken it out. He'd given her two numbers, actually, and the one she called was answered by the same brisk, businesslike woman who'd called to set up that dinner.

Luke wasn't available. When Emily started to leave her name to have him return the call, though, the secretary asked her to hold—which left Emily with nothing to do but try to concentrate on the Muzak instead of the vague sense of panic gnawing at her stomach. She'd tried to not count on the promotion. She'd even made herself think all along that she probably wouldn't get it. The mental diversionary tactic hadn't worked, for she had been clinging to some nebulous hope. She who knew better than to count on anything.

"Just another moment, Ms. Russell," she heard the secretary say. "Mr. Montgomery is leaving his meeting to take your call."

"He doesn't have to . . ." *do that,* she finished silently, then sank down in the chair at her desk.

"Emily?" came Luke's deep voice. "Why are you calling?"

The tone of the question was concern rather than demand. Emily wasn't into making such distinctions at the moment. He simply sounded brusque to her, and she just wanted to get this over with. Just as she wanted to get the day over with before anything else went wrong.

It was only nine o'clock.

She pushed her fingers through her hair. The weariness of the movement was reflected in her voice. "I can't accept a washing machine from you."

She had no idea what his pause meant. Nor did she care that his tone went as flat as the cricket Cody had smashed in the driveway this morning.

"It's not for you. It's for Cody."

"Cody can't accept one from you, either."

"Sure he can. He's my son."

"Please, don't do this, Luke."

"Don't what? Don't see that my son has clean clothes to wear? Or don't try to help you out?"

She didn't have the energy to argue with him. She also didn't have the energy to go to the Laundromat again next weekend, which was what she'd have to do, because she really couldn't afford to call the repairman on Wednesday.

A new machine would be a blessing. Heaven knew the one she had sucked up money faster than it drained itself of water. With all the money she'd put into repairs in the past year, she could almost have bought another one by now.

"All right. I'll keep the machine. But I'm paying you for it." If she couldn't afford a repair bill, she could hardly afford a payment. Later, she told herself. She'd worry about it later. "How much did it cost?"

"Twenty dollars."

"It's brand-new, Luke. Come on. How much was it?"

"Ten-fifty. If you ask again, it's going down to five."

"Then I can't accept it."

"Damn it, Emily. Are you always this stubborn?"

"Yes. And don't swear at me. I have a headache."

"You make me crazy, lady. Do you know that? It's just a blasted household appliance. The way you're going on, you'd think it was a mink."

She hadn't intended to smile, much less laugh. But the thought of Mr. Lucas Montgomery sitting there in his three-piece suit being driven crazy by the likes of her did something very freeing to her spirit.

Dear God. He was making her crazy, too.

The faint laugh had actually sounded like a sob.

He must have heard the strain in her tone. His own became cautious. "Is there anything else you're calling about? Is everything all right there?"

"Everything" meant his son. "Cody's fine. I was just calling about the washer."

"What about you?" The line hummed faintly with static. "Are you all right?"

She cradled the phone tighter. "I'm not getting the promotion."

She hadn't realized until she actually said it that the part of her that didn't want anyone to know of her failure was infinitely weaker than the part that needed to share the disappointment. Not that she thought Luke would be disappointed for her. He was just the only one who had known. The only one who might in any way have cared. And then only because of Cody.

"I'm sorry, Emily," she heard him say. "I really am."

She'd once thought she preferred talking with him on the phone, because she was safe from his too-intimate scrutiny. He saw so much, somehow, when he was with her. Now she was grateful for the physical distance, because his words reminded her of the gentleness in his touch when he'd captured her hand yesterday, and the thought of being held in his strong arms was dangerously tempting.

"Thanks, Luke. And thanks for the washer." She would pay him back. Every single penny. "We'll see you Saturday."

"You sure you're okay?"

She tried to smile. "I'm always okay."

Chapter Seven

I'm always okay.

Emily's softly spoken statement echoed in Luke's mind that evening as he sat at his drafting table staring at the lights of the Denver skyline. Those same words haunted him two days later as he traded his briefcase for a hard hat to inspect the progress of his San Diego sports-arena project, and they made concentrating on Friday's meeting in Dallas over the warehouse-conversion project next to impossible.

No one was ever always okay. Especially someone who was trying to do as much as Emily was all by herself. It was almost as if she were trying to prove something. But to whom? And why?

Luke didn't like unanswered questions. In business they could be nasty nuisances that posed risks, held up deals and slowed progress. He paid good people to stay on top of his interests so that when questions arose, the answers were there. But with Emily the matter was strictly personal. And while he didn't like not having the answers, he would bide his time until he got them. It was essential that he understand her. He didn't want to talk to her about going to court until he had to. Courts tended to bring out the worst in people, and, if she had a bad side, he wanted to discover it before they started discussing custody. So far, he could fault only her ridiculous refusal to let him help her out financially—something Jeff would no doubt tell him to regard as a blessing. That he would deal with in his own way.

Luke would help support his son whether she liked the idea or not. In the meantime, he'd spend as much time as he could manage with the little boy who was making him subtly shift the priorities in his life. Up until a few weeks ago, Luke couldn't have imagined taking off the weekend before a major presentation. Ordinarily he'd be fine-tuning facts and figures, getting every last detail down to perfection. Instead, he went to the zoo. With his son.

That monumental event was overshadowed, however, by Emily's presence.

Emily didn't mean to put a damper on his day. Luke was sure of that as they wandered along the zoo's winding paths with what had to be a small army of other parents and children. If anything, she was making every effort to see that both he and Cody enjoyed themselves. She hung back a little, letting them explore and discover at their own pace. And while she didn't openly encourage Cody to interact with him, she didn't discourage him, either. She simply left them to establish their own opinions of each other, and Luke, aware of her in ways that were neither prudent nor wise, knew that the effort cost her.

He saw it every time he met her eyes. And every time he met her eyes, her gentle sensuality taunted him with the same predictability as the reserve in her smile.

Even with that reserve in place, he couldn't keep his eyes off her as she laughed with Cody over the antics of some of the animals. He found her delightful to watch when she felt free to be herself. Her smile was like sunshine, and her expression openly radiated the affection she had for the little boy laughing with her. But her smile would fade the instant she caught Luke watching her, and she would turn away, seeming suddenly very self-conscious and very anxious to draw Luke's attention away from her.

She had a very effective way of accomplishing that, too. All she had to do was point out some new animal to Cody, and Cody, as if on cue, would pipe up with a dozen questions, the majority he asked of Luke, who had to turn to the information plates on the cages for answers.

At the moment, the habitat housing orangutans had Cody's attention. He sat leaning forward in his wheelchair, quite fascinated by the trio of hairy primates picking bugs off each other, while Luke finished reading about their dietary preferences. To Luke's relief, Cody had seemed guilelessly accepting of his presence today. None of the animosity or shyness he'd displayed before was present. It was even Luke's hand he reached for when the male orangutan broke away from its mate and offspring, startling Cody as it lunged forward to cling to the side of his cage, swinging and screeching as if telling them to go away.

"Cool," Cody muttered, wide-eyed. "It sounds like he's telling us to leave them alone. Doesn't it, Mom?"

With Cody's wheelchair between them, Luke glanced at Emily. She stood with the breeze teasing the curls about her face, her arms hugged over her loose sleeveless white shirt despite the eighty-degree heat.

That's what you wish about me, isn't it? Luke silently asked her, and even as his heart knotted up at the feel of Cody's small, soft hand tucked so securely in his, he wondered how long it would be before the stress of his involvement in their lives caused their tentative arrangement to break down.

As if he'd spoken aloud, she glanced toward him. Her attention was immediately drawn to Cody's outstretched arm, and to the hand that was so trustingly clasping his father's. For a moment, she looked wounded, as if he or the child had somehow betrayed her. But when she looked up and met Luke's eyes, he saw only a soft, sad smile.

She knew what Cody's acceptance meant to him, and understood as no one else could. And for all that, he was left with the feeling that he was taking something away from Emily that he could never replace. The feeling only compounded the guilt already plaguing him. But, as bad as he felt about what he might be doing to her, he couldn't turn his back on his son—despite the fact that such a decision would no doubt cheer her immeasurably.

By the end of the day what would have cheered Emily was a long bubble bath and eight hours' sleep, both of which were luxuries she had long ago abandoned. As it was, she had to try to hide her relief when Luke left after dropping her and Cody off late that afternoon, saying he'd only be able to visit with Cody for an hour on Sunday.

As nice as it was for Cody to get out, her time on weekends was precious. She couldn't be spending it on a man who seemed bent on cramming a lifetime of father-son bonding into forty-eight-hour chunks. That was why she dug in her heels the following Saturday when Luke showed up and wanted to take Cody to a baseball game. While Emily had no philosophical objections to baseball, she did have chores to do and a huge stack of typing to attack. Emily had asked Jan for a little extra work and received enough to keep her busy through a month's worth of insomnia. But Emily wasn't about to tell Luke that that was why she preferred he visit with Cody at home instead of taking him to the game. What she told him was that she didn't feel Cody needed to do something exciting every time his father showed up. As young and impressionable as he was, Cody might come to expect it, and she didn't think that was the kind of relationship Luke wanted with his son. She knew for certain that wasn't the relationship she wanted Cody to have with him. That conviction had nothing to do with how little spare time she had.

Whether or not Luke saw through her rationale didn't matter to Emily. What did matter was that, while he could easily have pointed out that she would have more time if she'd give up the typing and let him help her out, he kept that conclusion to himself. By some unspoken agreement, certain subjects simply weren't addressed, and neither of them was willing to be the first to upset the delicate balance they'd somehow achieved. Sooner or later, something would tip the scales. Each of them seemed to know that the other wouldn't be ready yet for the repercussions when that happened.

Therefore, on that Saturday, Luke ignored her insistence that he didn't have to pick up a pizza for lunch, and spent the day watching movies about mutated reptiles with black belts in karate and got his socks beaten off by a little boy who proved to be a real ace with a joystick. He didn't know why he was so proud of the fact that his son could beat him at Nintendo. He had the feeling Emily knew, though, and it was by watching her that he began to

understand what it means to see your child master a new
skill or reach just a little farther then he'd reached before.
Especially when that child had so much to overcome just
to get to the starting line.

Sharing the joy of accomplishment was a new experience for Luke. It was also a humbling one. Actually, it was
Emily who humbled him, he realized. Emily never thought
of Cody as a burden, which was how Luke had first
thought one would regard a child with such special needs.
She never complained of the work or the worry, and when
he was around she even tried to hide the weariness she
earned with both. But what Luke noticed the most was
that, little by little, they were settling into a routine.

Luke usually arrived by noon on Saturday. Saturday
night, when it was time for Cody to go to bed, he returned
to his hotel. He then spent the evening alone, trying to
catch up with reports and papers he hadn't had a chance
to get to during the week, and tried to get a jump on the
week ahead, though the latter was pure fantasy on his part.
By Monday afternoon, he was usually already two days
behind. He'd never minded the long nights and even longer
days before. He'd thrived on them. But this particular
Saturday, he very much dreaded the evening ahead of him
as he watched Emily come from Cody's room and hold her
finger to her lips.

Slowly she closed the door and motioned him ahead of
her. "He's exhausted. I think he was out before you finished saying good night."

Luke pushed his hands into his pockets. This was his cue
to go.

He was really beginning to hate hotels. "I'm not surprised that he's tired. He must have gone at it over an hour
on the swings, trying to go higher than the crossbar."

"He has a real competitive streak, doesn't he?"

"I'll say."

"I can't imagine where he gets it."

With a smile that seemed strangely nervous for the teasing behind it, she moved into the living room. In another minute, she'd be hanging around the front door. Resigned, Luke followed.

He had taken Cody to the park today, alone, which was a real first as far as he was concerned. Emily hadn't really even balked at the idea. The fact that the neighborhood park was only two blocks away and that Luke had pushed Cody there in his wheelchair instead of taking him in the car was beside the point. What mattered was that they seemed to be making some sort of progress.

Or so he had thought.

Usually, when it was time for him to go, she walked him to the door, then stood behind the screen until he pulled away from the curb. He would wave and she would wave and the ritual would seem very civil and uncomplicated. It was a sham, of course. There was nothing uncomplicated about their situation. The slightest deviation from the norm seemed to signal a potential problem.

Instead of heading to the door, Emily stopped at the counter that divided the kitchen from the dining room. The way she was running her nail along a chip in the surface made her seem decidedly unsettled.

What Emily was doing as she frowned at the crack was gathering courage. All day long she'd thought about it. All week, actually. And now that the time was here, she wondered if she shouldn't take the coward's way out and mail his contribution back to him. Preferring not to think of herself as Emily the Chickenhearted, she squared her shoulders.

"I have something of yours," she said before she lost her nerve. "Just a minute and I'll get it."

She felt his eyes on her back as she retrieved her purse from the cabinet under the counter. She never knew what he was thinking when he watched her that way. Sometimes, lately, it felt as if he were mentally disrobing her. Other times it felt as if he were trying to see inside her to figure out what made her tick. Right now, she was too worried about how he was going to react to be either annoyed or flattered.

She closed the cabinet door with a click that sounded terribly loud in the too-quiet room. Envelope in hand, she returned to where she'd left Luke standing by the sofa.

The sun was setting, replacing the light in the room with a faint pink glow. In minutes, the glow would be gone and the gray twilight would fill the room with shadows. She hadn't turned on any lamps, and wouldn't have yet, had she been alone. She loved that fleeting transformation between daylight and darkness. But the gathering glow made the space feel too intimate, and she wished that she'd turned on a light somewhere.

It was too late to do so now. Luke, his expression one of abject curiosity, was obviously waiting. So, in that fading evening light, she held out the envelope.

Without her having said a word, he seemed to know what was in it.

His jaw tightened, and his eyes grew infinitely cooler than they had been only moments ago. "If that's what I think it is, I'm not taking it."

She expected as much. "I can't accept it. And don't tell me that Cody can." She inched the envelope closer to him, distressed to see that she was trembling. It didn't matter. She wouldn't back down on this. She couldn't. "If you want to be part of Cody's life, I'll work around that. I have been working around it. But we don't need your money."

"It's just his tuition, Emily."

"I know what it is," she returned with utmost patience. "I knew what it was when I received a receipt for it from the registrar's office. I also knew, since this quarter's tuition isn't due until the first and I hadn't paid it, that you must have."

He didn't seem at all impressed with her powers of deduction. That was about all that she could read in his maddeningly enigmatic expression.

"Is that your check or mine?" he wanted to know.

She hesitated, wondering what difference it made. "Mine." His had no doubt been deposited by the time she'd received the receipt. "It's good, if that's what you're worried about."

She couldn't tell if it was frustration or anger darkening his eyes. It actually seemed to be a combination of both. "I wasn't worried, Emily. I was simply going to tell you to keep it if it was yours, or to give it back to the school if it was mine. The tuition is paid. Why don't you just leave it at that?"

"Because I just can't."

"Now there's a defensible position."

She deserved his sarcasm. She probably even deserved his irritation. But she couldn't tell him she didn't want his money because by accepting it she would be acknowledging the responsibility he claimed for Cody. She needed to keep Luke on the periphery of their lives—part of their weekends, and nothing more. For Cody's sake, as well as her own, she couldn't let Cody come to rely on Luke too much. And it seemed to her that if she accepted Luke's financial help, Luke would be buying the right to have Cody count on him.

Emily wasn't proud of the way she felt. But then, she wasn't crazy about the powerlessness she felt because of Luke, either, the awful feeling that at any time the other shoe would drop. She hated the way she guarded her words to keep from saying something that might anger or upset him out of fear that he might threaten to take Cody. He'd never done anything of the sort, but the implied threat was always there, anyway. What she hated most, because it seemed to be something she could somehow have avoided, was the way she wanted him to hold her.

She hadn't yet withdrawn the envelope. Refusing to admit defeat, she'd just decided she'd mail the check to him when she felt him tug the envelope from her fingers.

"It's not worth arguing about." Sounding disgusted, he stuffed the envelope into his back pocket. "What time can I come by in the morning?"

Despite his capitulation, this wasn't the end of this particular matter. Something in his expression warned her of that. She wasn't going to worry about it. After all, it wasn't as if he could force her to take his money.

"Whenever you want," she said, not feeling as comfortable with her conclusion as she'd have liked. She had the strange feeling that somehow she'd just made a very big mistake. "We'll be here. You could come for breakfast, if you'd like."

Luke considered her in the fading light, appreciating her conciliatory gesture, yet a little skeptical of it, too. Eggshells. He felt as if they were always walking on eggshells around each other.

"Could I just stay for a drink?"

She looked surprised by the suggestion. Surprised, and as skeptical as he'd felt a moment ago. "A drink?"

"You know. Coffee. Wine. Water?"

"You don't have to get back to the hotel?"

"Not unless you want me to go."

She couldn't honestly say that she did. For all the discomfort he could make her feel, for all the uncertainty he caused in her, she always missed his presence when he left. When he was around, the house seemed more like a real home. Not the kind she'd grown up in, but the kind she'd longed to have. There was a certain security in the sound of Luke's deep voice when he would call her to come and see what he and Cody had done. She found that same security in the sight of him helping his son with his arithmetic flash cards or sitting shoulder to shoulder as they worked on a puzzle or read a book. Maybe she was just catching glimpses of what it must feel like to be a real family. Maybe, to anyone who had bothered to notice them among all the other mothers and fathers and children in the various places they'd been together, they had even looked like they belonged to each other. In some bizarre way, she supposed they did.

Like his presence, that thought tantalized her as much as it disturbed her.

The silence stretched between them. He hadn't moved, his eyes holding hers as he waited for her to respond.

Say something, Emily. His glance moved to the fullness of her mouth, narrowing slightly as he imagined how soft it would feel against his own. *Say something before I really mess things up and do what I've been thinking about for weeks.*

His eyes met hers again, dark and intense. Shaken by his visual caress, she looked away. "I'll see what I can find."

Emily hadn't expected him to follow her into the kitchen. But then, he'd done quite a few things lately she hadn't expected of him—such as mowing her front lawn last Sunday, and helping Cody with his bath. Now, he pulled the cork on a bottle of wine Jan had given her last

Christmas, while Emily got the glasses. They moved with surprising ease around the kitchen, executing a carefully choreographed dance in which they neither touched nor brushed against each other. Neither of them was willing to break the unspoken agreement that had somehow gone into effect not fifteen feet away, in her laundry room. Neither of them had touched each other since that afternoon.

Luke had already crossed one line when he'd asked to stay. Apparently he wasn't as reluctant as she to test the strength of their "rules."

Emily's sewing basket sat on the end table. Picking it up, along with a pair of Cody's pants she intended to mend, she settled on the far end of the sofa. She had just dug out a spool of thread when Luke's hand suddenly covered hers.

"Not now." Turning her hand over, he opened her fingers and retrieved the spool. Dropping the spool into the basket, he took Cody's pants from her, set everything aside, then picked up her wine and pressed the glass into her hand. His touch wasn't gentle, but then, neither was his expression. If anything, he looked quite determined. "You've been working all day. Give yourself a break and relax, will you?"

She was thinking how impossible it was to relax with him looming over her when he reached toward the lamp on the end table. The lamp had three settings. Emily had turned it to the highest one. Luke set it on the lowest, throwing the corners of the room into shadows.

Feeling her heart bump against her ribs, she watched him pick up the glass of wine she'd left for him on the coffee table—and slowly released her breath when he settled at the opposite end of the sofa.

He had something on his mind. Emily felt certain of that when he leaned forward, dangling his glass between his knees. He stared into his wine, his thoughts looking light-years away.

"Does Cody ever ask about me, Emily?"

There was an edge in Luke's expression, a combination of defensiveness and hope that she understood far better than he probably realized. He needed to know that he mattered to his son. But, to Emily, the more he mattered to Cody, the more Cody might want to be with him, and that could make it easier for Luke to take him from her if he should decide that was what he wanted to do.

Luke obviously had no idea how hard any of this was for her.

"Sometimes he asks when you're coming to visit. Or if we're going anywhere when you do." She never mentioned Luke unless Cody brought him up himself. While she had no intention of deliberately undermining his father, she wasn't going to encourage Cody's affection for him, either. The more Luke mattered to Cody, the easier it would be for her child to be hurt. "That's about it, though."

Even that much seemed to please Luke. His broad shoulders relaxed a little, eased of their ever-present tension. Her own tension increased, though the casual observer would have thought her quite relaxed already, curled up as she was in the corner as she sipped her wine.

"Nothing else?" he wanted to know. "No questions you haven't been able to answer?"

"Not so far."

"He hasn't asked about Andrea?"

"Since he hasn't been told about her, he doesn't know *to* ask. He's only six," she reminded him. "Children relate pretty literally to their surroundings. Since Cody's background hasn't been what some would consider normal, I don't think he associates mothers and fathers in pairs. Until he was three, he lived in hospitals and group homes. Since then it's just been the two of us. I don't think he's figured out that if he has a biological father and an adoptive mother, there had to be another woman out there somewhere."

"He's a smart kid. He'll figure it out eventually."

"Is there something you want him to know?"

Emily knew she had no reason to be jealous of a dead woman. If anything, she should be grateful to Andrea. She wouldn't have Cody if the woman hadn't given him up. But as she waited for Luke to finish frowning at his wine, she experienced a twinge of something distinctly like envy toward the woman. Something that had nothing at all to do with Cody.

As if to make up for that shortcoming, she waited until it was apparent Luke wasn't going to answer, then made herself ask, "What was she like?"

His focus was on his glass. "Attractive. Socially connected. Possessive."

"So that was it."

He raised his eyebrows at the flatness of her tone. All Emily did was smile. "When I asked you at dinner a few weeks ago why she broke your engagement, you said it was because you had different priorities. Sounds more like there wasn't room for two of you in the relationship."

"What do you mean?"

"A space could get pretty crowded with two possessive people in it."

"You think I'm possessive?"

The point was easily proven. "What's that on your shirt pocket?"

He glanced at the pale yellow polo shirt he wore. The letters LJM were neatly embroidered in brown. "My initials," he returned, in a tone that clearly said, So what?

"Your initials are also on the buttons of the blazer you had on the other day, and they're on your briefcase." She'd noticed that when he'd brought some work over to finish while Cody watched a movie. "They're on your pen, too." They were also in the name of his company. "You brand things, Luke. Maybe you brand people, too."

There was no accusation to the observation, and she concluded with a shrug. The motion caused the strap of her loose tank top to slip from her shoulder. Barely aware that she was doing it, Emily slipped the inch-wide strap back up.

Luke watched her hand slide away, his focus remaining on the swell of her breasts where the soft green fabric draped over them. Her movements were provocative in their innocence. Artless. Enticing.

Her comments were provocative, too, and he couldn't help but wonder if maybe she wasn't just a little bit right. He'd never thought of himself as being possessive before. But he was. Not about people, though. Never about people.

"Was she the clinging type?"

Luke shook his head. Andrea hadn't been a clinging vine at all, though he had once thought her so. That was because he'd felt stifled by her. Now he had to admit that she probably hadn't wanted anything more than any other woman would reasonably expect of a relationship or marriage. "She just wanted more of my time than I wanted to give her."

For several seconds, the only sound in the room was the rhythmic ticking of the clock. Luke sat there, studying the poster of the dancing children on the opposite wall as if the thing held the mysteries of the universe. There was more to be said, and Emily could see him struggling with whether or not to say it. It was apparent enough that he needed to talk. And because Emily knew how lonely it could be when there was no one to listen, she encouraged him.

The simplicity of her quiet "Why?" somehow reduced the enormity of his decision.

His sigh was heavy. "I suppose it was because what I was doing mattered to me more than she did. It doesn't feel very good to say that. But it's the truth." He could give Emily no less. He just hoped she didn't think less of him for it. "I made love to her, Emily. But I didn't *love* her. Not the way she needed me to. But the act produced a child. A child I didn't even know about until six years later."

And now she was dead and there was nothing he could do to change what had happened.

Emily's tone was as calm as it was certain. "She was the one who made the decision, Luke." She remembered the anger in him when he'd first told her how Andrea had kept the knowledge of the child from him. The anger and the hurt. "According to the letter you told me about, she didn't know she was pregnant when you broke up, and she didn't tell you when she found out because she was afraid you'd push marriage and make her keep the baby. It sounds to me like your relationship was over before her pregnancy could have become an issue. Even if she hadn't already made her decisions, marrying her wouldn't have been the solution. Cody would still be handicapped, and she'd still have become ill and died."

"But in the meantime he'd have had a mother and father."

Cody had a mother. *She* was his mom.

"In the meantime," she corrected, trying to overlook how her part in Cody's life was being dismissed, "you'd probably have all been miserable. I was raised in a marriage like that. My parents got married because my mother got pregnant with me. My father never wanted to marry her, and he certainly didn't like being married to her. Divorce isn't the worst thing that can happen to a child. Having only one parent isn't the worst, either."

"What about being given up? How do I explain that to a six-year-old?"

"You don't have to." Emily had already taken care of that a year ago. "You only have to come to grips with it for yourself. Then forgive her for it. Giving up a child couldn't possibly be an easy decision to make."

It was strange, but to Luke her words were like a balm. Her voice drew him, bathing him in the forgiveness he hadn't been able to manage himself. She would never give up a child of her own. Of that he was absolutely certain.

Luke set his glass down and pushed his fingers through his hair. He hadn't meant to get into this. All he'd wanted to know was if Cody had had any questions. He wasn't even sure now why he'd wanted to know that. Or maybe he'd just needed an excuse to stay. There was no one he could talk to about any of this except Emily. No one he cared to talk with anyway. Other than Andrea's attorney, Jeff and the private investigator, no one else knew about Cody. Certainly no one else knew about the guilt or remorse or whatever it was that he'd just dumped in Emily's lap. He was confused, and he didn't like being confused.

Yet there were times, when he was with Emily, that everything seemed very simple. Very clear.

He turned to her. "If you could only accomplish one thing in your entire life, what would it be?"

She smiled. The ease of her reaction to his seemingly off-the-wall question would have seemed odd to anyone but him. With that smile clinging to her lips, she considered him, her green eyes lacking the guile he might have seen in anyone else trying to come up with that one grand accomplishment.

"To raise Cody to be happy and self-sufficient."

As soon as she said it, she wished she hadn't. Luke could keep her from that goal.

Luke wasn't interested in reminding her of that. He was thinking more of the simplicity and selflessness of her objective when he heard her ask, "What about you?"

Did she know that he felt compelled to leave his mark? Or was she merely returning the question because he'd asked it of her? It didn't matter. Without much effort at all, she made him analyze things he had taken for granted for a very long time. Matters that he hadn't questioned because it hadn't seemed necessary. Until now.

"I'm not so sure anymore," he said, and the admission shook him. "I used to think I needed to build the tallest building, or something equally obscene."

His work wasn't just what he did, it was who he was. His way of identifying himself. That he hadn't been pursuing his ambitions with his usual obsessiveness in the past few weeks should have bothered him more.

For a long time, Emily watched the play of emotions in Luke's features. With the insight of one who had survived the struggle, she had the feeling he was discovering more about himself than he was comfortable with. Luke Montgomery was a man who measured himself by his accomplishments. Yet he was discovering that he found as much satisfaction building a toy town for a bunch of plastic dinosaurs as he did in building a skyscraping office complex. What he was discovering, too, was how important a child could be in one's life.

And the more important Cody became to him, the more insecure Emily felt.

"Who are you trying to impress with these skyscrapers, anyway?"

She meant the question to be teasing, an attempt, however feeble, to lighten the conversation. But as Luke reached out to pick up his wine and took a healthy swallow, she realized she'd hit on something very close to home. His jaw hardened, the muscle clenching. It was as if he were trying to figure out just what he wanted to say. Or if he wanted to say anything at all.

He decided to let it go. He had enough on his mind without dragging up ancient history. He'd been trying to prove something his entire life—that he was worthy of his father's attention. Such a simple thing, really. But it was hard to impress someone who didn't care in the first place. Even harder to impress someone who was no longer even alive. Yet, still, he kept pushing himself. Out of habit as much as anything else.

His jaw relaxed. Ease up, he told himself, then glanced over at Emily. The way she was all tucked up in the corner made him smile. Sometimes she looked impossibly young to him. All too often she simply looked like temptation.

"Cody's impressed with my skyscrapers. Isn't he?"

"Definitely."

What about you? he wanted to ask. But didn't. He didn't want to impress her with buildings and design awards and all the trappings of his accomplishments, anyway. Even if she could be swayed by them—and he didn't think she could—he wanted to impress her more with the fact that he was a decent human being who wanted to do right by his son. And if he were to be totally up-front with her, he wanted to impress her with how difficult it was for him to sit on his end of the sofa and do absolutely nothing when what he wanted to do was push her back into the cushions, wrap her long legs around his hips and kiss her until they both ran out of air. He wanted nothing more than to lose himself in her softness, to make her ache for him the way he ached for her sometimes when she did nothing more than smile at him.

Knowing that a man could drive himself crazy with thoughts like that, Luke dragged his gaze away from where her legs were tucked under her nicely rounded bottom. He had work to do back at the hotel, and whether he thought it necessary or not, he knew she would head for her typewriter after he left. He'd be back tomorrow, and tomorrow he would do exactly what he'd done today. He'd try to keep his hands to himself and his thoughts off her body. He'd wanted to take her to bed almost from the moment he'd met her, but, as tenuous as their relationship was, he didn't want to jeopardize it. If he scared Emily off, he might have an even harder time seeing Cody. Spending weekends with his son—and with Emily—was something he'd come to look forward to.

It had been a long time since Luke had looked forward to much of anything. That was why his mood was so lousy when he had to call Emily the next morning to cancel their picnic.

Chapter Eight

Luke had left Phoenix too early to call Emily, so he had called from Denver, reaching her just about the time he was to have been at her house. She'd actually sounded disappointed that he wasn't coming.

Luke consoled himself with that thought as he hung up the telephone in his office. When he'd returned to his hotel last night, he'd found a message from one of his contract managers waiting for him—a problem with the San Diego project. By midnight, Luke had realized the problem was too big to take care of by phone and booked himself on the first flight back to Denver Sunday morning. Now, with the blueprints for the sports arena spread out on his drafting table, the contract specifications spilling all over his desk and a copy of a geological report in hand, he had four hours in which to study the problem, trade the clothes in his suitcase for fresh ones and get back to the airport to catch a flight to San Diego. The soil under the east end of the arena had turned out to be of a different type than that indicated in the geological report. The twenty-two tons of concrete that had been poured Friday would have to be blasted out and a different stress system designed.

Before he started any of that, though, Luke had to call Jeff to cancel the handball game they'd scheduled for tonight. He was punching in Jeff's number when he remembered the envelope Emily had given him yesterday. He'd put it back in his pocket this morning as he'd dressed. Jeff had just come on the line when he pulled it out.

As they talked—Jeff far more interested in the potential lawsuit Luke had against the geological survey company than in a forfeited game—Luke tore the envelope open and stood staring at Emily's small, neat script. There was nothing flowery or fancy about her writing. It was completely unembellished, except for the sweeping stroke of the Y at the end of her first name. He didn't know why he liked that. He just did.

What he didn't like was that she'd also added her first "installment" on the washing machine to the amount he'd paid for Cody's tuition.

The check was slipped into his top drawer. Since he already had Jeff on the line, he told him to draft whatever it was that had to be filed to reopen Cody's adoption. He'd be back sometime next week to look it all over.

"He's not coming?"

When she heard the unhappiness in the question, Emily's hands slipped from the steering wheel. She had just picked Cody up from school, and he was buckled in on the passenger side of the car. His eyes were wide, and his bottom lip threatened either to quiver or to poke out another inch. With his recent abhorrence of anything babyish, she figured he was going for the pout.

"No, honey," she said gently. "I'm afraid he's not. Luke is really busy. He said to say hi to you, though."

This was the second time she'd had to break the news that Luke wasn't going to be able to make it. Last Sunday, Cody had accepted his early departure with little more than a fleeting frown, then promptly asked if *she'd* take him outside to catch bugs, since Luke wouldn't be there to do it. Now he looked genuinely disappointed.

"I wanted to show him what I made."

"You can show him in a few days. He said he's going to stop here on his way to Dallas this week." She gave him an encouraging smile. "You can show it to me, though. I'd like to see it."

Cody considered her offer as he scratched at the spot where his brace put pressure on his black high-top tennis shoe. This morning he'd had her change the laces from neon orange to a bilious yellow-green. Apparently Luke had said he liked the garish color. "You can see it. But it's for Luke."

Since Emily never referred to Luke as "your dad" or "your father," she figured that was probably why Cody called him by his first name, too. Whatever reason, the omission was deliberate on her part—a subtle way of inserting a little distance in the relationship until Cody could protect himself with a little distance of his own, if he needed it. A child could be hurt so easily.

He held a sheet of paper toward her. It was heavy with blue poster paint. "Do you think he'll like it?"

The picture was a handprint, the kind children usually gave their moms to tack up on the refrigerator. Cody looked terribly proud of his work, and terribly anxious that he please Luke.

It was a really stupid thing to feel bad about, but as she stared down at the little work of art, she wondered why Cody hadn't made a handprint for her, too.

"He'll love it," she promised, and felt something crumble inside.

Luke didn't stop to see Cody on his way to Dallas. He didn't make it on Saturday, either, though Cody insisted on waiting for him until two o'clock and missed the horse at Billy's birthday party. Luke hadn't said he'd be there that weekend, but he'd set a precedent by having been there every Saturday for the previous six weeks, and Cody had been "absolutely positive" Luke would show up.

Cody didn't say much when Emily finally convinced him that Luke wasn't coming. After all, he hadn't said he would, she reminded him in Luke's defense. But Cody was disappointed nonetheless. He'd been counting on him, and he hadn't been there.

It was because Cody had been so disappointed that she didn't mention Luke's call that night to tell them he'd try to make it the following weekend. *Try* being the operative word. He couldn't promise anything, he told her. Two of his projects were at critical stages, and he had an important bid out on a third. To Emily there was no sense in getting Cody's hopes up over a possible visit. When the weekend passed and Luke hadn't been able to firm up his plans, she was glad she hadn't mentioned that he might come to see him.

She wished she hadn't mentioned the next three tentatively scheduled visits, either. The only reason she had was that Luke had sounded more positive about being able to get away, but those visits all fell through at the last minute, too.

Emily didn't know whether to be angry or relieved. She had hoped to keep him on the periphery, to keep him from really being involved in their lives. Yet, even when he wasn't around, he made an impact—and, like it or not, he had become a very important part of Cody's life. A part that wasn't there. Try as she might, Emily couldn't feel grateful for the man's absence. What she did feel was an odd sense of loss and a lot of annoyance with herself. For a while, she'd almost started to count on him herself. She certainly didn't now, though—which was why she hadn't planned on him showing up when he'd said he'd try to get to Phoenix on Wednesday. Since it was almost ten o'clock at night, she'd stopped listening for his car a couple of hours ago.

Emily sat on the floor with her back to the sofa, strumming on the guitar. She'd been typing until she'd had a question about one of the forms and had to call Jan. She probably should have gone back to it, too. Or taken a look at the new book catalog Vanessa had given her. Or cleaned out the refrigerator. There were any number of things she could do to get her mind off the uneasy sensation in the pit of her stomach. But the guitar had beckoned, and she'd needed its comfort.

She was worried about Cody. When Luke hadn't shown up by bedtime, Cody had asked if he could call him. He had an appointment with Dr. Hamilton tomorrow, and he wanted to tell Luke that he might be getting new braces— something the doctor had mentioned at his last visit. Because it seemed to important to Cody, she had let him try to call. Luke hadn't been home, though. He never was. It had almost killed her to see how Cody had tried to pretend it didn't matter. She'd seen the tears in his eyes and had almost felt like crying herself when he'd shrugged off her attempt to comfort him. He'd even gone to bed without letting her read to him. He'd never refused a story before.

Emily understood "busy." She knew what it meant when a problem arose and a person couldn't get away. But it had been three weeks since Luke had seen his son, and surely in that time he'd had a day to spare. All she cared about was Cody, and what Luke had done to him wasn't fair. It also wasn't fair of him to leave her to cope with the hurts he caused, because she was the one who had to explain to the little boy why his father wasn't coming to see him—the little boy who kept his handprint on his desk, waiting to give it to a man who'd been around just long enough to matter to his son, then couldn't make time for him anymore.

The knock sounded lightly. So lightly she wasn't quite sure she heard it over the softly strummed chords that filtered into the otherwise quite room. She lay her hand over the strings, stilling their vibration. Had the sound come from Cody's room? she wondered, and even as she did, the knock came again.

She scrambled to her feet, tugging at the tie of her short cotton robe, and stared at the front door. Anticipation and anxiety met as she peeked out the window, her heart beating a little faster at the sight of Luke's familiar profile.

He frowned the moment she opened the door. With his brow lowered over his glittering gray eyes, his glance swept from the smooth skin revealed by the V of her robe to the length of her legs exposed by its thigh-length hem.

"Were you in bed?"

The thoroughness of his scrutiny was unsettling, and the bold approval in his expression was even more so.

"What are you doing here?"

The question was stupid. It was also defensive, but she couldn't help it. What she could help was the way she was staring at him. She'd become accustomed to seeing him in worn jeans and casual shirts. Now, the jacket of his dark gray suit hung open. His tie was loosened, and the top button of his shirt was undone. He looked beat, his fatigue lending a cragginess to his features that made him look very formidable, very dangerous. His eyes grew shuttered, his expression that of a man who'd been pushed about as far as he could go. A man who was in no mood to stand on a front porch at ten o'clock at night answering idiotic questions from a woman in a bathrobe.

"May I come in?" he asked, in a tone so polite she almost cringed.

The hinge groaned as she pushed the screen door open and stood back for him to enter. With him came the balmy evening air. Emily took a fortifying breath of it, and caught a hint of spice in his subtle after-shave. The breath proved anything but stabilizing.

"I didn't think you were coming." The door closed with a solid click, and she slipped the latch back in place. "Cody's already asleep."

Luke pushed his fingers through his hair, his glance sweeping the room as if he wanted to see if anything had changed since he'd last been there. He seemed somehow relieved to find the comfortable room the same as he remembered it.

"I was afraid of that," he said. "Mind if I just go look in on him?"

"Actually, yes." Her arms crossed protectively beneath the soft swells of her breasts. A sliver of ice-blue lace peeked from the neckline of her robe. "I do mind."

With some effort, he pulled his glance to her face. "Would you mind telling me why?"

Luke saw her chin come up. Instead of answering him, though, she walked right past him, her bare feet moving soundlessly over the cool tiles and her arms crossed so tightly he wondered how she could breathe. A moment later, he heard a door close softly—presumably the door to Cody's bedroom—and she returned, still clutching her middle, as if to protect herself from his reaction to whatever she was about to say.

Her voice was quiet. Her eyes were clear and certain. "I mind because you haven't shown up the last three times you said you'd be here. I didn't think tonight would be any different."

His glance jerked from her mouth. "I said I'd *try* to be here. I never promised. And I always called when it didn't work out."

"After Cody was asleep," she pointed out. "He waited for you, Luke, and you didn't show up."

"Did you tell him I called?"

"Of course I did. But that didn't keep him from going to bed disappointed. He even missed most of a birthday party because of you. He'd been looking forward to riding that pony for over a month."

"What pony?"

"Oh, never mind," she muttered, and turned away, because if he didn't remember, then the situation was worse than she thought.

Luke glared at her slender back, wishing she didn't look so appealing in that skimpy robe and wondering if it would be possible to leave, come back in and start over again. One minute, he'd been standing outside, looking forward to the peace he seemed to feel only in this house. The next thing he'd known, he was being accused of depriving his son of a ride on a pony.

Luke groaned. Billy's birthday. He'd forgotten all about it.

"Did he miss the party?" he asked, not sure he wanted to know.

"Not all of it. But the pony was gone by the time we got there. He made it in time for the cake."

"I'd said I'd take him."

"I know."

With his hand clamped over the back of his neck, Luke kneaded his knotted muscles. He wondered even as he did if Emily's shoulders felt as stiff as they looked. Judging from her starched stance, she was upset about more than a missed birthday party.

"Look," he began, knowing he couldn't start over, but taking a shot at it anyway. "I told you I was coming tonight. You said it was fine. I'd honestly planned to be here by six, but I couldn't get an earlier flight. I tried calling you to tell you that, but your line was busy." So far, she hadn't so much as blinked. "I'm sorry I'm late," he added, irritated by the necessity of yet another apology. "All I've got is about twenty hours before I have to be someplace else, and I'd like to spend as much of that time as I can with Cody."

He'd also hoped that he could crash on her sofa, because he hadn't felt like facing another hotel room. When she turned slowly, eyes narrowed, he didn't think now was the time to mention that.

"I'm not about to wake him up at this hour."

"I thought he'd still be up."

"You know as well as I do that he goes to bed between seven-thirty and eight."

All right. So I wanted to see you, too, he admitted to himself as the muscle in his jaw bunched.

Emily kept her voice low. The last thing she wanted was for Cody to hear her and Luke arguing. Her tone would remain reasonable. No way would Cody be subject to the stomach-knotting sounds she remembered from her parents' battles.

"You wanted to know once if Cody ever asked about you. He asks about you now, Luke. All the time."

She took a step closer, not to challenge him so much as to make it easier to keep her voice down. "Every once in a while he'll come up with a question about how far away you live, or how big your house is. Mostly he asks about whether or not you're coming to see him. And when you don't show up, he wants to know why."

"Haven't you told him that I've been busy? You know that I've got problems on a couple of my projects. Those projects are fifteen hundred miles apart, Emily." The end result of that logistical complication was a work schedule that had broken down on both ends and a personal schedule that had gone out the window. "I asked you to explain that to him."

"Yes, Luke," she told him, her voice growing quieter in direct proportion to her desire to make him understand. Heaven help her, as irritated as she was, she didn't want to anger him. But she couldn't let him do this to Cody. Or to her.

She pressed her finger against her chest. "*I've* told him, because you haven't been around to do it yourself. I'm the one who has to see his disappointment and try to make him understand that the reason you're not here isn't because you don't care. A child doesn't associate things like obligations and responsibilities with the fact that you aren't around. All he knows is that he misses you, and that you aren't there for him. When you tell a child you'll see him soon, that's exactly what he expects. Soon. Not in ten days or two weeks or whenever it's convenient for you. Every time you don't show up, you let him down."

He'd thought at first that it was anger darkening her eyes. It wasn't anger, though. It was protectiveness. And hurt.

All Luke felt was defensiveness. She was accusing him of the very things he'd resented most about his own father. The fact that he'd never been there, that his work and his pleasures had been more important. Luke refused to consider that there was any similarity at all. "I've been trying to find the time," he began, attempting to justify his actions.

"You aren't getting it, are you?" She matched his glare. "You don't find time. You have to *make* it. There aren't many people Cody has been able to count on to be there for him, Luke. He doesn't have grandparents or aunts and uncles or any brothers or sisters. Until you showed up, all he had was me. It's only going to hurt him if he starts building a lot of false hopes where you're concerned. You've either got to be in his life or out of it. You can't have it both ways."

The instant the words were out of her mouth, Emily knew she'd made a mistake. Issuing an ultimatum to a man like Luke was about as smart as poking a stick at a rattlesnake. Luke's expression turned as ominous as a thundercloud. The tension in his body was so tangible that she could almost feel it coiling around her.

Emily's stomach felt queasy.

Luke's jaw clenched.

Cody's muffled voice drifted into the tense silence. "Mom? Is that Luke? Is Luke here?"

Her whole body felt deflated with the breath she released.

"It's me, sport," Luke called back when her silence wisely indicated that she wouldn't try to stop him. "I'll be right there."

Emily would have thought Luke most anxious to remove himself from her presence. But for several very long seconds he remained where he was, staring at her with eyes as hard as obsidian and his glance moving deliberately over her face. She didn't know what he was looking for, but the way he was looking at her made her feel very edgy and very uncertain.

"It's late, Luke. He has school in the morning."

"Don't worry. I'm not going to stay long."

He didn't. He stayed only long enough to get a bear hug from Cody and *promise* him that he would stop by school to see him at recess in the morning on his way to the airport. He wasn't going to impose on Emily by asking if he could stop in while Cody had breakfast or insist on taking his son to school himself. In her present frame of mind, he doubted she'd find either request reasonable.

Tired and frustrated himself, he had to admit he probably wasn't capable of having a rational discussion about much of anything, either. He'd never met another woman who could spark anger and desire in him at the same time. And he'd certainly never known a woman who had made him so mad that he'd seriously considered shutting her up with a kiss. He hadn't been half as angry at Andrea when she'd broken their engagement with much the same arguments about how his work always interfered with *her* plans.

But even as Luke left Emily standing by her front door and headed for the hotel he'd wanted to avoid, he had to admit that Emily hadn't been upset for herself. Instead of the relief he'd felt when his engagement had been broken, what he felt as he pulled away from Emily's house was the desperate need to settle this crazy setup with her and his son.

His glance darted to the passenger seat. Beneath Cody's handprint was a copy of the pleading Jeff had filed with the court. Luke had intended to talk to Emily about it tonight. After the crack she'd made about him either being in his son's life or out of it, he decided it was her own damn fault that he hadn't had the chance.

For a long time after the sound of Luke's car faded into the night, Emily sat curled up in the corner of the sofa. She knew little of his life apart from what he had told her. But it wasn't difficult for her to believe he could easily be consumed by whatever it was that he did. He was that kind of person. Intense. Dedicated. Driven. Unfortunately, when a person directed that much energy toward his ambitions, there was little left over for people. Luke kept the part of himself that cared aloof, separate. At least she had the feeling he had done so until Cody had come along. Now she truly believed he wanted to be part of his son's life, and as long as he was part of Cody's life, he was also part of hers.

She'd caught glimpses of the man beneath the power and the wealth. She'd seen his soul raw with pain and had been touched by it. Knowing he'd trusted her with that had made her begin to trust him. Just a little. She had begun to care about the odd friendship they'd begun to form. Had begun to need it. It was only a self-protective device, she knew. But she'd always thought that if she didn't acknowledge what mattered to her, she couldn't be hurt if she didn't have it. Yet she did hurt, because whether she liked the idea or not, Luke was becoming important to her.

Dr. Cleo Hamilton made Cody giggle by running her thumb over the bottom of his foot. He wiggled his toes again, enjoying the temporary freedom of being without

braces and shoes and, in that way children have of leaping
from one subject to another with baffling ease, blithely
announced that he had a daddy now. "He's the smartest
man in the whole world," he said, squinting into the bell
of the stethoscope the doctor had hung around Cody's
neck. "'Cause he makes really big buildings and stuff. He
bought me a big blue electric car to ride around in but
Mom says I might not get to keep it."

Cody frowned at his mom to let her know he still wasn't
happy with her about that. Emily said nothing. Luke had
told Cody about the car when he'd visited him at the
school this morning. Apparently his gift was to be delivered in a day or two. Atonement, she was sure, for the
missed pony ride.

Dr. Hamilton watched the silent exchange with open
curiosity. She was a tall woman, large-boned and solid.
Her dark hair was cropped close to her oval face, and her
brown eyes revealed a quick intelligence and infinite compassion. She also had a smile that came easily and often.
"I'm sure she has her reasons," she replied to her patient,
then winked at Emily, who stood at the foot of the exam-
ining table. "Now where would you have found a daddy?"

"Mom brought him to me."

The woman's eyebrows rose as she glanced toward Emily. Dr. Hamilton had known Cody almost from birth. She
and Emily had met when Emily began going to the pedi-
atric unit to read stories to the children there and started
spending extra time with the little boy. "A special man in
your life, Emily?" the doctor asked.

Preferring not to consider the implications of such a
question, Emily shook her head. "He actually is his father. He tracked Cody down a couple of months ago."

The smile faded. A moment later, as if nothing had been
said, the doctor's attention was back on Cody. "Okay,

young man. You and I are all finished, but we're going to get some pictures of your hips and legs. Do you think you could go with the nurse and leave your mom here with me for a few minutes?''

It was only with Emily's assurance that his trip with the nurse wasn't going to result in a test or procedure that hurt—and the bribe of a cherry sucker—that Cody agreed to be wheeled off with the nurse for his X rays. After promising that she'd be along in a while, Emily turned back into the room.

Dr. Hamilton sat at the small desk, writing in Cody's three-inch-thick file.

''He's looking good, Emily. He's grown out of the brace on his right side, though. I think that one's been extended about as far as it'll go. There's been no measurable growth on the left side. But we didn't expect there would be. Do you have any questions?''

Emily didn't. This was just a routine examination, one of many Cody had to monitor his progress and catch problems before they had a chance to become serious.

''Okay, then.'' Dr. Hamilton laid down her pen and motioned Emily to sit in the chair next to the desk. ''Do you want to tell me what's going on?''

Apart from the staff at Cody's school—who had all wondered that same thing when Cody had told everyone that he now had a dad of his very own—Emily had told no one about Luke. She wasn't exactly sure why. Possibly it was because talking about Luke somehow validated his claim to Cody. Or maybe it was because talking about him made her think of him, and she did far too much of that already.

But she was thinking about him anyway, his claim to Cody was very real, and Cleo Hamilton was probably the one person in the world who would understand how insecure Emily felt. So Emily told her how Luke had found them, and about Andrea's letter, and about how Luke had been coming to see Cody, and then how he'd stopped. Then, because she was worried about it, she told her that she was afraid she'd blown their whole tentative arrangement by telling him he had to make a choice about either being in Cody's life our out of it.

"It was such a stupid thing to say," she concluded, verbalizing the thought she'd been beating herself up with for the past eighteen hours.

"I don't think the statement was stupid at all." With that quick reassurance, the doctor moved straight to the heart of the matter. "Obviously you're worried about custody. I have no idea how a court would determine something like this, but you might well be worrying for nothing. Why would a single man as busy as you say he is want custody of his son when he's got you taking care of him?"

The question made perfect sense, but Cleo Hamilton didn't know Lucas Montgomery. Even if she had, there wasn't anything she could say that would change the circumstances or make them go away. What she did do, however, was try to get Emily's mind on to something more constructive.

"Is it possible that one of the reasons he's stayed away is that he doesn't know how to cope with Cody's disabilities? That maybe he's become busier suddenly because he's needed some distance from the situation?"

It was on the tip of Emily's tongue to deny that possibility. There had been a time, back in the beginning, when she could have easily believed that to be the case. But what the doctor said next made her keep silent.

"He might not even realize what he's doing himself, Emily. In his mind, every reason he has for not seeing

Cody might be irrefutable. Or," she said with a pixielike smile, "maybe not. I have an idea." She absently tapped her fingers atop Cody's file. "We're starting another support group here at the clinic. You've been through the drill before, so you know it can help to talk to others in the same position. As hard as it is for a woman to deal with all the emotional and physical challenges of a handicapped child, it's even harder for a man.

"You adopted Cody, so you didn't have to go through blaming yourself for what happened to your child. And being a woman, you didn't have to suffer the ego-bashing most men put themselves through because their body produced an imperfect human being. I know that raising Cody is just as difficult for you in all the other ways, so you understand the rest of it. Since you've been willing to go along with his visitations up until now, suggest a meeting or two to him and see what he does. In the meantime, maybe you should cut him a little slack on this.

"Even if he can't make it," she said, smiling, "if you have a few spare hours during the week, we could sure use you. I assume you've been tied up with other things lately or we'd have seen you at our weekly meetings. It would be nice to have you back as an anchor."

Anchors were the old-timers, the parents who'd lived through some of the problems new parents of handicapped children were only beginning to face. Some of those parents, especially those whose children had learning disabilities, faced enormous challenges. To Emily, their courage was so much greater than her own.

"I'll see what I can do," Emily said, because she never had any problem helping out someone else. It was accepting help herself that was so hard for her. "And thanks," she added, because it did feel better to get a different perspective on the situation. It was entirely possible that Dr.

Hamilton was right. Maybe she was worrying for nothing. And maybe, in her desire to protect Cody, she hadn't given his father a fair chance. A couple of months wasn't very long to get used to the idea that he even had a child, let alone to adjust to Cody's physical problems. And he had been terrific with Cody when he'd been around.

Not sure why she was making excuses for him, if that was what she was doing, she told herself that at the very least she should call him and apologize for coming off like Shakespeare's shrew. So after she and Cody got home that afternoon, she did. His office was closed. All she got at his home was his answering machine.

It was just as well that she didn't talk to him. She probably wouldn't have slept all night if she had. As she checked her mail that evening, there was a notice from the post office that she had a registered letter to pick up. When she picked it up the next day after work, she discovered that a petition had been filed to reopen Cody's adoption case.

Chapter Nine

Emily scarcely remembered leaving the post-office parking lot after she opened the envelope and read the document it contained. Somehow, though, she got to the school to pick up Cody, and then home, where she parked him in front of the Nintendo and dragged the telephone by its long extension cord into her bedroom.

There, with the door closed, she hugged the phone to her stomach, receiver pressed to her ear, and paced between her bed and her dresser while she learned that the caseworker who'd handled Cody's adoption no longer worked in that department. The gentleman she would need to speak with for further information was already gone for the day. Emily didn't know who else to call.

She sank to the edge of her bed, her whole body trembling. According to the document crumpled in her hand, Luke was challenging the court's termination of his parental rights. If that termination was overruled, then the adoption would be invalid.

Emily closed her eyes and drew a deep breath. The panic hadn't subsided. It was still there, compounded now by the sense of helplessness she'd felt when Luke had first come into their lives, and by an awful sense of betrayal. Luke had promised he wouldn't do anything without talking to her about it first.

The telephone rang, the sound so jarring that she nearly jumped out of her skin. For a moment, she just stared at the thing as if it had grown teeth, then snatched it up when the second ring nearly made her heart quit.

It was Luke.

"Emily," he said, almost as if he were relieved to hear her voice. "I need to talk to you. Can I come over?"

He was obviously in town. It didn't occur to her to ask when he'd arrived. "Why?"

"I just told you. So we can talk."

"You said you'd talk to me before you did anything."

When he heard the accusation in her tone, Luke swore. "You got the papers," he said flatly.

"About an hour ago."

He swore again, under his breath this time, but she caught the drift of his displeasure. "I meant to tell you about them the other night. I *was* going to tell you," he repeated, as if he knew she didn't believe him. "I just didn't have a chance."

Had Emily been thinking more clearly, she'd have realized that his wanting to talk to her about the papers the last time he'd been there meant he'd already decided on his course of action before she'd come unglued. And had she realized that, she would have stopped blaming herself for pushing Luke to do what he'd done. All that mattered to her, though, was that she might lose Cody, and how frightened she was at such a possibility. Her only claim was that she loved him as if he were her own. She had no right by birth or by blood. She didn't need a caseworker to tell her that. What she needed was an attorney. But even had she been able to afford one, she wouldn't have known who to call. It was already after five o'clock.

Her hand tightened on the receiver. More than once during the past hour, she'd considered packing up Cody and getting as far away from Luke as possible. The thought wasn't worth the energy it took to create it. She had no place to go, no money to get there, and no way to defend herself when Luke found them again. And she didn't for a moment doubt that he would.

There was only one practical thing to do. Talk to him. Find out what he intended to do next and deal with it from there.

"You can come over after Cody's gone to bed," she finally told him. "I don't want him hearing any of this."

With a calmness that would have worried him had he been there to notice it, Emily quietly hung up the phone. She could almost hate Luke for what he was doing to her and to Cody, for what he was making her feel. Mostly, she resented that, once again, someone else had more control over her life than she did.

It was nearly nine o'clock when Luke arrived. The evening was pleasantly warm, as it tended to be in Phoenix in April, and Emily decided to lead Luke into her tiny backyard rather than stay cooped up inside. At least the pleasant weather was the excuse she gave Luke when he asked why they couldn't sit in the living room to talk. Another reason was that being outside afforded her more personal privacy. With only the faint light from the porch spilling out into the stucco-fenced yard and a sliver of moon for illumination, she didn't feel quite so exposed to his scrutiny, or quite so sensitive to it. Even as she moved out into the night, stopping by Cody's birdbath, well away from the house, she could feel his glance moving up her back.

She was beyond the reach of the porch light now, the soft yellow glow extending only as far as the palm trees and an ancient wrought-iron settee the house's previous owners had left behind. Emily had painted it white a couple of years ago, and a pot of red geraniums sat in the grass near one gracefully curved leg. In the sparse light, the settee looked rather ghostly, the flowers and the graceful palms now a deep forbidding gray.

Rather like the gray of Luke's eyes when he stepped in front of her.

His glance skimmed her face. The moon was sparing with its light, and he could discern little in the shadows. Deliberately he moved to one side, letting that faint light stream over her.

"How's Cody?" he asked, sounding every bit as edgy as Emily felt.

"He's fine." Actually Cody had been agitated tonight, as if he'd known something was wrong, despite her efforts to act as if everything were normal. "He had a checkup yesterday. All the test results aren't back yet, but Dr. Hamilton didn't expect any surprises."

"I wish you'd told me he had an appointment. I want to meet his doctor."

Cody *had* tried to tell him. "I would have. But our conversation the other night didn't allow it."

"It didn't allow for a lot of things, Emily."

She'd expected the defensiveness in his voice. What surprised her was the regret. She couldn't tell why it was there. Was he sorry he hadn't had a chance to warn her about what he was going to do? Or did he regret that her involvement in his son's life had made the step necessary in the first place? If it hadn't been for her, if she hadn't adopted Cody, there would be no legal claims to untangle, no court order to be overturned. Cody would be his. And his alone.

Emily pushed back the curls the evening breeze tugged across her cheek. It was difficult enough standing so close to Luke that she could feel the tension in his body. It was harder still to be so close and yet be so very far apart.

"I don't know what I'm supposed to do, Luke." Her voice was quiet, as soft as the shadows that protected her from his eyes. "I can't put Cody in the middle of a tug-of-war between the two of us. I've been in that position myself, and no child deserves to be treated that way. But I can't let him go without a fight."

A scowl entered his tone. "I'm not asking you to fight for him."

"You expect me to just walk away?"

"Of course not." He sounded puzzled. Exasperated, too. "All I want is a little cooperation. I'm trying to do what I think is right here, Emily. That's all I've tried to do from the time I found out about Cody. You didn't come from such a hot family. Well, neither did I. I happen to know all about flaky fathers, and I'm trying my damnedest not to be one. But you keep blocking me. I just want to help with Cody's expenses. To be able to buy things for him without you feeling you have to pay me back. I wouldn't be surprised if you've even thought about sending back the car I bought him."

He moved closer, the faint light of the moon revealing the distress in her features.

"You didn't return it, did you?"

"It hasn't been delivered yet."

"But you're thinking about returning it. Right?

"That's what I thought," he concluded, when her silence confirmed his suspicion. "Well, don't. The reason I told Cody about it instead of just letting it be a surprise is because I wanted him to know it was coming. I figured that way, it wouldn't be so easy for you to send it back."

"You have no right...."

"I do have the right, Emily. And all this only adds weight to the point I'm trying to make. There are things I can give him that you can't. Yes, even unnecessary things like electric cars," he added, because he knew she was going to protest the extravagance. "It's bound to be more fun for him to ride up and down the street in a miniature sports car than to be in his wheelchair all the time.

"That car's not the problem, though. The problem is how unfair you're being to deprive him—" and yourself, he mentally added "—when I can afford to make things easier for both of you. I'm not sure why you have such a problem with me supporting my son, but I'm going to do it whether you like the idea or not."

Finally giving in to his frustration, he pushed his fingers through his hair and turned away. A second later, he turned back. "You know what's so laughable about all this?" he asked, not really expecting a response. "My attorney has been warning me all along that I had to be careful of you. He would have bet his corner office that once you found out I had a couple of bucks you'd be digging for all you were worth to get what you thought was Cody's due.

"You know what's even more frustrating?" Not expecting an answer to this question, either, he paced back the other way. "I can't figure out what it is that you do want. You're willing to let me see Cody, but you won't let me take over any responsibility for him. The fact is that he *is* my responsibility."

"All I want is Cody," she said, although there was more she could have wanted, had she allowed herself to dream. "I want what's best for him. I'd think you'd want that, too."

"Of course I do."

"Then why do you want to take him away? It's been hard enough for you to get here to see him lately. If you take him, who's going to take care of him when you're gone? I'm the only parent he's ever really known, Luke. He isn't going to understand why I'm not there for him if he's living with you. I know you could hire a nanny or a nurse, but Cody needs to be with someone who cares about him. Not someone paid to be there."

Luke didn't move. For several seconds, it felt as if he didn't even breathe. In the silvery light, Emily's features were almost haunting in their delicacy. But it wasn't that ethereal quality he found so stunning. It was the anguish in her eyes, in her voice. The woman had no idea how far off base she was.

"Is that what you think this is all about? That I want to take him from you?"

Emily hadn't been prepared for Luke's confusion. It made no sense to her, given what he'd done. Yet he truly didn't seem to understand her conclusions.

Confused herself, she struggled to make sense of what she thought she'd already figured out. Her interpretation of the legalities had been pretty straightforward. "When I first asked about adopting Cody, the caseworker told me I couldn't do it until the rights of his natural parents were terminated. His mother had signed away her rights at birth, and because his father had been listed as unknown, his rights were terminated by the court. Maybe you know something I don't," she told him, afraid to hope. "But if the court acknowledges you as Cody's father and reinstates your rights, won't that invalidate my adoption?"

For several very long seconds, Luke simply stared at her, trying to make sense of what she'd just said and of what Jeff had explained to him when he'd signed the documents the attorney had prepared. Luke's only concern had been the acknowledgment of his paternity, and the papers filed in the case had to do only with overturning the court order terminating his rights. Jeff hadn't mentioned that all of Emily's rights would be taken away in the process.

"That's not what I intended to do at all, Emily. Honest."

"But that's what will happen."

It was the defeat in her voice that caught him like a blow to the gut. Or maybe it was the suspicious brightness in her eyes.

Oh, God, Emily, he thought. Don't cry.

Not considering what he was about to do, he reached out, his fingers curling over her shoulders. He felt the tremor in them, and the suppleness of her skin where his hand curved under the silky curls covering the back of her neck. Her hair was even softer than he'd imagined. "I never even considered taking him away from you." He'd needed to touch her, to assure her. "I'll talk to my attorney. We'll work it out. Okay?"

The last thing Emily thought she would feel at that moment was relief. Yet that was the sensation coursing through her as Luke drew a slow circle against the side of her jaw with his thumb. He seemed to be waiting for a response, some indication from her that she understood what he'd said. But the breath she'd drawn had brought his scent with it, and that coupled with the tenderness in his touch, had somehow short-circuited the relief she'd felt.

"Emily?" His thumb inched along her jaw, tracing its delicate shape. "You believe me, don't you?"

The leaves of the palm trees rustled dully behind them. In the distance, crickets called to each other, studding the darkness with night sounds that created an intimacy far different from what Emily had originally sought. It wasn't the intimacy that frightened her so much. It was Luke's need for her to have faith in him.

That he knew she didn't seemed to trouble him.

"You still don't trust me, do you?"

She wanted to pull back. At least she told herself that was what she should do. But the very gentleness of his touch made it imperative that she stay right where she was.

"It doesn't matter."

"It does matter," he countered. "If we're going to make this work, we're going to have to trust each other."

She thought he would add "for Cody's sake." But his glance slipped to her mouth, and all she heard was his slow intake of breath when her lips parted. She'd thought to tell him she didn't know how to trust him. That she was afraid, because trusting someone gave them the ability to let you down. But when she saw the feral gleam in his eyes, the words stuck in her throat, and she shook her head instead. The slow motion rubbed his fingers against her skin, creating a frisson of heat as provocative as it was disturbing.

His voice became as dark as the night. "For what it's worth, it's not always easy for me, either." His thumb skimmed upward over her cheek. "But I don't see that I have any choice."

With that, his head inched closer. "Maybe neither of us does," he whispered, and she felt his breath warm her skin.

His lips brushed hers. Once. Again.

It was the gentlest of kisses, more promise than provocation. He raised his head, studying her in the pale light. She wasn't sure what he saw, but she felt tension suffuse his body. His fingers pushed into her hair, splaying over the back of her head. A moment later, he drew her against him and his mouth covered hers.

It was a mistake. Luke knew the instant he heard the tiny moan catch in Emily's throat that he shouldn't have touched her. No, he'd known before that, in those unguarded moments when her soul had been bared by the pain in her eyes at the thought of his taking Cody away. He'd never wanted to hurt this woman. He'd needed her to know that. That was why he'd reached for her.

Now, feeling the shape of her mouth molding to his as he drew her closer, he wasn't sure it mattered how she'd come to be in his arms. He was aware only of the feel of her, the sweet taste of her, as she hesitantly opened to him. He was aware, too, that for both their sakes he should let her go.

Soon, he promised himself, angling her head to deepen the kiss. Soon, he would step back from her and allow perspective to sort need from want, desire from duty. But right now, he could feel her body go lax, its slight weight shifting forward to lean against him. He groaned when she did that, and drew his hand up her side to trap her hands against his chest. She wasn't pushing him away, but he could feel her hesitation. He'd felt it the instant he'd grazed the tantalizing slope of her breast.

He didn't want her to be sorry she'd let herself respond. And he wouldn't take advantage of the amazing fact that she had. It didn't matter that his whole body felt as if it had gone up in flames at the touch of her tongue against his. It didn't matter that just brushing his palm over her breast made him so hard he hurt. His only concern was that she not pull away from him first.

Luke brought his kiss to her temple, breathing in the clean scent of her hair, and pressed his forehead to hers. He held her hands to his heart. The thing was beating like a trip-hammer. He found it infinitely reassuring that her breathing was no calmer than his.

"I said we'd work out something," he reminded her, because he didn't want her moving away from him. "We will, Emily. I promise."

She believed him. She didn't want to, but she did. On the matter of Cody, anyway. She knew something else, too, as she felt the heavy thudding of his heart beneath her palms. It was not only Luke she didn't trust completely. It was herself, for she was vulnerable to him in ways she'd been afraid to imagine. There was hunger in him, a raw, elemental need that pulled at something deep within her soul. She'd felt it the moment his lips had touched hers. Nothing in her experience had prepared her for that. Though she'd never thought of herself as innocent or naive, she'd been with only one man in her life. The boy she'd married. And his fumbling attempts at lovemaking had borne no resemblance at all to the heady seduction in Luke's kisses.

She needed some distance. It was difficult to think when his thumbs were rubbing her neck as they were.

She stepped back, giving herself the space she needed. It was a little frightening to be so susceptible to his touch. Especially when she wasn't at all certain what he was thinking. There was a certain caution in the way he regarded her, as if her reaction puzzled him. Or perhaps he knew how he had affected her, and that possibility was more unsettling still.

He touched her hair with his fingertips, his expression quizzical.

Emily swallowed and crossed her arms around her middle. She wanted badly to believe they could reach a compromise about Cody. ''What do you suggest we do?''

Luke could see her closing up on him, drawing back within the protective little shell that he should probably just leave her in. Frustrated with himself, and with her, he reluctantly released the curl clinging to his finger.

''We could just keep doing what we have been. Hell, I don't know,'' he muttered, when that suggestion met with little more than a blink. ''But for all the hassles we have, we might as well be married.''

''I don't think sarcasm is the solution.''

The comment had been nothing more than a sardonic observation about the whole unorthodox situation. But, though Luke was a little surprised by his own words, the idea, when he considered it, wasn't really all that outlandish. In fact, it seemed a very practical solution.

''It's not such an off-the-wall idea,'' he said defensively, thinking it certainly had its advantages. ''It might actually solve a lot of problems.''

''You're not serious.''

''Why not?'' He watched her face in the moonlight, saw incredulity meeting disbelief. ''You wouldn't have to worry about money. You wouldn't have to work at all unless you wanted to. I could see more of Cody, too. When I came to see him, I wouldn't have to stay in a hotel, so he and I could spend more time together.''

''You'd just sleep here when you're in town?'' she asked mildly.

''Of course.''

''Where?''

"With you. You'd be my wife," he said flatly. "I don't think sleeping with each other would exactly be a hardship."

The thought of making love with him conjured up mental images that did nothing to relieve the warmth still lingering deep in her stomach. That the images were so provocative shamed her. Not because they were particularly shocking, but because they held so much appeal.

"This isn't even worth discussing, Luke. We can't get married. We don't love each other."

"What's love got to do with anything? My parents were married for forty years, and they certainly never loved each other."

How sad, she thought, and in that moment she had a crystal-clear picture of what marriage meant to him—and possibly why he had so little respect for it. His role models had obviously been no better than hers.

She didn't share her odd disappointment with him. With her realization had come an equally clear picture of how he felt about her. She could never mean anything to him. That knowledge hurt far more than she would have expected. Suspecting it was one thing, having it so bluntly confirmed was another matter entirely. All he wanted from her was that she care for his son. If a little sex got thrown in with the agreement, well, she supposed every deal had its perks.

Had Emily been alone, she might have laughed at the irony of it all. She'd thought her dreams of love and romance and happily-ever-after had died shortly after she stopped believing in the tooth fairy. How infinitely sad that they should be resurrected by the one person who could destroy them again.

Her voice was remarkably calm. "We'd probably get farther if we'd concentrate on a more realistic solution.

You said you'd talk to your lawyer. Maybe he'll have some advice.''

If there was anything Jeff had, it was advice. His latest, after two canceled meetings, had been for Luke to get out of Emily and Cody's lives and get on with his own. Luke had considered Jeff to be completely off base in all his thinking about Emily and Cody. Now he wondered if he shouldn't take his advice and get out of Emily's life anyway. He'd really done nothing but upset her all along.

"I have to go back to Denver tomorrow afternoon," he said. "I'll talk with Jeff then. Do you mind if I see Cody in the morning?"

"Would you like to take him to school?"

He thought it wouldn't have killed her to look a little less relieved at the change of subject, but this was the first time she'd ever trusted him to take Cody anywhere in a car without her. Had he finally proven she could trust him enough not to run off with his child? Or had she made the offer because she no longer had a choice?

It didn't really seem to matter to him now. He felt oddly deflated. "What time?"

"If you're here by seven, you can have breakfast with him."

He gave her a nod, wondering at the emptiness filling his gut. He knew they would have no time to talk in the morning. It was probably better that way. "Call me if Cody needs anything."

"I will."

"I'll let you know what Jeff says."

She nodded, her throat feeling oddly tight. Feelings she didn't want to consider were getting too close. For weeks she'd defended herself against him by refusing his help, his money. I pay support, she remembered her father yelling. That gives me the right to see how my daughter is raised.

She'd thought she was denying Luke that power. But his wealth wasn't the source of his power over her and Cody at all. His power came from the fact that both she and Cody cared about him.

"Take care of yourself," he said.

"You, too."

Two minutes later, after brushing a kiss across Cody's forehead, he was gone.

What Jeff had to say didn't please Luke at all.

"Of course I knew it would invalidate the adoption. That's what you wanted."

Jeff had been leaning back in his leather chair, threatening to tip himself right through the wall of window, with its view of another glass-and-steel office building across the street. Now he popped forward and stood, because that was what Luke was doing, and it made him uncomfortable to have the taller man looking down at him.

"What I wanted," Luke said as he paced, his hands in the pockets of his slacks, "was to establish my own rights. Not interfere with his mother's."

"His mother was Andrea."

The look Luke sent sailing across Jeff's huge black lacquered desk was barely civilized. In response, Jeff merely blinked and leaned against his matching credenza.

Luke continued pacing across the plush Aubusson carpet. "All right," he conceded. "His adoptive mother, then. Whatever you call her, I never intended to end Emily's relationship with Cody. If we get this termination order overturned and the adoption ruled invalid, where does that leave her?"

Jeff shrugged. "Nowhere."

"Terrific." Luke turned his scowl to the view. When he'd left Phoenix, the sun had been shining. Here in Denver it was raining. There seemed to be something symbolic in that. "So we draw up some kind of joint custody agreement or something. Okay?"

"You can't do that. I mean, you could, but you'd have trouble getting a court to accept it."

"Why? Divorced people do it all the time. Hell, you did it. You and your first wife have joint custody of your daughter."

"It was my second wife, and yes. But that's different. You and this woman aren't going through a divorce. There's no legal relationship at all between the two of you."

"There's got to be some way."

Luke could be impossibly single-minded. It was a failing Jeff had pointed out on more than one occasion. Luke had the feeling Jeff was preparing to make that point again as the attorney moved toward the wet bar adjacent to a wall covered with leather-bound law books.

Jeff held up an empty highball glass.

"Sure," Luke muttered, accepting the silent offer of a drink, and turned back to the drizzle. Ten stories below, umbrellas bobbed like colored mushrooms along the sidewalks as commuters headed home for the evening.

Jeff joined him at the window, staring out, too. He handed Luke a scotch and took a sip of his own.

"Tell me something," Jeff began, proving to Luke that he'd been right about Jeff's next approach. "Say you did somehow wind up sharing custody with this woman. Does Cody continue to live with her?"

He'd expected a trick question. This was easy. Luke wouldn't even consider having the boy stay with him, then leave him in the care of a stranger. He'd known that last night when Emily's remark about hiring a nanny or nurse had reminded him of how often he'd been left in such care himself as a child. From the time he'd seen his son, he'd felt some indefinable need to make things right with the boy. It had something to do with honor, he supposed, and a lot to do with responsibility. Mostly it had to do with a desire to see that his child had what he'd never known—a real relationship with his father. He'd never felt like explaining that to anyone, though. Not even to the woman who might very well understand if he did.

He certainly didn't feel like explaining it to Jeff.

"Absolutely," Luke said. "Cody needs her."

"And you'll do what? Visit once or twice a month?"

Luke rubbed the back of his neck. "More often than that. I'm thinking about getting a place in Phoenix. It would make it easier to spend weekends, and I could use it as a base for projects in the Southwest. I figure that way I can see him midweek, too, once in a while."

"She'll just let you come and go pretty much as you please?" Jeff scratched his neat, dark beard as he considered his own question. A moment later, he shook his head. "That won't last long."

Considering the question himself, Luke had to admit that Jeff's conclusion was probably more realistic than his had been. Aside from the fact that it would be asking a lot for her to go along with such a loose arrangement, she had a routine in the evenings, and his presence could easily be disruptive. He could help with Cody's exercises, though, he thought. That would free up some time for her.

Or maybe not.

"We'd work something out."

Jeff nodded his balding head, pleased that his client had come to a more realistic conclusion. "You'd pay support, of course. I know." His hand shot up, palm out, when Luke's scowl cut toward him. "I'm not going to say a word about financial liability right now. I'm willing to concede that I was wrong about her. I've never heard of any woman turning down support from a child's father, and frankly, I think it's pretty unbelievable, but this doesn't appear to be an ordinary case.''

"She isn't an ordinary woman."

With that, Luke went back to his perusal of the gray city. Jeff's eyes narrowed.

"All right," the attorney said, as if his perspective on the situation had somehow changed. "Let's say you're contributing to the boy's support and you're seeing him on a schedule that suits you and Emily and everything is all fine and wonderful. Then, all of a sudden, a third party enters the picture. What happens if one of you wants to get married? Will she have a problem with another woman being the kid's stepmom? Even if she does, will that matter to you? Wouldn't you want your wife to adopt Cody so that you could have your family with you?''

"You're talking nebulous possibilities here."

"Hey, buddy, you need to consider them. You're prime right now. You're thirty-seven years old. You aren't going to want to keep up this pace forever. And what about her. How old is she?''

"Twenty-nine."

"I couldn't tell much from her picture. She a dog, or what?''

Studying a raindrop tracking its way down the glass, Luke didn't even bother to be annoyed by his friend's crudeness. "She's beautiful.''

"Then she'll probably be off the market before you will. If she gets married, are you going to have a problem with another man living with your son? Even if she doesn't marry. If she just has some guy move in?''

The raindrop Luke was watching took a sharp turn. An instant later, it converged with another, and the two slid straight down the darkening window. It occurred to him then that Emily could wind up with another man just that fast. It wasn't likely, given how she kept to herself, but anything was possible. The odds against those two particular drops merging had been astronomical. Yet it had happened. It could happen that Emily could wind up with some other guy, too.

As disturbing as Luke found the idea of having someone else help raise his son, equally unsettling was the thought of Emily sleeping with another man.

Jeff was not an overly sensitive guy. He was, however, a friend. "I just want you to be sure you know what you're getting yourself into here, Luke. Hell, I know what I'd do, but we both know I run a little short on noblesse oblige. You, on the other hand—" he chuckled and gave Luke a sympathetic slap on the back "—I wouldn't be surprised if you'd thought about marrying her to share custody of the kid."

Luke didn't laugh. If anything, his silence only grew more brooding in the moments before he tipped back his glass and finished off his scotch.

Jeff's hand fell. His expression was one of abject disbelief. He'd only been joking. "You didn't."

"Yeah." Luke set his empty glass on the credenza beside him. "I did."

"And?"

"She told me she didn't think sarcasm was the solution."

"Is there something going on between the two of you?"

That, Luke thought, was one difficult question. There was something there. But he'd be damned if he could figure out what it was.

Not knowing how to explain to Jeff what he couldn't explain to himself, Luke chose not to respond to the question at all. "Just hold off on everything for a while. Except the trust. Go ahead and set that up. But wait on the custody part. Okay?"

"No problem. The hearing hasn't even been scheduled yet. You okay?"

"Sure. I'm fine." *I'm always okay,* he remembered Emily saying, and wondered if she'd felt this odd sense of isolation when she'd said it. "Thanks for the drink."

"Anytime. And Luke?"

"Yeah?"

For a moment, Jeff looked as if he'd been about to say something nice. He was obviously uncomfortable with the thought, and he seemed to catch himself before he could ruin his reputation. "I'm up for handball if you're into a game tonight."

The only thing Luke was "into" was another scotch. Alone. But that evening, as he sat in his den, a room that felt as if it belonged more to the decorator who'd put it together than to him, he found himself wishing very much that he wasn't alone. If he'd wanted to, he could have remedied the situation by calling any of the acquaintances he'd neglected for so long. He just wasn't up to the small talk, or the gossip, bragging and maneuvering that went on in those circles.

Where Luke wanted to be was back at Emily's. Where he really wanted to be was back at Emily's with her lying beneath him in her bed, her sweet voice whispering his name and her body damp from lovemaking. But Luke wasn't going to frustrate himself any more than he already had by dwelling on that. After the proposal he hadn't quite made, she'd made it pretty clear that their interest in each other was best confined to what they were going to do about Cody.

Last night he'd told her to call if Cody needed any-thing. He'd reminded her of that again before he'd taken Cody to school. As he sank back in a chair he didn't like but was sure must have cost him a fortune, he truly doubted that she would.

Chapter Ten

"His doctors say it can't wait?"

Emily took a deep breath and looked up from her glass of iced tea. She hadn't meant to stay when she'd dropped off the typing, but Jan had insisted. Cody had, too, once the offer had been made. Now he could be heard in the Bartells' family room, engaged in friendly fire with Billy over a video game.

"Dr. Hamilton said we really couldn't." Emily paused. "We've known all along that he'd need surgery if he was ever going to get up on crutches. I've been prepared for that. As much as I can be, anyway. But I thought we had a while yet. At least another couple of years." They still had that time before they would begin the process of lengthening the bones in his legs. They didn't, however, have the luxury of waiting to repair what had shown up in Cody's X rays and the additional tests he'd been through in the last few days. "I always get a little lost when they start using medical terminology, but what it boils down to is that they have to change the angle of his left hip socket before he grows much more, or it will be harder to help him later."

Jan, her elbows propped on the table, offered no sympathy. Not the verbal kind, anyway. Being familiar with the numb sort of acceptance the parent of a chronically ill or disabled child develops when learning of yet another complication, she let her silence speak for her.

"I still haven't told Cody," Emily said with a sigh.

"Have they already scheduled him?"

"He goes in in a couple of days. That's why I can't promise when I'll get this typing back to you." As Jan sometimes did when she left the office early, she'd brought the files with her for Emily to pick up on her way home. It was closer for Emily that way. "I'll work on it tonight...."

"Will you forget the typing?" Jan waved her hand, smiling even as she admonished. "Just do what you can of the correspondence, and I'll muddle through the rest. I can hardly expect you to be thinking about insurance endorsements when you've got a little one to worry about. I understand these things. You just concentrate on Cody. Here, let me get you some more tea. And eat some of those cookies, will you?" She motioned toward the plate on the table, half-empty now that the boys had attacked it. "I don't know about you, but calories always make me feel better."

Emily passed on the cookies, but she was glad to stay a while longer in Jan's big country kitchen, listening to the giggling and squabbling going on in the other room. This was good for Cody. Even though he saw Billy every day at school, playing at Billy's house was a treat, one he wouldn't be able to indulge in for a while after today.

She positively dreaded the thought of telling Cody what was coming up. Jan knew that, too, and told Emily point-blank she didn't envy her the dilemma of when to break the news. It was good for Emily to know someone like Jan. Someone who understood the anxieties she faced without having to have them explained to her.

Sometimes, though, Emily wished she could go beyond the anxieties, wished she could share her fears for Cody with someone the way other parents had shared their fears with her. She had, at first, but she'd found her concerns minimized because Cody wasn't her biological child. She knew people didn't mean to be insensitive, but in their preoccupation with their own problems, hers didn't seem to count quite so much. After all, as had been pointed out to her on any number of occasions, she'd known what she was getting into when she adopted Cody. They, on the other hand, had had no choice but to live with the disabilities of their natural children. Some support systems, she'd discovered, could be pretty lopsided.

Jan had never dismissed her. But then, Emily hadn't given her the chance, either.

"I suppose I should call his father."

Pitcher in hand, Jan sat back down at her round oak table, with its handcrafted centerpiece and the makings of another craft project pushed to the side. "You know," Jan said with a little laugh, "when Billy first said Cody had a dad, I thought Cody was just indulging his imagination."

"Oh, Luke's definitely not Cody's imagination. He's very real."

Making sure her own glass was refilled with tea, and that the activity in the other room was seemingly still under control, Jan propped her elbows on the table. Jan wasn't the type to pry. She also wasn't the type to ignore another person's obvious distress. "I assume, from what I hear through Billy, that he's visited with Cody quite a bit. Is he a problem?''

Emily frowned at the beads of water that had collected on her glass. ''He's very good with Cody, if that's what you mean. I'm just not sure I'm up to having him at the hospital.''

''You've been in the hospital with Cody before, so you know as well as I do what kind of strain you're going to be under. It's all the worse when surgery is involved. If you want my advice, do what will be easiest for you. Personally, I do better when Bob is with me. But Bob is my husband, and we need each other for support. If Cody's father wants to be there and can be supportive, then having him around might not be a bad idea. If his presence will make the time harder for you, then ask him not to come.''

Jan's advice seemed remarkably simple. Unfortunately, utilizing it was a little more complex. If Emily was to think of herself first, she would just wait until Cody was recovering to tell Luke what was going on. In three or four days, she could call and tell him to go to the hospital to see Cody instead of coming to the house—then hold her breath until he either accepted the way she'd handled the situation or came unglued.

Despite the fact that they were being polite enough with each other to gag Miss Manners, Emily knew Luke would not appreciate being informed of Cody's surgery after the fact. She certainly wouldn't, and, to be fair, she had to admit that his right to know about what concerned his son probably did outweigh her ambivalence about Luke himself. His attitude toward her had deteriorated into a sort of polite indifference within the past couple of weeks, and the thought of having to cope with his coolness, on top of having to deal with Cody's surgery, held as much appeal for her as having a root canal.

Of course, there was always the chance that Luke might not want to come. Emily clung to that hope. The man was, after all, doing his level best to avoid her.

He'd been polite but distant when he'd come to take Cody to the park last Saturday, and hadn't even asked to come in when he'd brought him back. On Sunday he'd stayed for less than an hour, and he'd been outside with Cody the entire time, catching bugs that she'd refused to let Cody bring in. The only other contact she'd had with him was a phone call the evening after he'd told her that, for now, the custody situation was status quo. His attorney had said there was a possibility that someone from the state might contact her, since it had also been served with the pleading, but she wasn't to worry. Emily had hung up thinking she'd forgotten how *not* to worry, and spent the rest of the evening wishing she hadn't recalled the last time they'd been together. She'd been having enough trouble sleeping as it was without remembering how it had felt in his arms.

As it turned out, it didn't matter what Emily thought she could or couldn't handle. By the time she checked Cody into the hospital late Thursday afternoon, Cody had made it quite clear that he wanted Luke with him.

"You called him, didn't you?"

Cody sat in the middle of the elevated bed, his braced legs sticking out from beneath a miniature version of an adult hospital gown. As unhappy as he was to be in the hospital, he was unhappier still with his mom. She had failed to produce the man he wanted to see.

"Yes, Cody," Emily said, not wanting to sound exasperated, but fearing she did anyway. "I called him. I left a message on the answering machine at his house, and one with his secretary. He just hasn't called back."

Emily expected Cody to become more demanding. It wasn't unusual for him to cop an attitude with her when he first arrived at the hospital. Children shouldn't have to deal with what he and so many others like him had to face, and a little protest wasn't exactly out of line—especially since this was about as bad as it got with Cody. To her consternation, though, the insistence left his expression, along with the accusation. For several moments, he was silent, studying the tiny blue and red animals printed on his gown. With his pale eyebrows drawn together, he looked very serious, very small, and far wiser than any child should have to be.

"It's like before, huh, Mom? He doesn't have time for me again."

"Oh, Cody." Smoothing her hand over his head, she sat down next to him on the bed and drew him to her side. "That's not it at all. He's still coming to see you Saturday. At least that's what he said last Sunday, and he hasn't called to say otherwise. That's just the day after tomorrow."

Cody wasn't listening.

It was a clear sign of his distress that he hadn't treated her like a leper at her show of motherly concern. She didn't doubt for a moment that in more secure surroundings he would have tried to wriggle away, especially since there were other people around. Specifically, a boy a couple of years older than himself in the next bed.

The boy, an incorrigible-looking little kid with round cheeks and a face full of freckles, had one leg in a full cast—the result of an attempt at bungee jumping from the roof of the family garage. Emily had learned that from his harried-looking mother, who'd just departed a few minutes ago to grab a bite to eat. The devil-child, Jason, had the television's remote control, and kept flipping through the channels as if the action were a game in itself.

Emily ignored him.

The only concession Cody made to the boy's presence was to lower his voice.

"I think I made him mad when I told him I wished he could live with us. He didn't yell or nothing. But we stopped having fun."

Emily's hand stilled for a moment before she continued stroking his hair. "When did you do that, honey?"

"Last time he came to see me."

That would have been Sunday. The day Luke had left after about an hour without coming back into the house. "Is that all you said to him? That you wished he could live with us?"

Picking at one of the straps on his brace, Cody nodded.

"Do you remember what he said?"

"He said that you wouldn't like that."

"That's all?"

"Uh-huh."

"I don't think you made Luke mad, honey. Don't worry about it, okay?"

Cody was worried, though. His voice grew quieter still. "I guess I did something else that made him not want to see me."

Outside the room, a doctor was being paged over the intercom system, and a telephone was ringing at the nurses' station. The sounds filtered past the television's constantly changing audio. Emily scarcely noticed. Her concerns centered completely around one dejected little boy— and the man who was making him feel that way.

She gathered Cody to her, holding his little body close and protecting him as best she could from hurts that he didn't deserve to feel. "Honey, you didn't do anything.

Luke's not being here has nothing to do with something you said. He probably just hasn't gotten the message yet.''

Cody lifted his head. It was apparent that nothing she said was making one iota of difference. ''If I promise to be good, do you think he'll come?''

It nearly broke Emily's heart to see the hope in Cody's eyes. What made her heart ache even more was how badly he was coming to need his father—a father who couldn't always be there for him. At least, not as long as she remained his mom.

Impossible situations. She seemed especially gifted at finding herself in the middle of them. But, instead of dwelling on that dubious talent, she chose to impress upon Cody that his parents' love for him—Luke's and her own—had nothing to do with how bad or how good he was, that sometimes parents just got so caught up in themselves that they didn't stop to think how their actions were affecting the people they should care about the most. As she talked, she rubbed his back, taking comfort from him, as well as giving it. If Cody thought about it at all, he probably thought she was talking about Luke. And she was. To a point. But Emily was talking about herself, too, as she sat on the edge of the bed, rocking Cody as she had when she used to come to this same hospital to read to him—back before they belonged to each other.

When seven o'clock arrived and Luke still hadn't called, Emily tried to reach him again.

There was no answer at his office, though she hadn't expected one at that hour of the evening. Likewise, there was still no answer at his house—not that she expected him to be home, either, since about the only thing he had said to her was that he'd be in Texas part of this week. The messages she'd left before were simply to ask that he call. Since the last he'd heard about Cody was that his checkup had been fine, a message about him having surgery was bound to be alarming. Now, though, she didn't have much choice. She only hoped he'd called back in time to talk to Cody before he went to sleep tonight.

Unfortunately, she and Cody were in the playroom at the end of the ward when Luke did call back. Cody's roommate's mother didn't know where they were, though. It wasn't until much later that the lady, looking relieved to be leaving for the night, mentioned that Cody's dad had called and said to tell her he was on his way.

Cody had been asleep for hours when Emily finally dozed off herself on one of the two sofas in the waiting area outside the ward. She had promised Cody she wouldn't leave, and it made more sense to her to stay, anyway, since they would wake him at five-thirty for his seven-o'clock surgery.

The sofas, remarkably uncomfortable things covered in turquoise vinyl, faced the elevators. They were separated by a table littered with outdated magazines read by people who paid little attention to their content anyway. Most of the visitors who used this distinctly Spartan area were concerned only with the child or grandchild or niece or nephew in the ward beyond the double doors farther along the wall.

The mechanical whir of elevator cables preceded the *ping* of the floor indicator. Such sounds were barely noted during the day and early evening. It was only in the wee hours, when the elevator's use was less frequent—and some parent or relative was hoping for sleep—that the soft sound was at all disturbing.

Hearing it now, Emily sighed into the crook of her arm, where it rested on the back of the sofa, and felt the muscles in the back of her neck knot in protest when she raised her head. With one hand at the back of her neck, she used the other to push herself upright just as the elevator doors slid open.

Luke saw her the moment he stepped into the waiting area. The lighting was dim—in deference, he supposed, to the hour—but he could see her anxiety when she pushed the tangle of cinnamon-colored curls from her face and slowly rose to face him. She looked as if she'd been sleeping, or trying to, and he had the craziest urge to simply fold her in his arms and hold her before he had to listen to whatever it was she was going to tell him.

"What's wrong with Cody?" He posed the question even as he dropped his flight bag at the end of the sofa and tossed his suit jacket on top of it.

"He's all right, Luke." She offered the assurance quickly, needing to dispel the worst of his fears. "It's not an emergency. It's just a corrective procedure for his hip," she explained, then realized she was searching his face, hoping for some sign that he was glad to see her.

Feeling utterly foolish, she sank back down on the sofa. When he did the same a moment later, leaving the width of one slightly cracked cushion between them, she quietly told him what the doctors had told her and how the testing Cody had been through this week had confirmed their conclusions.

At first, Luke simply listened as she spoke, leaving her to explain procedures he'd never heard of until he'd gathered enough information to form questions of his own—such as how much danger Cody would be in during the surgery, and how long it would take for him to recover. His features were drawn, worry having etched itself into his brow. But even as Emily felt his relief at discovering the situation less than critical, she also began to feel his irritation.

It was in his voice when he looked up from where his hands were clasped between his knees. "I don't suppose it occurred to you to call me when all this started?"

Guilt kept her attention focused on the creases her attempts at sleep had ironed in her cotton pants. "I didn't think it was necessary. If the tests had proven he didn't need surgery right now, you'd have been concerned for nothing."

"It's not up to you to decide what I need to know about my son's health. When those first test results came back as being questionable, you should have let me know. I told you to call me if Cody needed anything. God, Emily—" he sighed, out of either disappointment or exasperation "—I thought you'd know that included stuff like this."

Her twinges of guilt seemed to be closer, a little like labor pains, and probably just about as comfortable. She'd known all along she should have let him know sooner. If she hadn't known, she wouldn't have wrestled so much with the decision.

Now she was wrestling with defensiveness. She'd almost have felt better if he'd been more upset with her. His weary acceptance of what she hadn't done was unnerving. "It's not like I didn't try to reach you earlier. I left a message with your secretary at nine o'clock this morning. She must not have gotten it to you."

The look he sent her over the short distance separating them was remarkably patient. "She got it to me, Emily. She's very good at tracking me down. She's also very good at getting messages correct, which is why I'm sure she would have told me it was urgent had you mentioned it yourself. Apparently all you asked is that I call you back."

Emily looked from the odd disappointment in his expression to a crack in the vinyl of the sofa. She began tracing it with her fingernail. She couldn't explain that she hadn't wanted to alarm him with some impersonal message saying that his son was in the hospital. He'd only point out that, because she hadn't done it sooner, she'd had to do it later, anyway. "As it was, you didn't get back to me until almost eight o'clock. At least that's when Cody's roommate's mom said you called."

"So that's who that was," she heard Luke mutter as he ran his hand over his face.

When his hand fell, his eyes narrowed. He couldn't care less about the addle-brained woman he's spoken with earlier. He wasn't going to let Emily get away with shifting blame here. Not with something as important as this. If they were going to share custody of Cody, they were going to share it all.

"When I got your message," he said, his words lacking the irritation they could have held, "I was on the thirty-second floor of a building with open air for walls and bare steel girders swinging by on crane cables. So let's say I wasn't in a position to give your message to call much thought just then. When I did think about it, I thought maybe it was because you or Cody had some plans for the weekend that would affect my plans to visit with him. So I called on my way to dinner, but you weren't home. Then, after dinner, I went back to the hotel instead of staying with the rest of my party for a drink and tried to call you again."

Since he'd been in Dallas for three days, he went on to tell her in that same matter-of-fact tone, he'd then called his house to get the messages off his answering machine. That was when he'd gotten the message to call her at the hospital, but the woman who'd answered the phone in Cody's room hadn't known anything other than that Cody was having surgery in the morning. So he'd gotten on the phone to the airlines, found a red-eye flight from Dallas to

Seattle with a stop in Phoenix, and here he was. Whether she liked the idea or not.

Luke didn't say that last part. Not exactly. Emily knew he was thinking it as he watched her curl herself into the corner of the sofa and rub at the knots in her neck.

Jan had suggested she should do what was easiest on herself. The easiest thing to do right now would be to leave the conversation right where it was. To simply accept that she'd been wrong not to call him sooner, to accept that he was here, and just let the matter rest.

"I wouldn't have called you if it hadn't been important, Luke. Why would you assume I only wanted to talk about your visiting Cody this weekend?"

With his elbows on his knees and his hands clasped loosely between them, he suddenly looked tired. He hadn't seemed so at all to her until now, despite the fact that it was after three o'clock in the morning. Yet, with her question, fatigue crept over him like a shadow, and he didn't seem at all interested in fighting either it or her.

"Honestly?" he asked.

She wasn't so sure she wanted to know when he put it that way. Still, gamely, she nodded.

Luke's sigh sounded strangely like regret. "I guess it's because of what I know you'll never do. I told you to let me know if Cody needed anything, and even though you said you would, I knew you'd just keep on doing what you've always done. Handling it all by yourself. The only thing you've been able to force yourself to ask me is that I spend regular time with Cody. And it probably hurt like hell for you to have to do that much." He shook his head, neither wanting nor expecting a reply. "So when you called, it just seemed that whatever you wanted must have something to do with that. I couldn't imagine any other reason."

He turned his head toward her, the dimmed overhead lights catching hints of silver among the shades of wheat in his hair. There was none of the accusation she'd expected to see in his eyes, only a dispassionate curiosity that was somehow far more cutting. "What were you going to say when you reached me, Emily? Were you just going to tell me that Cody was having surgery and that you'd let me know how it went?"

That she'd considered just such a scenario must have been evident. The awful disappointment was back in his face again, harder for her to take than his disapproval would have been. She didn't want him to be disappointed in her.

"I was going to ask you to come to the hospital," she told him, because it was the truth. At least it had become so eventually. "Cody wanted you here."

"But you didn't."

It was impossible to meet his eyes and deny what he somehow knew. "No," she admitted as he studied her face. "I didn't."

"What did you think I was going to do?"

"I don't know, Luke. I don't suppose I thought you were going to do anything." It was simply his presence she'd wanted to avoid. "For a while, I didn't think you'd even want to come yourself."

"Why wouldn't I?"

He was clearly thinking of Cody. She was considering all of them. "You've got to admit that the last couple of times you and I have been around each other things have been a little . . . tense," she concluded, unable to come up with a better word. "The last time you came to see Cody, you were only with him for an hour, and you said all of a dozen words to me. That didn't leave me with the impression that you were anxious to rush back."

Recollection swept over Luke's features. His voice lowered. "I just didn't have much time that day."

"Cody thought you were angry with him."

There was no accusation in her tone. She was simply telling him something she thought he needed to know. Luke seemed to realize that. He also seemed at a loss as to how Cody could have gotten such an idea.

"He said he asked you to live with us," she reminded him. "Apparently you told him I wouldn't like that, and he got the idea you were upset with him for asking."

Luke's expression grew oddly pensive. "I wasn't upset with him. The question just threw me a little. He was full of them that day." In the quiet, the *ping* of the elevator stopping a floor below could be heard. "He also wanted to know if he could have a new brother. He wanted one for Mike, too."

Emily went completely still. Cody had asked Luke for a brother? "For Mike?"

"His turtle, Michelangelo," he returned, as if she should know that. "We had him outside with us. Remember?"

Actually, she didn't. She wasn't trying to recall anything about the day at the moment, either. She was too busy wondering what Luke had thought of Cody's request. "What did you tell him? About the brother, I mean."

"For Mike, or for himself?"

She swallowed when she saw the hard edge creeping across Luke's features. "For himself."

"Actually, I told him he'd have to take up both matters with you. If you said it was okay, we'd get him another turtle. As for the other, that one's strictly up to you."

He stood then, his frame shadowing her as he pushed his fingers through his hair. "I need some coffee. Can I get any around here?"

Emily shifted on the sofa, wincing a little when the movement irritated the persistent kink in her neck. "There's a machine right around the corner."

He said nothing else. He simply turned away, ending the discussion in much the same way she assumed he'd ended the one with Cody. She was left feeling much the same way she suspected Cody had felt, too. Luke didn't seem angry, or even upset. Yet, as he disappeared around the corner, she was under the impression that he was displeased with her. Or maybe, she thought, as the image of her pregnant with Luke's child sprang unbidden to her mind, the displeasure had only been with the subject.

Luke hadn't asked if she'd wanted coffee. He brought her a cup anyway, handing it to her as he passed the sofa on his way to the window at the end of the waiting area. He stood with his back to her, his thoughts as closed to her as his expression had been when she'd thanked him for the coffee.

He hadn't come right out and said so, but it was clear enough he was staying. As much as she'd fought the idea, Emily found herself far more relieved by that circumstance than she'd thought she'd be.

She just couldn't stand the silence.

"I'm afraid that's not a very exciting view out there."

The window he stood before overlooked a curving multilevel parking structure and the street below. As dark as it was, there was little to see.

"I guess that depends on what excites you. The design of that structure is very fluid. Its lines are clean and unbroken. To me, that's exciting." He turned to face her. "For some people it's the opera or great paintings. I get turned on by structures."

He looked calmer, as if losing himself in what lay beyond the window had helped alleviate the tension that had brought him to it. She marveled at that ability.

"Has this been a lifelong affliction?"

"Only from about seventeen." His chiseled features softened slightly with a self-deprecating smile. "I was pretty normal before that."

She met his smile as he sat down beside her appreciating his attempt to ease the strain that always permeated their conversations. She wished it didn't have to be there, that strain. But it was. And now, because they would be together for the next several hours, it was her turn to try and ignore it, too.

Angled sideways, she propped her elbow on the back of the sofa and absently worked at the muscles in her shoulder. "What were you doing when you were seventeen?"

He took a sip of his coffee, forever ruining her image of him as a gourmet when he didn't so much as grimace. The furrowing of his brows was simply from thought.

"At seventeen I was a senior in high school, trying desperately to get into Dartmouth and a cute little blonde named Judith Holt. Not necessarily in that order. If I recall correctly, I was somewhat obsessed with relieving myself of my virginity that year."

Emily almost smiled. "I shouldn't have asked."

"But you did," he pointed out reasonably. "And no, I didn't get Judith. I did get into Dartmouth, though, and managed to solve my other problem the summer in between. What about you? What were you doing when you were seventeen?"

With the question turned on her, she was now absolutely positive she shouldn't have posed it. Of all the years in her life, that was the one she chose to think about the least.

"I forget." There was a dent in the lip of her foam cup. Emily turned her focus there. "That was a long time ago."

She wouldn't look at him. That in itself was enough to raise Luke's suspicions. It was the weakness of the reply that actually gave her away.

"You know, Emily, I think that's the first."

Her glance came up, and the delicate wings of her eyebrows lowered. "The first what?"

"The first time you've ever lied to me."

The sofa creaked as she started to turn away. His hand on her arm held her in place.

"Stay put," he told her. "I'll just come after you if you leave, and I don't feel like getting up. I'm not going to push, Emily. If there's something you don't want to tell me, just say so."

She sank back onto the hard cushion. "I just don't like thinking about any of it. Besides," she added, because it was a consideration, too, "I'm not sure what you'd think of me if you knew."

"Does it matter what I think of you?"

The dent had her attention again. "I suppose so."

"Why?"

"Because I need for you to believe I'm a good influence on Cody."

"And if there were no Cody? Would it still matter what I thought of you?"

The air felt rather heavy all of a sudden. As if someone had pulled all the oxygen out of it and it was suddenly hard to breathe. Emily didn't know if it was the late hour, the place, or some Freudian thing that had made her admit what she had. But, as she watched him study her face, she knew there was an import to his question that went far beyond her anxiety over having to answer it.

Her glance fell to the second button on his dress shirt, open and revealing a tuft of golden brown hair. Yes, it would matter. Very much. "There is a Cody, Luke." She wouldn't play hypothetical games. "And you really might not like what you hear."

"Perhaps," he admitted, seeming strangely disappointed with her response. "There's one way to find out."

It wasn't what he could do with the knowledge that kept her silent. He couldn't use it against her. Not to get Cody, anyway. The court already knew all the nasty little details. Her concern lay solely in what he might think of her.

That, ironically, was what finally made her answer him. She'd never deliberately hidden her past. She wouldn't start now.

"When I was seventeen," she began, determined to get through it quickly, though not in great detail, "I was busy dropping out of school, running away from home, getting married, getting divorced and getting out of juvenile detention. Not necessarily in that order."

Luke didn't even blink. "What about when you were eighteen?"

She watched him watch her, searching for his disapproval, his disgust, his shock. All she could see in his expression was quiet interest, and a patient insistence that she continue.

The defensiveness she hadn't even known was there left her tone. "I was working as a waitress and going to night school to get my GED."

"Is that how you put yourself through college, too? Being a waitress?"

"That, and typing other people's term papers."

"Now." The tip of his fingers grazed the side of her neck as he nudged her curls aside. "Was that so hard?"

"Yes."

His fingers slid along her nape, and his thumb roamed upward, into her hair. "Why?"

"I don't want to do this, Luke."

She hadn't been conscious of the way she was rubbing her shoulder until she felt his hand nudge hers aside. His palm splayed over the back of her neck. It felt warm and strong as he flexed his fingers against the knots in her neck.

"You're not doing anything but sitting here." The misinterpretation was deliberate, a subtle attempt on his part to keep her from pulling away from him. "What's not to do?"

"I don't want to get into all that—" she lifted her hand, then let it fall ineffectually to her lap "—all that stuff. And don't ask me what stuff. You know what I mean."

Luke knew exactly what she meant. She was talking about the emotional baggage people dragged around with them and either tripped over or hid behind when a relationship threatened to get too complicated. What he didn't understand was why the two of them had stacked that baggage so high between themselves. Or why it felt so imperative that he understand whatever it was that kept her from trusting him enough to tear down a few chunks of that wall.

It was time, he knew, that he found out.

Chapter Eleven

Emily didn't want to move. Luke's hand gently rubbing her shoulder was pleasant, seductive in a way, but mostly just nice to feel. The motion eased the ache sleeping in the pretzel position had produced and conveyed an offer of support that she badly wanted to accept. Yet, even as his touch soothed, it enlivened. That, combined with the tension created by a conversation she didn't want to have, gave her no choice but to slip from him.

She sought her solace as Luke had earlier—in the view out the window.

"They should be waking Cody in another hour." She rubbed her hands over her arms, a purely physical reaction to the loss of Luke's touch. That she wanted his touch so badly didn't even alarm her anymore. "I think I should go sit with him."

"He's asleep, Emily. You told me yourself that some-one would come get you if he woke up. You don't have to go in there to avoid me. I told you I wouldn't push."

He had come up behind her, standing close enough that she could feel the heat of his body. He didn't touch her, though he could easily have laid his hand on her shoulder and turned her to face him. Instead, he simply watched her reflection in the night-darkened window—and waited for her to decide whether or not she believed him.

With a sigh, she realized that she did believe him. Maybe that was part of the problem. More and more, she trusted what he said, what he did. As disconcerting as it was to realize that, she let herself feel the tantalizing security that came with it. For now, anyway, because it seemed he trusted her, too. He hadn't turned away when she'd rat-tled off her list of sins. If anything, his reaction had been that of a man who wasn't learning anything he didn't al-ready know.

"The private investigator you hired to find Cody," she began, watching Luke's reflection in the window. "Had he told you everything I just did?"

"He'd found out you were divorced. You know that. As for the rest of it, I know only what you've told me."

In the darkened window, Emily saw his shoulders mimic the verbal shrug she'd heard in his voice. It wasn't indif-ference she sensed in him. It was something more like pa-tience. He seemed willing to accept her whether or not she chose to elaborate. That was what finally gave her the courage to trust him with a glimpse of a past that she'd overcome in many ways, but that still subtly influenced every day of her life.

"I hadn't really wanted to run away," she quietly told him. "It was just that, at the time, it seemed like all I could do."

She felt his fingers touch her hair, then drift away.

"Where did you go?"

A small rather wry smile curved her lips. She'd gone from the frying pan into the fire. "I knew a girl who'd graduated the year before. She had an apartment." Emily touched the glass of the window with her fingertips. "She also had lots of friends. Kids naturally gravitate to their own kind, you know. The misplaced and the misfits accept each other simply because no one else will."

When she'd met Jimmy Ashton, she'd found them to be kindred spirits in that respect. Though it had taken Emily a few years and the insights of a juvenile probation officer to discover, she'd eventually come to realize that she'd dropped out of school and married Jimmy because she was looking for affection from parents who were too wrapped up in themselves to care about her. So she'd gone looking for that caring elsewhere, and she'd wound up with the first guy who said he loved her.

But Jimmy had never loved her, she told Luke. He'd been a year older than she, spoiled and angry with his parents for the rules they'd tried to impose on his life. He'd always been looking for a way to show them he was his own man—which was why he'd married her. He'd always been looking for a new thrill, too—which was why he'd wound up in jail on charges of auto theft after taking her for a joyride in a car Emily hadn't known was stolen. Being only seventeen at the time, she'd been put into juvenile detention. Jimmy got off.

His parents, pillars of the Scottsdale society, had hired a lawyer, bailed Jimmy out and worked out some deal to which she wasn't privy. They'd also bailed her out, once Jimmy had gotten around to mentioning that they were married. But as soon as they had, they'd threatened to disinherit him if he didn't get a divorce—presumably so that he could later marry the "right" kind of girl—get back to school and clean up his act. Given a choice between her and the loss of Daddy's money, her knight in shining armor had ridden off into the sunset in his Porsche.

She, on the other hand, had been given probation for being an accessory and in possession of stolen goods. Fortunately, because of the nature of her "crime" and because she was a juvenile, she'd had no police record after she turned eighteen a few months later. It was that record that she'd worried about the most when she'd applied to adopt Cody.

As she told Luke all of this, she remained facing the window, seeming to find some kind of strength in the coral dawn edging away the blackness of the night. Luke remained behind her, hearing so much more in her words than she actually said. She'd been emotionally abandoned, first by her parents and then by an immature husband, and left to make it on her own.

He had to respect her tenacity and her drive. Yet he had the feeling she gave herself little credit for what she had accomplished. He cared little about who she'd been or what she'd done so many years ago. God knew he'd made his share of mistakes. It was who she was now, the woman she'd become, that was important. And the woman she'd become, he was coming to realize, might very well be unreachable.

"You know, Luke…" Her voice came softly, hinting of a tiredness that had nothing to do with physical fatigue. "I was a pawn for my parents, something they could use against each other. It wasn't that whoever had the upper hand got me, it was that whoever got me had the upper hand. I could just as easily have been the house or the furniture. As for Jim, I was just a way of defying his parents." She paused, adding certainty to the resignation in her tone. "I hated the way they made me feel. I'd rather have nothing and be alone than be nothing to someone."

Headlights arced across the window as a vehicle moved through the top level of the parking structure. The white light caught Emily's face as Luke turned her toward him. He hadn't known what he'd see in her expression; sadness, perhaps, or anger over having been used by the people who should have cared the most. What he saw bore no resemblance to those deserved feelings. All her delicate features betrayed was a quiet sort of acceptance that told him more than he'd been prepared to know. The look in her haunting green eyes actually made him hurt inside.

It was no wonder she'd closed herself off from certain types of relationships. As long as she was doing the giving, and as long as she expected nothing in return, she was fine. It was when she started to become vulnerable that she began to pull back.

But she already was vulnerable. To his son.

As his hand moved up her neck and he saw the flash of awareness darken her eyes, he suspected that she might be just a little vulnerable to him, too.

"Ms. Russell?" A young nurse, her long blond hair held back in a ponytail, held open one of the double doors leading to the ward. "It's time to wake Cody now. You said to come get you."

Beneath his fingers, Luke felt the tension creep back into Emily's shoulders. Anxiety replaced the jolt of awareness she'd scarcely acknowledged. His hand fell, and a strange disappointment filled him when, an instant later, she slipped away as if what she had just shared with him didn't matter in the least. The instant she'd heard the nurse's voice, he'd lost her. Her thoughts now were for Cody.

Though he would have been hard pressed to justify it, Luke actually felt a little jealous of his son at that moment. This woman was getting to him in ways he hadn't counted on. In ways he wasn't sure he knew how to handle. Right now wasn't the time to consider that, however. His own concerns for his son had just taken over.

The wide hallway was quiet, and all the doorways were dark as they followed the nurse with clowns on her smock to the room just beyond the nurses' station. The room was dim, and someone had drawn the curtain between Cody's bed and the one near the window to minimize the chances of waking the other boy. Emily wondered if Luke even realized there was anyone else in the room as he moved to the head of Cody's bed and looked down at the peacefully sleeping child. From where she stood opposite him, she saw his hands clench where they curved over the side rails.

A moment later, Luke bent forward, his hand looking huge as it covered the top of his son's blond head. "Hey, sport," he whispered, then bent lower and added something Emily couldn't hear.

Cody never woke quickly. He would stretch, and groan, then stretch again, and maybe open his eyes if the effort wouldn't take too much energy. More often than not, he'd turn his head away and pull his pillow over his face—which usually meant that Emily would have to stick her face under the pillow, too, so that she could tell him it was a nice try but he had to wake up anyway.

There was none of that reluctance now. Cody's eyes opened, and his little brow puckered in confusion as Luke raised his head. A moment later, recognition cut through the fog of sleep.

His voice was still raspy with sleep, but there was no mistaking his delight when his arms came up to grab his father around the neck and he all but squeaked, "Daddy!"

It was the first time Emily had ever heard him call Luke that.

From the way Luke's eyes squeezed shut as he wrapped his little boy in his arms, it seemed to be the first time he'd heard it, too.

Emily's chest constricted as she watched, her smile painfully tight when Cody finally glanced her way and grinned. She didn't deserve his smile, though it was there mostly, she knew, because he was so happy to see Luke. In her effort to protect herself from what she'd told herself *she* no longer needed, she had almost denied her precious little boy the security of his father's presence. And she had almost denied his father the satisfaction of being there for his son.

As she looked away, she knew Luke realized how bad she felt about that, too.

"I'm going to get him ready now," the nurse said in a near-whisper as she slipped past Emily. "You can stay with him until we take him down. The gurney's on its way."

Even as she spoke, two orderlies in surgical scrubs and wearing blue paper hats on their heads appeared at the foot of the bed.

Cody's smile turned upside-down. He was clearly worried. Not about where he was going, though he did look pretty wary of the guys in the paper hats. What had his eyes so big and his expression so uncertain was his concern about how long Luke would remain.

"You'll be here when I come back?" he wanted to know.

Luke's hand rested on Cody's small shoulder. "We'll both be here. I promise."

"You won't let him go, Mom?"

Deliberately Emily turned her glance from Luke to Cody's anxious expression. Rather than reply, she simply shook her head to indicate that she wouldn't, and leaned over to tell him she loved him as one of the orderlies lowered the side rail and the medical staff took her baby from his bed and covered him up on the gurney. Two minutes later, the entire entourage was at the elevator. A minute after that, Emily was telling Cody to be her brave little boy and bracing herself to do what she always did when something moved beyond her control. She pulled inside herself, gathering her defenses against whatever might happen and shutting out everything else.

It was only when she noticed Luke still staring at the closed doors after Cody had been taken down that she knew she wouldn't be able to shut him out. Not the way she would once have done. Cody was his, too.

"He's going to be all right," she said, offering him the same assurance she had his son. She had to believe Cody would be okay. He was all she had. "Really. He'll be fine."

If Luke heard the catch in her voice, he didn't let on. He simply met her eyes with a look that said he knew she was worried, too, and gave her arm a squeeze when he walked past her.

So it was that they paced the waiting room, taking silent comfort in the fact that they weren't having to do this alone and avoiding any subject that might add to the stress that seemed to cling to the very walls of the place. The waiting seemed a little easier when other parents began to show up, the presence of others taking the burden of talking, or not talking, from them. For the most part, though, Emily and Luke simply stood together at the window, trying to watch something other than the clock.

That was where they were when Dr. Hamilton stepped off the elevator, three long hours later.

Luke saw her first. He didn't know who she was, because he'd never met her. But the tall woman's strides held purpose, and she was headed straight toward Emily.

He touched Emily's arm. Lost in whatever thoughts had kept her from him for the past hour, the contact startled her.

Easy, honey, he silently soothed, then nodded toward the approaching woman.

The instant Emily made eye contact with her, Cleo Hamilton smiled. She was still in her blue surgical scrubs, her mask hanging around her neck, but she'd removed her cap to let her short, dark hair frame her round face. "The surgery went beautifully," she said, coming up to them, her smile growing wider. "Cody's in Recovery right now, and he's doing just fine."

Luke's expression didn't betray the knee-wilting relief that was evident in Emily's. He simply closed his eyes and took the first easy breath he'd drawn in three hours.

"It will be a while before they bring him back up," the doctor was saying, her smile fading to speculation as she glanced at him. "Once they do, he'll probably sleep for the rest of the afternoon." Her brow furrowed. "How are you doing, Emily?"

"Fine," she returned, meaning it now that she knew Cody was all right. "Fine," she repeated, and watched the doctor's eyebrows lift ever so slightly when Luke's hand protectively cupped her shoulder.

The doctor was very good at detecting subtleties. Emily was never so sure of that as when she introduced Luke to her, then fell silent as the two of them spoke. Dr. Hamilton immediately picked up on Luke's concerns, seeming impressed both by the nature of his questions about what Cody might eventually be capable of doing and his willingness to accept that this was only one of a very long line of operations that came with no guarantees.

What Emily missed, though, was that underlying Luke's interest in his son was concern for her, too. It was there in the way he kept glancing toward her, frowning at the dark circles the lack of sleep had formed beneath her eyes. It was there, too, in the way he drew her closer when he felt her trembling now that it was all over.

Cleo Hamilton missed none of it.

"You might feed her," she said, with a nod toward Emily. "I know when she gets in this place she forgets about food. She also forgets to sleep. Which," she added as Luke rubbed his unshaven jaw, "seems to be a lesson she's teaching you. I'll tell you what I tell all the parents of my patients. You won't do your child any good if you get sick yourself. Cody will be fine. Once they bring him back up, he's going to spend most of the day sleeping off the rest of the anesthetic."

She turned back to Emily. "Go home after you see Cody. He really did do very well. Our boy's a real little trouper."

It wasn't her intention to slight Luke with her last remark. Luke was sure of that when the doctor, a bit belatedly, included him in her smile. He'd have to be as dense as stone not to understand that there was a bond between this woman and Emily and his son that couldn't include him. These two women had been through a lot with Cody. They had been there for him, and cared for him, while Luke had gone on about his life, concerned only with making his next project more notable than the last.

In the past couple of months, his priorities had begun to shift. But not until he felt that moment's exclusion did he appreciate quite how much.

Cody was brought up half an hour later. As the doctor had indicated, he was awake barely long enough to know they were there before drifting off again. Another half hour of watching him sleep and Luke was hardly able to stay awake himself. It wouldn't have been so bad if he'd had something to do, but just sitting there was the worst.

"Come on," he whispered to Emily when she started to lay her head on her arms at the foot of Cody's bed. "I'll take you home."

Emily didn't want to go home. Despite the fact that she'd managed only bits and snatches of sleep the night before, she wanted to stay with Cody. But she knew Dr. Hamilton was right, and her eyes felt as if lead weights were attached to their lids. As for Luke, he hadn't slept at all, and she knew he wouldn't leave until she did.

He also happened to be starving. Or so he said as they waited for the elevator.

She suggested the hospital cafeteria.

Luke didn't even bother to reply. He simply gave her a look that told her to try again.

Emily dug in her heels. "I can't go anywhere else like this. They expect people to look terrible in the hospital cafeteria. I look like I slept in my clothes."

"That's probably because you did."

He knew he was smiling when she glared back at him. He didn't care. She looked fine to him. Better than fine, actually. Beautiful. Enticing. Exciting. But Luke knew better than to argue with a woman about how she thought she looked.

He stifled a yawn. "Look. I don't want to eat here, and you don't want to go to a restaurant. What do you suggest we do?"

As tired as she was, she just wanted to be home. So that was what she suggested—that she fix something for them to eat at her house. After the hours of worry they'd spent together, sharing a meal didn't seem like such a big deal. "But I'm warning you," she added as they headed through the hospital lobby and out into the noon sun. "I'm not much of a cook."

Luke took Emily's warning in stride. He clearly remembered the roast she'd put in the oven the day her washing machine had broken down. When he reminded her of it, she seemed surprised that he'd been at all impressed by something so basic. Not sure what she meant by that, but certain that, as tired as they both were, he might be borrowing trouble by asking, he traded that memory for another. He'd very nearly kissed her that day. Now, knowing how her body felt against his, he found himself thinking of an entirely different sort of hunger and wished he hadn't recalled that particular day at all. But as with all the other days he'd spent anywhere near her, the details were burned in his brain. He could no more forget them than he could forget her.

The realization shook him.

He shared none of those thoughts with her. He kept them to himself, much as she kept her thoughts concealed behind her closed eyes during the twenty-minute drive to her house. He'd thought time would make things easier between them. All time had done was show him how much more complicated the situation could get.

Since it had been faster for Luke to grab a cab than to get a rental car at the airport, he was driving Emily's car. By the time he pulled into her driveway, he thought Emily had fallen asleep. The moment he cut the engine, though, she raised her head. Pushing back her hair, looking a little sheepish, she gave him a soft little smile. It occurred to him then that she was actually too tired to care that he hadn't said anything about going to a hotel. His flight bag was in her back seat. He hoped she wouldn't have a problem with him cleaning up before they went back to the hospital tonight.

"Mind if I bring this in?" he asked, and when she indicated that she didn't, he followed her in and dropped the bag by the front door. He'd clean up later. Food and sleep were his first priorities.

"You have your choice of eggs, a grilled cheese sandwich or a cheese omelet. Which would you prefer?" Tired, but hungry now that she thought about it, she glanced over to see Luke watching her. The speculative look in his eyes was so familiar by now that she forgot to be wary of it. Her mind was on other things, anyway. "Do you think I should call and see if Cody's okay?"

He opened the cabinet behind him. "They have the number here, Emily. He was sound asleep when we left, and he probably still is. Sleeping is also what I'd like to be doing, so what can I do to help?"

"You never said what you wanted."

Deliberately he kept his attention on the bowl he set on the counter. "The omelet."

A moment later, he was at the stove and taking a small frying pan from the cabinet beside it.

Emily's frown moved from the bowl to the pan now on the stove. It finally settled on Luke's unreadable expression when he turned around.

"How did you know where I keep everything in here?"

"I've watched you."

Silverware shifted with a dull clatter as he opened a drawer. Out came silver for the table and a fork for the eggs. "You don't have a whisk," he said, as if to explain the extra utensil.

"You've watched me?"

"Put dishes away," he said, thinking of the times he'd seen her in this room doing something or other while he and Cody put a puzzle together at the table or he helped him with his homework. "You know, when you empty the dishwasher."

"And you've remembered where I put everything?"

"I think I remember everything I've ever seen you do," he admitted, and turned her by the shoulders so that she could start the eggs. "What else do you want with this?"

He seemed so much more efficient in her own kitchen than she did. Certainly he was at the moment. Facing the counter, feeling almost dizzy with fatigue, she wasn't sure she had the energy to eat what they were preparing, much less make any decisions about what that might be. "Toast?" she heard herself suggest. Then she heard him moving about behind her while she took a deep breath and started in on her appointed task.

It didn't occur to her to be at all annoyed with the way he'd taken over. All she thought was that it was really nice to let someone else be in charge of a meal for a change.

She had no idea why that thought brought tears to her eyes.

Blinking away the unexpected moisture, she started cracking eggs. The first two made it into the bowl. The third slipped from her fingers and landed on the floor.

She'd just knelt down with a paper towel when she felt Luke's hand on her shoulder.

"Let me get that."

"No. No," she repeated, her voice not nearly as strong as she'd have liked it to be. "I can do it."

"Emily. Here. Why don't you finish the toast—"

"I said I can do it."

His hand left her shoulder, and she closed her eyes to draw a deep breath. She hadn't meant to snap at him. She really hadn't. He was just so bloody efficient, and she was feeling foolish for having dropped the egg in the first place.

Rising, not so much as glancing toward Luke, she dumped the mess into the trash, gave the floor another swipe with a damp towel and opened the refrigerator. She wasn't sure what she was getting, she just knew she had to keep moving so that she wouldn't have to think. But the thoughts were there anyway—the thoughts she'd avoided the whole time Cody had been in surgery. Thoughts of Luke. Of his son. She couldn't avoid them now any more than she could avoid breathing.

She rested her forehead on the edge of the door.

The chill air from the refrigerator made her shiver. Or maybe it was the feel of Luke watching her—of knowing how easily he seemed to see through her—that made her feel so shaky. Somehow, when she hadn't been looking, she'd fallen in love with him. Hopelessly. Completely. Irrevocably. She'd fallen in love with his sense of honor, his strength, his love for his son. Even with his stubbornness. Yet, as painful as his presence was because she'd realized how very much she cared, she was so very glad he was here.

That thought had just registered when she felt him turning her around. "You just put the salt in the refrigerator. Do you want me to fix the eggs?"

Her throat tightened, so much that she didn't dare speak.

She wouldn't meet his eyes. She didn't have to for Luke to know that the strain of the day was finally getting to her. She was doing what Cody's turtle did sometimes, pulling into her shell to protect herself when the going got rough, even though she knew she'd be vulnerable once again when the trouble was past. She was vulnerable now. He knew that when he tipped up her head and saw the suspicious brightness in her eyes. The movement of the slender cords of her throat as she swallowed betrayed all she was holding back. I'm always okay, he remembered her saying.

Sure she was.

He gave the door to the fridge a nudge to close it, then let his arms slide around her. "It's all right, honey," he told her, because he knew she didn't want him to see her this way. "You're just tired."

The feel of his arms closing around her was more than Emily could handle. She was tired. But not tired the way he meant it. What she felt had to do with so much more than physical fatigue. It had to do not with handling it all alone, but with being alone. With having no one to share with, no one to turn to.

She'd thought she could handle the demands of Cody's disability. She had honestly thought she was strong enough to see herself and him through the rough times she knew lay ahead. She hadn't expected it to be easy. Nothing ever had been for her. But maybe she'd misled herself into thinking she had the strength to help them both cope. She certainly didn't feel she had it. Not at the moment, anyway.

His lips feathered over her cheek, her temple. "Why don't you forget about eating and just go to sleep? I'll stretch out on Cody's bed. Come on. We'll fix something later."

He took her lack of protest as agreement. Still keeping his arm over her shoulder, he put the eggs back in the refrigerator and led her down the hall to her room. The weight of his arm felt good, protective and maybe just a little possessive. She did want to sleep. But she wanted his arms around her even more. She felt inexplicably safe, sheltered against his side, and very cared for when he sat her down on the edge of her bed and pulled off her tennis shoes.

"You don't have to do that."

"Sure I do. You don't let Cody take a nap with his shoes on." He rose, one hand hanging loosely at his side, the other raised to push back her bangs so that he could see her eyes. "What is it?" he asked when he saw the question forming there.

Her glance fell to her knees. "I don't want you to go."

"I'm not going anywhere."

"You said you were going to Cody's room."

With the tip of his finger, he nudged her chin up. There was hesitation in her weary expression, along with a quiet plea he couldn't have begun to refuse.

"Do you want me to stay here with you?"

"Would you?" Her voice sounded very small. "Please?"

From somewhere beyond the pale pastel walls of the bedroom came the faint sound of a car door slamming and from somewhere nearer the sounds of a radio being played a little too loud. Neighborhood sounds that Luke barely noticed. He thought only of the woman who looked very much as if she needed to be held.

"Move over," he said, and a moment later he was stretching out with her atop the eyelet comforter on her bed. "Give me your back."

Without another word, Emily turned onto her side. Luke fitted himself behind her, draping one arm over her waist and curving the other over her head. He thought he heard her sigh. Or maybe the faint, satisfied sound had been his own.

Luke had known he was tired. They both were. Yet he wouldn't have believed it possible to fall asleep so quickly with the bass of a neighbor's radio pounding away—and with Emily's sweet, seductive body nestled so securely against his.

* * *

The feel of Luke curved behind her had carried Emily into sleep. That same feeling was what woke her.

For the briefest moment, Emily thought she hadn't slept at all. Then she realized that the sunlight slanting through the shutters and making a pattern over the bed wasn't nearly as bright as she'd remembered it being when she and Luke had first lain down. He was awake now, too.

She felt his hand push the curls away from her neck, and a warm, liquid sensation filled her at the touch of his lips to the curve of her shoulder. "It's almost six," she heard him whisper, and she relaxed against him, because it wasn't as late as she had feared.

That she could relax at all with Luke in her bed was remarkable. It felt like heaven to be held the way he was holding her. In his arms, caught somewhere between sleep and full consciousness, she felt secure, protected. But it was the feel of his hand pressing into her stomach to pull her closer that created a sensation far more provocative.

His warm breath feathered her hair. "Did you sleep?"

She nodded, snuggling deeper against him. "Did you?"

"Uh-huh." His lips brushed her skin again. "I don't think either of us moved. Come here."

He turned her in his arms. His features were softened a little from sleep, and his hair was appealingly mussed. Without thinking, she pushed back the strands that fell over his forehead—and watched his eyes darken as they scanned her face.

His hands skimmed her hip. "We need to get up in a few minutes."

She thought she said something in agreement. She couldn't remember what it was, though, when his gaze locked on hers. She was conscious only of the feel of his hand as it slipped over the curve of her bottom, and the hard feel of him when he pulled her against his groin. Beyond that, she knew only that his eyes went inky dark in the moments before his breath fanned her cheek and his mouth slowly closed over hers.

Emily almost forgot to breathe. He tasted hot and sweet as his breath mingled with hers. In a movement so subtle that she scarcely noticed it, he changed the slant of her head to take her tongue into his mouth, drawing it in to tangle with his own. There was no urgency as he pulled her closer, only an earth-shattering tenderness that was far more powerful than any demand could have been. Stunning, liquid sensations filled her, and she reached for him, touching as he touched.

She had no idea how long he held her that way, exploring, teasing.

Needing.

Wanting.

Denying.

"Emily." He whispered her name as he rained damp kisses over her cheek to her temple. "Don't do that."

Her hand had slipped around to the small of his back, urging him forward as he had coaxed her. Now, catching her by the wrist, he brought her hand between them. "Don't," he whispered, pressing her head to his chest, quieting her, quieting himself.

Two deep breaths, and he nudged her chin upward.

His voice sounded raspy. "Do you mind if I use your shower?"

Emily shook her head, her heart pounding. She didn't know what she'd done, but he was pulling back from her, his gaze glittering hard on her face as he smoothed back her hair. A tortured look swept through his eyes just before he closed them and pressed his forehead to hers.

"Good." He let out a long, deep breath. "Then that's where I'd better go."

Disappointment robbed the light from her eyes. He would have kissed her again, had he been able to trust himself to stop there. But he didn't trust himself at all at the moment. That was why he'd stopped. And now she was rolling away.

It occurred to him then that she had gotten the wrong idea.

Catching her by the waist, he pulled her back. "Where are you going?"

"I'm just getting up," she said. She wouldn't look at him.

"Why?"

"Because you are."

"The only reason I am," he told her, making her tip her head back to look at him, "is because of what will happen if I don't."

She didn't so much as blink.

Luke felt his whole body grow rigid.

He framed her face in his hands. Bearing his weight on his elbows, he slid himself over her. Even fully clothed, the feel of her beneath him was enough to make him groan. He actually did when she shifted against him and touched her fingertips to his cheek.

"I don't want you to go, Luke."

Sweet heaven, he didn't want to, either. But as he'd been mentally burying himself inside her, he'd been struck by the possible consequence that neither of them needed right now. As oddly erotic as the thought was to him of having his child growing inside her belly, they had enough problems without him getting her pregnant.

Capturing her hand, he pressed a kiss to her palm. Another kiss was pressed to her jaw. She turned her head, meeting his mouth, but he drew back before what he ached to do could sabotage his little remaining common sense. "Are we okay?" he asked, and felt her go still.

He drew back to see her suddenly troubled frown. It was all the answer he needed. She wasn't using any birth control. Without having to be told, he knew that she'd probably had no reason to. The knowledge fueled more than just desire for this woman. It made him feel possessive, protective; feelings that were becoming more familiar every time he thought of her.

His hand slipped from her cheek, lingering to graze the slope of her breast. A moment later, taking a deep breath, he slipped away from her.

Emily listened to his heavy footsteps over the heavier thudding of her heart. She sat up, pushing her fingers through her hair, only to have him nudge her right back to her elbows after he set his shaving kit on the nightstand. That he carried protection with him should have bothered her somehow, she supposed. He even waited for her to say something about it. Or, perhaps, what he was waiting for as he leaned over her, his eyes searching her face, was for her to change her mind.

All Emily considered as she touched the hard line of his jaw was that he'd thought to be careful with her. For that, she was grateful.

"Hold me," she whispered, reaching for him.

She saw his nostrils flare with his deeply drawn breath. Yet, for all the heat in his eyes, the touch of his lips to hers was infinitely gentle.

"Anytime." He guided her head back to the pillow, following her down. "Anytime," he repeated, then said nothing else as he coaxed her lips to part.

The tenderness she'd felt before in his kiss was still there, a gentle seduction of her senses. It was in the slow, exploring touch of his tongue to hers, and in the feather-light caress of his hand from her neck to her shoulders. He drew that gentle touch to her waist, to her stomach, and then up to her breasts to fill his palm with her softness. He taunted and teased that tight bud until, long moments later, he grew frustrated with her shirt being in the way and pulled it over her head.

His shirt hit the floor, too.

The feel of his bare skin against hers was exquisite. Emily strained toward him, needing his touch to become bolder. His deliberate restraint as his hands roamed her body awakened a hunger in her unlike any she'd ever known. She wanted to feel him against her. All of him. But instead of drawing her closer, he feathered his lips down her throat, seeming quite content to drive her crazy as his fingers and his lips brushed over her bra. His teeth nipped at the point straining against the thin fabric, dampening the lace and creating little waves of heat that shot straight down. Only when he heard her tiny moan of frustration did he finally get rid of the lace and pull the hard nipple into his mouth.

Emily's hand moved into his hair. The silky strands slipped between her fingers, and she drew him closer. The first time he'd kissed her, she'd been frightened by what he could make her feel. Now she was frightened at the thought of not feeling it. She had thought she could live without this. That she could survive without a physical relationship, because what she had known of sex had more to do with youthful experimentation than anything resembling lovemaking. But what Luke was doing was making love. The hunger in his kiss spoke of need rather than want. Of desire rather than lust. And as he pushed his hand under her hip to draw her pants down her legs, she knew she was very tired of only surviving.

Her pants landed on the floor. His joined them, along with everything else that separated hard flesh from soft skin. His kisses deepened, taking her into a dark place of swirling sensation, where nothing existed but the length of him pressed to her and the feel of his hands creating little lines of fire everywhere he touched. She returned those caresses, mimicking his movements and glorying in the way his body tensed at her touch.

"That's it," he told her, loving the greedy feel of her hands on his body. "Touch me as I touch you. Don't be afraid of me. Don't ever be afraid."

She wasn't. For the first time she could remember, she was actually not afraid of being close, of being vulnerable. Right now, with Luke, she felt safe and whole and desired. For now, she mattered to him.

That was the only thought encroaching upon the sensations as she felt his harder, rougher body moving over hers. She mattered to him. And as he coaxed her fully beneath him, filling her, consuming her, nothing else made any difference.

He should have slept. Heaven knew he needed to. But what Luke seemed to need more as he lay with Emily in her bed when they returned from the hospital that evening was to acknowledge the feeling that had been haunting him for as long as he could remember. Loneliness. He'd never wanted to admit that emptiness, that lack of connection to another person. But it had been with him for so long that he hadn't recognized it for what it was. All his adult life, he'd filled that lack with his work. Yet even the people surrounding him there—the business associates he talked with nearly every day, even the women he'd known over the years—had touched him only on the surface. But with Emily, it was different. She touched him in a place that made him feel far too much, and that scared the hell out of him.

He pulled her closer. For now, he wouldn't analyze the depth of his feelings too closely. For the next few days, he'd simply do what he'd never really done for anyone else. He'd just be there—for her and for Cody.

Chapter Twelve

Three days after Cody's surgery, his discomfort had subsided enough for boredom to set in. There wasn't much he could do flat on his back, but Emily was pretty good at devising games children could participate in even from a hospital bed. The games were always better when other children were included. So, as she once had done when she'd volunteered her time in this same ward a few years ago, she gathered children in wheelchairs and pushing portable IV stands from up and down the hall, and began playing games and telling stories.

She was in the middle of one of those stories when Luke returned from a quick trip to San Diego. He'd flown over, met with city officials to confirm in person that his project there was back on schedule and returned in less than six hours. Ordinarily, he would have looked forward to such a meeting. Today, it had seemed a monumental inconvenience.

Seeing her, he realized why.

He'd missed her.

He realized something else in the moments before she looked up from the children surrounding her. She was smiling. An easy, bright smile that he hadn't seen since he'd first watched her pushing Cody on the swings at the park. He'd robbed that glow from her smile himself the very next day, when he'd told her who he was. Now it was back again. Not because of him. Because of the children. There were six of them—all boys—gathered around Cody's bed. But in her lap she held a somber little girl of two or three.

Incredibly, that smile stayed on her lips when she saw him.

"I'm glad you're here."

"You are?" he asked, after giving Cody's arm a squeeze and ruffling his hair.

Mischief danced in her eyes, making her look like a child herself, as she pulled a new book from beneath the one she'd been reading. The little girl in her lap snuggled closer, and Emily automatically began rocking the child, as if she knew exactly what it took to soothe her.

The sight of that child clinging so trustingly to Emily created images in Luke's mind that were far too compelling.

"We need another voice for this story. You'll be perfect."

The boys in the group, most of them too young to read, immediately recognized the masked reptiles on the book's cover. Excitement lit their faces.

From her right came a cry of "Cowabunga!" from a boy in a neck brace.

"Cool, dude!" was the comment from the little guy with two legs in casts.

Cody, his bandages and braces concealed beneath a sheet, punched the air with his fist. "Awesome, Mom!"

Luke grinned. He couldn't help it. It was good to see Cody doing so much better. For that matter, it was good to see all these kids having a little fun. He knew from talking with the father of the boy in the neck brace that the youngster had been having a real rough time of it. Right now, though, he had a smile stretched from ear to ear.

He found a chair and pulled it up behind Emily. There had been a time when Luke couldn't possibly have imagined himself reading to children in an orthopedic ward. But Emily had gently prodded him into many things he once wouldn't have considered, and though he'd fought himself most of the way, he'd learned in the process.

Because of her, he had learned to get as much pleasure out of building a sandcastle as a corporate tower, to feel as much pride over a child's accomplishments as he did his own. He had learned to relax by watching a bug crawl up a leaf with a little boy, instead of trying to run Jeff Eller into the floor on the handball court. Most importantly, though, Emily had given him the gift of knowing his son. Without her, Luke didn't think he would have let himself discover what a special child Cody was. For that he would be forever grateful. He told her as much that evening, as he pulled her into his arms. But then he kissed her, and he forgot everything but the sweet oblivion they created together. He'd never known how good it could be to love someone. And he did love Emily. It was as simple and as complicated as that.

The days blurred together for Emily, time taking on a surreal quality that made her feel as if she were moving about inside a small, isolated capsule of space. It was comfortable there, but it was also an illusion, and she was practical enough not to let herself dream. She simply got

through the days of working and running back and forth
to the hospital as best she could, and let herself look forward to the nights because that time with Luke was infinitely precious to her. She relied on Luke more than she
probably should. But it eased the burden a lot to share the
responsibility of Cody with him. Especially when Cody's
independent streak made him decide that only boys could
help him with his new physical therapy routine—which
meant that only his male therapist and Luke were allowed
the privilege of helping with the exercises.

"Don't worry. I'll show you what you're supposed to
do," Luke told her that evening over deli take-out. "Cody
and I have his routine nailed. We can teach it to you in no
time."

The pride in Luke's eyes filled her. He had come so far
from the day he'd first set eyes on his son. She remembered the fear, the anger. Mostly she remembered his pain.
Now it was hers to feel. The past two weeks had drawn
Cody and Luke even closer. It would be harder than ever
on Cody when his father left this time.

Emily didn't think it would be long before that happened, either. Luke had been out of town overnight only
four times in the past two weeks. He handled most of his
business from her telephone or the one in Cody's hospital
room while she was at work herself, though several times
he'd flown out, just for the day, to San Diego or Dallas.
Then there were the days when Luke didn't leave town but
didn't go to the hospital, either—at least not until Emily
went when she got off work.

It was on those days, when Luke said the least about
what he'd been doing, that she would notice a vague agitation about him. He would spend a lot of time pacing, or
staring out windows, and when the agitation only seemed
to grow worse, he would turn to her. There would be such

urgency in his touch, such need. And when they came together, Emily would be left with the awful feeling that it
might be the last time he would hold her. Their lovemaking became bittersweet, a tender b(ediction to the fragil-
ity of their feelings. Maybe that was why she always felt a
little desperate when he touched her now. The nearer the
time came for Cody to come home, the more Luke pulled
away. And, because she could feel his emotional with-
drawal, she began to pull into herself, too.

At least she tried. And never had she tried so hard as the
morning Cody was due to be discharged. It was early still,
too early to be up, but she'd awakened to find Luke gone
from her bed.

She found him at her kitchen table, watching the sun-
rise make prisms through the glass hummingbird in the
window.

"Luke?" Her voice was quiet, like the dawn creeping
over the rooftops. "Are you all right?"

He was wearing nothing but a pair of faded jeans, and
the muscles in his back flexed smoothly as he turned to
face her. He had made coffee; its rich scent filled the room,
and he had a steaming mug in front of him.

His glance skimmed the length of her legs as she belted
her short pink robe, but he turned away before he met her
eyes. "I didn't mean to wake you."

It was clear that he wanted to be alone. Wishing she
hadn't imposed, hoping that he didn't need to be alone
because of her, she started to back away.

"There's coffee." His head tipped toward the coffee
maker near the sink.

"That's okay. I'll just go get in the shower...."

"We need to talk."

He was still facing the window, and his head was bent.
Tension knotted his shoulders, the beautiful shoulders she

had clung to last night when he had buried himself in her and made them both forget about tomorrow. But tomorrow was here. As Emily went through the motions of pouring coffee into a mug, she had the very certain feeling that she didn't want to face it.

"We can't keep going on like this."

Slowly she sat down across from him. "Like what?" she asked, in the faint hope she might not know what he was talking about.

For several moments, all that could be heard was the ticking of the clock and an occasional hiss from the coffee maker as Luke pushed his fingers through his hair. Emily folded her arms over the knot in her stomach. Knowing something like this was coming still hadn't prepared her for it. It hadn't been easy for him to juggle his responsibilities the past couple of weeks, and the strain showed. He had a life away from here and that didn't include her.

Finally he met her eyes. His were cool as he searched her face for something she couldn't identify. Hers were guarded, but not to much so that he couldn't see her scrambling for her shell.

He let out a deep breath. "I can't keep staying here, Emily. Especially now that Cody's coming home. We haven't talked about what we are going to do, but I'll be in town for a few more days, so I can still help you with him. What time do you want me to meet you at the hospital?"

His manner was impersonal, almost businesslike. As if she were nothing more than a loose end of a business deal that hadn't worked out. As if she were nothing more than a detail.

A responsibility.

Her stomach clenched at the thought. That was the last thing she wanted to be to him. "Dr. Hamilton said Cody could be discharged anytime after his therapy session this morning. I'm taking the afternoon off.''

''Why don't I meet you about eleven, then? I'll settle up the bill, then meet you in his room.''

She said nothing about the money. Now that the state was aware of Luke's paternity and financial resources, it had cut off financial assistance with Cody's medical bills. She had no choice but to let him pay.

That didn't matter now. Not as it once had. He'd more than earned the right to take care of his son.

Emily's throat felt tight. Her nod was even tighter.

''What time is the lady you hired to stay with him coming in the morning?''

''I asked her to be here at eight.'' She didn't bother to ask why he wanted to know. As numb as Emily was beginning to feel, she didn't really care.

''Give me her number, will you? I'll come stay with Cody in the morning. She doesn't need to get here until noon.''

The legs of her chair scraped against the tiles as Emily stood, the sound jarring in the too-quiet house.

Quickly she wrote out the woman's name and number. Absolutely refusing to let him see she was shaking, she tossed the dinosaur-shaped slip of notepaper in front of him.

''You could have told me last night, you know.''

She saw the muscle in his jaw bunch. He knew exactly what she was talking about. ''I would have, if I'd known what to say.'' He stood, taking the notepaper and stuffing it in his pocket. ''We've both just been coasting these past couple of weeks, Emily. We've had to because of what's been going on with Cody. But he's okay now, and we've both got lives to get back to. Or at least get on with.''

''You couldn't have said that last night?''

Her defenses were up. She knew it. He knew it. And she didn't care.

Luke's hand cupped the side of her cheek. "I could have," he admitted, in a voice so smooth it sent shivers up her spine. "But I didn't want to believe it was necessary. When I touch you, I tend to forget about everything but the way you feel. The way you make me feel," he added, drawing his thumb toward her mouth. "But we're going to have to make some decisions soon, about Cody. About how we're going to handle his custody. Like I said, we can't keep going on like this."

It was difficult to think when he was touching her the way he was. But it seemed imperative that a solution be found before either of them walked out the door this morning. "The most obvious would be for us to go back to doing what we were doing before."

"Exactly as before?"

"I don't know, Luke. I haven't thought about it."

"Well, you'd better start. What we were doing isn't going to work anymore. It wasn't working all that great to begin with."

"We were doing all right," she protested.

The look he spared her was tolerant at best. "Come on, Emily. My showing up here on weekends was a strain on both of us."

"But we were working it out."

"Don't you think it's gotten a little more complicated lately?"

He was referring to their sleeping together. She was sure of it. And that certainly did complicate the issue. It was also the one issue they both seemed intent on avoiding, because if they didn't they'd have to talk about what they meant to each other. Emily was deathly afraid that she didn't mean enough to him.

"Maybe a little," she admitted, afraid to guess where this conversation was leading. "But we could probably work that out, too."

It scared her to think they might lose what they had. It frightened her even more that she'd allowed him to matter so much.

He watched her, half in disbelief, half in curiosity. "It wouldn't bother you to have me coming and going from your life like that?"

It would bother her a lot more if he wasn't.

She shook her head.

Luke shook his, too, and, wishing he had access to a crystal ball, brushed a kiss over her lips. She was no more prepared for another change in their relationship than he was. They really couldn't go on as they had, though. Something had to give. And soon. "I've got an errand to run this morning. I'll try to be at the hospital by eleven. Don't leave before I get there. Okay?"

She promised she wouldn't, looking as uncertain of the outcome of their conversation as he felt. Even as he watched, he could see her pulling back into herself.

The expression "back to square one" came to mind as he watched her head into the shower. But he didn't want to go back, and he wasn't sure how to proceed. He knew only that he had to. The key to the success of any venture was the timing.

In this case, he was also going to rely heavily on blind luck.

He'd asked her once before to marry him, thinking only of the practicality of it, and she'd turned him down flat. Given the benefit of hindsight, he now realized that hers was the only response a woman like Emily could give to such a proposal. Having been turned down once, he was wary of asking again—even though his reason for wanting her now had nothing to do with convenience. If anything, it was damned inconvenient caring about a woman who lived several hundred miles away from what he loosely thought of as home.

She had finally come to trust him. She might not realize it herself, but he knew she had. She never would have let him into her bed if she hadn't. Or allowed him to get as close to Cody as she had. Luke felt positive of that. All he had to do now was make her see it—and give her reason to trust him even more.

What Luke needed was the help of an expert. In business, a person hired all manner of professionals to teach him details he didn't fully understand. Luke knew he had no hope of fully understanding Emily—she was a female, after all—but he could get a better handle on some of the details. There was only one person with that kind of knowledge. As soon as Emily had left for work and Luke knew he wouldn't run into her, he headed straight for the hospital.

"You can't say anything to her until we get there. Got it?"

Cody, grinning, nodded his head. "It'll be a secret."

"Right." In the past few minutes Luke had learned that his son loved secrets. "Now, do you remember the afternoon we were feeding bugs to Mike? It was a Sunday," Luke added, trying to prod the child's memory. "No help, huh? Okay, that's not important, anyway. Do you remember asking me about getting a brother for him?"

Anticipation lit the younger pair of gray eyes, though recollection was still a ways off. "Did you get me a turtle?"

"Sorry, sport." Reaching across the hospital bed from where he straddled the chair beside it, Luke ruffled Co dy's silky hair. "Not yet. I told you to ask your mom if it was okay. Did you?"

"I forgot."

"I see. Then I don't suppose you asked her about the brother you wanted for yourself, either."

The expression on Luke's face didn't change by so much as the twitch of a muscle. Yet, mentally, he was holding his breath.

"I forgot about that, too."

"I see." Disappointed, Luke tried again. "What do you think she'd say if you did ask her?"

Little shoulders lifted in a shrug against the sheet, bunching Cody's gown up around his ears. Smoothing the gown back down, Luke let the matter go. If he said too much more, he might start getting Cody's hopes up about a brother, and that was definitely something he couldn't provide without Emily's cooperation.

He was no closer to knowing how Emily might feel about extending her family than when he'd arrived. The baby part could wait, anyway. What was important was that he now had an accomplice. That he was in league with a six-year-old probably should have told him something. But he figured that since he and that six-year-old both loved the same woman, his choice of cohort could be excused.

"I've got to go now," he said, leaning over the rails to give his son a hug. "But I'll be back in a couple of hours. Your mom will probably get here before I do, but don't tell her I was already here. Okay?"

Loving the conspiracy, Cody gave another vigorous nod. "Okay."

"Don't forget to ask if we can go for a ride when we get to your house."

"A long ride."

"Right."

"And I'm not supposed to ask where we're going, 'cause we're going to your house and she's not supposed to know. And when we get there, she'll be surprised."

Luke grinned. His son had all the details down pat. Good man, that little guy.

Not only did Cody have an excellent memory, he also proved quite the little actor. When Luke arrived shortly after eleven o'clock, Emily had already helped Cody dress in baggy shorts and an even baggier T-shirt—a style Luke had learned was de rigueur for the younger crowd—and Cody was patiently waiting for his dad as if he hadn't seen him all day.

"I haven't seen you for a long time," the little boy said when his arms were around his dad's neck.

"Don't be a ham," Luke whispered, and buzzed Cody's ear before he straightened to meet Emily's guarded green eyes. "Are you ready?"

She shifted the athletic bag containing the toys and games that had kept Cody more or less occupied for the past couple of weeks. "Ready," she returned, smiling for Cody's sake.

"I'll take Cody in my car. It's got a bigger backseat, and it might be more comfortable for him than yours."

A couple of months ago, the hair on her neck would have stood straight up had he said such a thing. Her first thought would have been that he might take Cody from her and speed off into the night and she'd never see her precious child again. Or some such thing.

It was a sign of how far they'd come that all she did was say that was a good idea, then let Luke take her bag as they followed Cody and the nurse pushing him to the elevator and out front to where Luke had left his car. Before he'd

left her this morning, he'd said they would have to make
some decisions about Cody's custody. The one thing she
knew he would not do was simply take him. Luke would
do the right thing by his son. By her, too, she supposed,
because he was that kind of man. But his idea of what was
"right" was probably light-years away from her own. To
her, there was only one solution.

She just didn't know if she had the courage to suggest it.

She was still trying to screw up that courage twenty
minutes later, when she pulled into her drive just ahead of
Luke and Cody. Stepping out of her car, she waited,
thinking Luke would be getting out of his any moment.

Instead, he lowered the window.

"Cody doesn't want to go in yet."

Frowning, the heels of her flats tapping on the drive, she
moved past the front fender of the shiny black sedan Luke
had been driving for the past couple of weeks. She couldn't
begin to imagine what he spent on rental cars.

With a quiet purr, the back window slid down as she
reached it.

Cody was propped up in the backseat, the new brace he
needed to wear for the next few weeks making it impossible for him to sit straight up. "What's the matter?" she
wanted to know.

Cody glanced at Luke, but Luke didn't say a word. He
just sat with his wrists draped over the wheel, staring
straight ahead. "I want to go for a ride," Cody said to his
mom.

"You just went for one."

"Not a long one."

"Cody, we need to get you inside."

"Why?"

Good question.

"Let's take him for a ride," Luke cut in, sounding as if he didn't want to sit there listening to them argue about it. "This is the first time he's been out in a while. It might do him some good."

Emily glanced toward the house, hesitating. Maybe a ride wouldn't be a bad idea. It would give her more time. More time to figure out how to approach Luke with her proposition. And more time before she had to be alone with him to do it.

"Come on, Mom," she heard Cody say in a half whine from the backseat. "Let's go."

So they went. For a short ride, Emily said. For a long one, Cody insisted, and all the while Luke said nothing. He seemed preoccupied to Emily. Distant. Tense. But then, she was feeling a little tense herself. Just because he wouldn't be staying at her house tonight didn't mean she'd never see him again. So it wasn't as if they had to come to a conclusion about what they were going to do about Cody this very afternoon. Or even tomorrow, for that matter. What they needed to decide was what they were going to do about each other.

Those thoughts occupied Emily to the point that she barely noticed where they were going. It was only when they'd turned off a main thoroughfare and were winding up the small mountain in the center of Phoenix that the locals called Camelback that she noticed how silent even Cody had become. That was unusual for him. In a car, he was usually tripping over himself with chatter.

They had neared the end of a narrow street with an incredible view of the valley below when Luke pulled into the drive of a newly landscaped house—a beautiful Spanish-style hacienda with beige stucco walls and a multilevel red-tile roof. Thinking he was only turning around, since the road dead-ended there, Emily paid no attention to it. At least not until he kept going down the drive and came to a stop in front of a three-car garage.

"Are we there?" Cody wanted to know.

"Are we where?"

Emily looked from Luke to the little boy in the back-seat. When Cody said nothing, she turned to Luke again. He looked a little uneasy.

"Luke?"

"Can I tell her, Dad?"

Luke cut the engine. "Go ahead."

"It's Dad's house. He has a big-screen TV and every-thing. Can we go in now?"

Without a word, Luke got out of the car and opened the back door. Letting Cody lift himself up by grabbing his neck, Luke carefully supported his hips and the heavier brace he now wore.

"Would you get the front door, Emily? The keys are in the ignition. It's the one with the blue circle on it."

"This is yours?" she asked, following Luke along a wide walkway to a pair of massive double doors.

"I bought it about a month ago. The sale just closed last week. There's not much in it right now."

He'd said he'd been thinking about buying a place. But it seemed to her that he'd just mentioned it in passing, be-cause he'd never said anything else about it. Apparently, with Luke, mentioning something once was all it took.

Using the key he'd indicated, she opened the door. "What about your home in Denver?"

"I've still got it."

He had a place in Aspen, too. For skiing. She knew that, because he'd mentioned it to her after a discussion with Dr. Hamilton about what kind of sports he could get Cody involved in. The doctor had seen no reason why Cody couldn't be fitted for a special ski board that would require only the use of his upper body. After he'd healed from his surgery, of course.

At the moment, Emily wasn't thinking of what Luke had planned for Cody next winter. She considered only that the acquisition of another house was apparently, to him, nothing to get excited about.

Therefore, she wouldn't let herself put too much importance on it, either.

Following Luke inside, she closed the door. The lock caught with a click that echoed in the huge white-tiled foyer. To her right was what she supposed was a living room, a great cavernous thing with a wall of arched windows. To her left was the dining room, judging from the chandelier handing in its center.

They crossed the entry and headed into the less formal area of the house, a large family room that opened on an expansive oak-cabineted kitchen. Beyond the wall of glass was a pool, and beyond that a view that went on forever.

A faint buzz came from down the hall, followed a moment later by what sounded very much like a typewriter in hyperdrive.

"It's the fax," Luke said when he saw her frowning down the wide hallway. "I've got an office back there. Go ahead. Take a look if you want. I'll take Cody in here."

The only furniture in the place was a large L-shaped sofa that still had cardboard packing on the ends and a television set that took up the better part of a built-in wall unit. Judging from the tools and pieces of wire lying on the carpet, someone had just installed the set and the electronic equipment in the wall surrounding it.

"Cool," she heard Cody murmur when Luke, having settled him on the sofa, handed him the controls to a video game and turned on the television.

"I told you it was big," she heard Luke say to the grinning boy, then glanced at the screen herself as Cody maneuvered the figures of a video math game across it.

Leaving Cody to his own devices, knowing he was perfectly content with his new toy, Luke shoved his hands into the pockets of his comfortably worn jeans. Emily hadn't budged from where she'd stopped.

"You don't want to look around?"

She hesitated. Then, realizing that he might want her out of earshot of Cody, she crossed her arms and gave him a nod.

As they walked through the house, Luke didn't seem in any great rush to bring up anything he couldn't have said in front of his son. It seemed he really did just want to give her a tour. Had Emily let herself look at him, though, she would have noticed how carefully he was watching for her reactions to the various rooms and areas. All she noted was that Luke had been doing a lot of work from the room with the drafting table and desk and now-silent fax.

"My southwestern branch," Luke called it, mentioning to her as he had to Jeff how much sense it made for him to have a base there. "I haven't made the decision yet, but I might make Phoenix my headquarters."

"So that's why you bought a house instead of just getting an office."

"That's part of it," he told her as they left that airy space and moved out onto the patio by way of a vast—and empty—master bedroom. "But I also wanted this house so that I could spend more time with Cody. That, and it had a pool. He'll need it for his therapy."

Of everything Luke had said in the past several minutes, his last statements, cautiously delivered, were the only ones that caused her any alarm.

It was one thing to adjust to the prospect of him living in the same town. It was quite another to consider what he would expect with that arrangement.

Through the large glass wall of the family room, she could see Cody waving at her. She waved back as he returned to his game, her heart beating in her throat. "It would be fun for him to come over here once in a while. When you're home," she added, desperately hoping she was misjudging his intentions.

He'd said they needed to settle the custody matter. With a sick sensation filling her, she suddenly knew that was his reason for bringing her here. She only hoped Luke didn't think it would be best for Cody to live with him just because he would now be in the same town.

Another thought encroached upon that unsettling one.

Just this morning, Luke had taken the number of the woman she'd hired to take care of Cody while she was at work. Had he asked that lady to come to work for him? Was that why he'd insisted it wasn't necessary for her to call her this morning?

Hating the suspicion, Emily tried to quash her panic. Luke was watching her, his eyes intent on her pale features. Because of how easily he could read her at times, she feared he could already see how she was trembling inside. She turned away from him, not wanting to believe what the feeling in the pit of her stomach told her might be true. That Luke had used her to gain the love and trust of his son, and now that he had, she wasn't necessary anymore.

"Emily?"

The weight of his hand settled on her shoulder, gentle, reassuring. There wasn't a time when he had touched her that she hadn't felt his strength or his tenderness. She closed her eyes against the glitter of the sun on the bright blue water of the pool. This was Luke. She'd come to trust him as she had no one else. He wouldn't hurt her that way. She had to believe that.

In a movement so familiar it made her ache, he brushed his thumb along the back of her neck. "What's wrong?"

She had to ask. "Did you call Mrs. Rosenberg this morning?"

The movement stilled. "Yeah. I did. Why?"

"What did you tell her?"

"To come to your house at noon tomorrow." Sounding puzzled at the mention of the sitter they'd hired together, he nonetheless told her what she needed to hear. "That I'd be there with Cody until then."

"You weren't going to have her come here?"

Luke didn't answer. Instead, hearing what had almost sounded like relief in her voice, he turned her around to face him.

He was frowning. "No. I wasn't. Why these questions, Emily?"

"I just want to know what's going on here."

The frown faded with the deep breath he drew. For several seconds, he wouldn't meet her eyes, his glance fastened on the motion of his fingers as he absently toyed with a strand of her curling hair. When he did look back at her, the muscle in his jaw bunched.

"Do you honestly want to go back to the way things were before?"

That was not the response she'd expected. That was also not a question she wanted to answer at the moment.

"What other choices do I have?"

The guilelessness in her eyes always unnerved him. Almost as much as the faint challenge that stiffened her shoulders. He admired that challenge almost as much as he was irritated by it. The woman was independent to a fault. He really couldn't blame her for feeling she'd needed to be. He could even appreciate that she might have needed to prove to herself—maybe even the world—that she didn't need anyone to take care of her. Or her son. *Their* son. But she'd proven it long ago, and there was nothing to gain by clinging to a stance she no longer had to maintain. If there was one thing she'd made him see, it was that standing on your own also meant standing by yourself. When there was no room for anyone else, it could get awfully lonely.

He hadn't realized that until he'd met her.

"Actually, you do. You could marry me. Don't say it," he cut in when her eyes widened. "The last time I brought this up, I was only thinking about being practical. And about Cody. Cody has nothing to do with this. I mean, he does, but he's not why I'm asking you. I love you," he said, because the word needed so badly to be said. "And I want you to be my wife. Not because Cody needs you, but because I need you." He was something so much better with her than he was without her. "You make me care, Emily."

Words deserted him. He felt he was expressing himself badly, anyway, but it didn't matter. He'd said what he needed to say, and now it was up to Emily to either dismiss his proposal—again—or let them live as he knew in his heart they all should. He just wished she'd say something. All she was doing was staring up at him as if he'd just lost all his marbles in the bottom of his new pool.

Her voice came softly, like the smile lighting her lovely face. "I've known for a long time that I wanted your son, Luke. I fell in love with him the first time I saw him." And because of his son, she had thought that the only solution to their problem—what she'd hoped for the courage to propose—was to ask Luke for a chance to change her mind about his earlier proposition. It seemed he'd thought so, too. And this time, it was for all the right reasons. "I think

I fell in love the same way with you. I was just so afraid to want you."

His hand moved up to trace her jaw. "You've got me, honey, and all the other sons and daughters you want. If you're interested."

With the grace of a dancer, she curved her arms around his neck. There was something truly irresistible about the Montgomery men. "I love you, Luke."

"Is that a yes?"

She grinned. "Absolutely."

Neither of them noticed Cody frowning at them through the window. Certainly neither heard his disgusted "Oh, yuck" when Luke's lips claimed Emily's a moment later. But each was very grateful for the little guy who had made it possible for them to find each other, and to be a family. A very special family who, just by being together, could meet each other's very special needs.

* * * * *

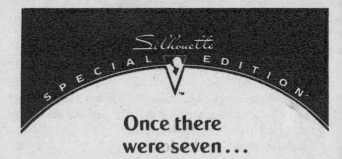

Once there were seven...

Seven beautiful brothers and sisters who played together, and weathered adversity too cruel for their tender ages. Eventually orphaned, they were then separated.

Now they're trying to find each other.

Don't miss Gina Ferris's heartwarming

FAMILY FOUND

Full of Grace   February
Hardworking Man   April
Fair and Wise   June

Available at your favorite retail outlet from Silhouette Special Edition

SEFF-1

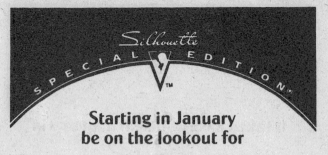

Silhouette

SPECIAL EDITION™

**Starting in January
be on the lookout for**

MAVERICKS

LISA JACKSON'S
MAVERICK MEN

They're wild...they're woolly...and
they're as rugged as the great outdoors.
They've never needed a woman before,
but they're about to meet their matches....

HE'S A BAD BOY (#787)—January
HE'S JUST A COWBOY (#799)—March
HE'S THE RICH BOY (#811)—May

All men who just won't be tamed!
From Silhouette Special Edition.

SEMAV-1

It takes a very special man to win

She's friend, wife, mother—she's you! And beside each Special Woman stands a wonderfully *special* man. It's a celebration of our heroines—and the men who become part of their lives.

Look for these exciting titles from Silhouette Special Edition:

January **BUILDING DREAMS** by Ginna Gray

February **HASTY WEDDING** by Debbie Macomber

March **THE AWAKENING** by Patricia Coughlin

April **FALLING FOR RACHEL** by Nora Roberts

Dont miss THAT SPECIAL WOMAN! each month—from your special authors.

AND

For the most special woman of all—you, our loyal reader—we have a wonderful gift: a beautiful journal to record all of your special moments. See this month's THAT SPECIAL WOMAN! title for details.

TSW1